Instant Ancestors

Preposterous tales sprung from a shoebox.

Acknowledgments

First, if you are reading these words, I'd like to thank you for taking a chance to read this book. It was a complete joy to imagine and write, and I hope you get a least a modicum of pleasure from taking a mental expedition with me. So again, thank you very much.

I want to thank my "story tumbler," Jay Fields, for his interest and contributions to the book. Like a rock tumbler, where you put your favorite rocks or minerals into and let them tumble with aggregate for a few weeks, polishing them to a high luster, Jay took my stories, tumbled them around in his brain, and knocked some of the rough edges off, revealing a much-improved gloss. Thank you, my friend.

Next, I'd like to thank my lovely wife, Fran, for being my "first reader." Her comments of "Where did these stories come from?" while maybe not a ringing endorsement, certainly was refreshing, as they caught her completely by surprise. And being an old ad guy, I know that anytime you can surprise someone with an idea that makes them look at something—in this case, me—in a new and different way, that is time well invested.

Finally, thanks to all my associates and neighbors who acted as early readers, offering similar responses to my work as Fran, for playing in the sandbox with me. Feedback and encouragement are good polishing tools.

I'll end where I started. Thank you for investing even a small amount of your valuable time with this cast of characters. They are among my favorite people, even though they never really were.

© 2023 Russell Allen Shuler

All rights reserved. Published in the United States.

ISBN– 979-8-9877048-0-6 Paperback

ISBN– 979-8-9877048-2-0 Hardcover

ISBN– 979-8-9877048-1-3 E-book

Cover and book design by Russell Shuler.

Studio portrait and front cover image created by Keith Wright.

The Genesis of Instant Ancestors

It's been said many times that you can pick your nose, but you can't pick your relatives. I believed that to be true until, not long ago, I came across a shoe box crammed with family portraits taken roughly a hundred years ago in a favorite antique store. The stall proprietor included an index card with the scribbled broadside: "Instant Ancestors!" It went on to say that with these pictures, you could conjure up a long-lost relative from God knows where famous for such and such, and no one would be wiser. To be truthful, the idea appealed to my lop-sided, passionate sense of humor, so I bought the box of photographs and began imagining the personal chronicles of these precious folks who had been relegated to the dustbin of history.

Of course, none of the characters I conjured are real, even remotely so. On the other hand, certain sayings and mannerisms flutter into the light of these tales from acquaintances in my past. Sorry about that—it's just that I largely went with zero impulse control in the tales that follow. I can't be held responsible if they resurrect someone buried in the annals of your very own family. And should there be no real likeness to anyone you know, buried or alive, consider yourself one incredibly lucky individual.

Russell Shuler

Table Of Contents

Cletus McHaggis

CLETUS
McHAGGIS

"So... are you gonna make a move any time today, or should I come back around tomorrow?" asked Willie.

Cletus answered with nothing more than a squinty stare. It was his not-so-secret weapon, and it didn't matter if he was playing a game of checkers or bidding on a steer down at the stockyard, and if you engaged with him, you were likely to fall victim.

After an uncomfortably long period, McHaggis responded, "When I'm darned good and ready, you'll know." He felt he now had Willie by the short and curlies, just like he liked it.

"Shoot then. I'm out! I can't be dragging ass for days on this chair while you make up your mind about whether to jump me." Wille snarled, kicked the chair over, and shuffled away.

Smiling on the inside, Cletus stared at the board as if carved from alabaster until Willie was out of sight, then intoned quietly to himself, "Gotcha again, you little shit!"

McHaggis discovered at an early age that if you weren't too quick to respond to people, they'd often proceed in the direction you wanted. And it didn't matter what kind of negotiation it was; the method was bulletproof.

Even as a baby bouncing along in a dusty covered wagon headed west with other homesteaders, he used this technique when breastfeeding Mammy. However, he was unaware he was doing so at the time. For example, she'd put her big old jug in his face, and he'd look at her, thinking, "Why do you have that pink-nippled, milk-smelly thing shoved in my face like that?" All of this, he said internally. All his Mammy heard was "Wah! Wah! Wah!" as he stared at her.

He'd continue to use the same gamut eating at the table with the big folk. Then, seeing his empty bowl, his Mammy would ask, "Clete, do you want some more porridge?" Of course, he did, but he wasn't about to let her know it, so he just stared at her for a few minutes. Then, after what became an uncomfortable moment, she'd heap another spoonful into his waiting bowl.

This technique also became invaluable when he started courting young girls. For example, when he and Maggie were rolling in the hay in the old barn, and she started getting as frisky and fiery as her red hair, she would sit astride him and sweetly ask, "Would you like to have a play with my little knockers, young Clete?" Thinking to himself, "What a stupid question. Of course, I'll be wanting to fondle and snuggle my face in your little cleavage and maybe in some other choice areas." But all he said was nothing. He just stared. Granted, it was a curiously intense and wild-eyed stare, but it was a stare nonetheless. Not sensing any reluctance from Cletus, Maggie removed her lacy under things and commenced satisfying her natural inclinations.

This formula of "non-response" responding seemed to have increasing power. The more Cletus didn't react to something and just stared away, the more people did as he wished. It was the darndest thing.

One day Cletus found himself in a bit of a pickle, though, and as you might guess, it involved a skirt.

Her name was Esmerelda, and she was like the famed literary figure in many respects, sans goat. She was a dark-haired beauty of Spanish descent, with eyes as green as the emerald coast of Ireland and dark olive skin. A singing and dancing member of a traveling medicine show. She loved to haggle and barter and was good at it, a traveling carnie her entire life. Moreover, she made exquisite use of her good looks. Purring and circling targets, letting her body do most of the talking as her prey fell speechless.

McHaggis first spied her riding into town, caroling sweetly to herself. He waited on the shady side of the street in front of the saloon. He cast his powerful stare her way, which was usually all he required to attract someone his way, and he felt Esmerelda would be no different. At least, that's what he thought as she pulled her one-horse cart in front of the saloon.

She stepped down from the cart, tied the horse's reins to the rail, dusted off her dark pleated dress, checking to make sure her frilly white blouse was hanging just right off her shoulders, adjusted her corset for maximum bosom effect, turned, and marched his way. Clete had never felt more optimistic about his prospects of bringing a hot-blooded filly under his command; all he had to do was bear down with his long, hard look.

But as she got closer, each step more provocative than the last, something captured his senses. Her fragrance was otherworldy! In a completely uncharacteristic move, he deeply inhaled her heavenly aroma and closed his eyes, almost floating up from his chair. Then, quick as a wink, the advantage shifted in Esmerelda's favor—she sashayed past him directly into the saloon without offering so much as a second glance. That she-devil!

This insult absolutely could not stand. Cletus jumped out of his chair, kicking over the checkers table, scattering checkers all over the street. Then, moving through the swinging saloon doors, he encountered a scene that stopped him cold. The entire population inside the tavern, men and women folk alike, were sitting or standing there, slack-jawed as wayward mules, rubbernecking this raven-haired vixen. The barkeep nervously cleaned a shot glass like his uneventful life depended on it. Finally, the piano player broke the spell when he started tinkling with the ivories, producing a tune no one recognized.

"I would like a glass of your best Madeira, kind sir," she lilted to the stunned fellow behind the bar.

"Ma-what?" he asked.

"Red wine! Like Bacchus pours out of his belly button," she spun as only a cunning temptress could.

"Why didn't you say so then? Sorry, we ain't got no wine. Beer and whiskey is all we pour here," mumbled the keep.

"Then pour me a quick whiskey, you gringo, before I smack your mouth!" she grinned.

Damn! McHaggis had never witnessed such a creature; truth be told, he was fearful about the whole prospect of engaging with her, yet he couldn't help himself. He had to get her attention and level up the playing field. But by what strategy? She was impervious to "the stare." And her anger was quick to rise. So whatever his next move was, he had to be sure, or it might be his last.

In a Fell Swoop

He casually strolled into the bar, never once taking his eyes off her, feeling that to do so would only increase her control. But unfortunately, even the back of her beautiful head seemed to have authority over him. Dropping down on a stool at the end of the bar, he ordered a beer and a beef jerky, thinking they might help stick courage to the post.

"Where are you coming from, lovely senorita?" he asked as gentlemanly as possible.

Looking straight ahead in the mirror behind the bar, she tossed her whiskey back in one fell swoop and said, "Same place I'm headed back to—what's it to you, mister?"

"Hold up! That's no way to treat a fellow, especially when I asked you all nice," Clete retorted, feeling dangled in space. "Here, let me buy you another tipple from the old jug. What do you say?"

Esmerelda turned on her seat to face him and said, "Pardon me, kind sir. Of course, I'll have a drink with you! Who knows what it could lead to?" She giggled, batting green eyes. Then, in a gush, she sauntered down to his end of the bar and nodded to the stunned barkeep.

"Name's Cletus. Cletus McHaggis. At your service, ma'am."

"Cleee-tus! So very lovely to make your acquaintance. You may call me Esmerelda, as everyone does." Then, whispering, she said, "Although a few handsome men have given me other names."

Feeling like he was gaining ground, Cletus sallied forth. "I'd like to propose a toast. To the indomitable Esmerelda and her secrets—may they be revealed to the worthy!"

"Why, Mr. Cleee-tus! You flatter me talking about secrets. I am but a shy, hard-working showgirl making her way in this big lonely world, singing and dancing to bring a moment's joy to people along the way. If those kind souls feel moved to bless me with a friendly word, a tasty meal, or, as you have so gallantly done, a tipple from the bottle, then the world is all the better for it," she exclaimed for all within earshot as she raised her glass.

"Cheers!" rang out across the bar as if she had pulled a puppet string dangling from everyone's back, and their tongues started wagging. The piano player suddenly found his hands again, unleashing a ragtime tune. The mob rushed to the bar like a tsunami to be close to Esmerelda and her intoxicating rapport.

The place surrounded her, everyone shouting and screaming to buy her another drink, a continental drift that filled Esmerelda with glee. Then, quick as a cricket, she jumped on the bar and started to sing and dance, swooping and swishing her long black mane for all it was worth. The piano player did his best to keep up. Everyone juked and jived to the rhythm of the moment.

Then everything got deathly quiet. Esmerelda stopped, tossed her head back in ecstasy, took a bow, stepped off the bar, and waded through the dumbfounded crowd and out of the saloon.

Cletus cautiously followed her out the swinging doors, unsure about his next move. Then, catching up, he escorted her across the street and up to her carriage.

Uncorking an inviting smile, she said, "Thank you kindly, Mr. Cleee-tus McHaggis. Our gang is staying just on the outskirts of town for a few days, and if you were to find yourself out that way for some unknown reason, Lord knows what mischief we might get into."

Swallowing hard, Cletus could only croak, "Yes, indeedy. Yes, indeedy. Good day, my lady."

He watched her leaving town, feeling a deep yearning for the very dust her wagon wheels kicked up. Feeling as if he had fallen into the tail of a random comet ripping across the night sky.

Doppeling the Ganger

When she returned to the Medicine Show, Esmerelda's identical twin sister, Desdomena, greeted her. The two were indistinguishable from each other, even to close family members, a likeness which came in handy when the two bestowed mischief on some poor, unsuspecting soul. Esmerelda hugged Desdomena, and the two climbed inside their covered wagon.

Esmerelda regaled Desdomena with her exploits in town, especially the winding up of Mr. Cletus McHaggis. This man, she felt certain, would be an easy mark, but they would have to plan carefully to bring him to his knees. The two would act like a mythical Janus, with one face setting Cletus up and the other taking him down a curved and humiliating road. Or, so they strategized.

All the years staring people down had taught Cletus one crucial fact: you had to concentrate intensely on what people said and, even more importantly, on what they didn't say. Through critical observation, you could unlock a person's innermost thoughts. This practiced discipline had created his ability to discern refined, almost incomprehensible details. Like how a person looked at you or not. How they breathed. Whether they hesitated at specific points during the conversation, as if waiting for information to fall into place before proceeding. And how was their body language? Did it change subtly from one moment to the next? All these clues painted a picture for Cletus to work with as he moved about his everyday world.

So, in this state of heightened awareness, Cletus proceeded out of town to the Medicine Show. The ride out clarified things to a degree. He had a chance to review the previous day's events, almost like watching one of those new-fangled moving pictures, and he fixed in his mind on as many details about Esmerelda as possible. Hair color and texture. Facial expressions. Eyes, mouth, teeth, everything. She would not catch him off guard again.

It was near dark, the golden hour, when he arrived at the campsite. The carnies had a fire roaring, and his mouth watered at the smell of smoking meat. He could hear someone plucking a guitar in a flamenco rhythm accompanied by a beautiful voice he recognized as belonging to Esmerelda. But, in the air, there were hints of something else: cannabis and peyote. This could get interesting.

"Hola! Welcome, Mr. Cleee-tus, to our humble campsite," came a voice he didn't recognize. It was Juan Carlos, a.k.a. "Sweetie" to family members, walking over to greet him.

"Gracias! Pleased to make your acquaintance," replied Clete, already cataloging Juan's particulars for later usage. "That was some mighty fine playing you were doing there, so please, don't let me stop you."

"You are kind, Mr. Cleee-tus," purred Esmerelda as she joined them by the fire. "Let me fetch you a drink. I hope you like tequila."

McHaggis replied, "I'd prefer Irish whiskey, but if tequila is what you're pouring, I'm obliged to follow your lead."

At this, Esmerelda ducked behind the wagon. Desdomena was secretly waiting there, taking in the conversation. She was dressed as a mirror image of Esmerelda, matching in every way. Desdomena whispered to Esmerelda as she poured the drinks, "So what's the play with this gringo? I'm assuming you want to loosen him up, and then what?"

Esmerelda replied, "I'm still trying to decide what prize awaits us at the end. He carries himself quietly, more steely-eyed than any man I've ever encountered. But we will strike when he feels the need to break his silence and make a move. It's all about timing. That is why we must loosen him up with tequila and peyote first. It will slow his reactions and give us an edge."

Cletus sat near the fire and cataloged the site. He could identify five to seven gypsies, guessing there were probably twice that number. Their wagons were covered with heavy canvas tops and splashed in bright colors with carnival-like markings. The wagon wheels had pinstripes; any sign painter would be proud to call the work his own. Clearly, this was a source of pride for the group.

"Juan, that is a mighty fine wagon you've got there," said Cletus. "Did you paint it yourself?"

"Ah no, that would be Esmerelda's handiwork. She has an eye for such things. Her mother, God rest her soul, was gifted in the same way," he replied. There was the slightest hitch in his response, like he was about to say another name, when "Esmerelda" clicked into place.

Esmerelda returned with drinks and sat down next to McHaggis. The combination of the crackling fire and the early evening sky, combined with the closeness of this fascinating creature, intoxicated the visitor. Any fire the tequila lit would be redundant.

"To our newfound friend, Mr. Cleee-tus McHaggis! May he be found worthy of much and suspected of little," Esmerelda smiled.

"My worth is yet to be determined. But if I am any judge of character, and I like to think I am, I suspect you'll make an appraisal, fair and square, of any values I possess," Cletus winked.

The circling had begun: like two well-seasoned wrestlers facing off in an unseen ring. One looked for innuendo, while the other looked to remain concealed and unsuspected until the jig was over.

After a couple of rounds of drinks, Cletus felt warm and fuzzy all over, but not defenseless.

He began to stare at Esmerelda as a wily crocodile with an extra pair of protective eyelids. And just like a croc, he would lay in wait, staring for as long as it took to disarm his prey, tequila or not.

The Thick Plottens

Sensing the moment to act was right, Esmerelda ceremoniously offered a recipe the carnies had shared for generations. "We must have our special tea now, so we might reach those rooms of friendship and unbridled passion that remain closed to most." And with that, she disappeared behind the wagon again.

Cletus' powers of observation were now on full alert, and he absorbed every move he could regarding Esmerelda. Nothing escaped his gaze. It was as if time had slowed down, and he could see her brain telling her feet and legs to move along at a sexy gait, her lungs to breathe expectantly, and her smile to conceal and deflect.

Desdomena had already prepared the peyote tea, and they quickly exchanged knowing glances. Switching places now, she would carry the baton for a while and set up the fleecing of one Cletus McHaggis.

Arriving at the fireside, Desdomena offered him a steaming cup of tea, "Here we go, Mr. Cletus. Enjoy our unique blend of peyote and other medicinal herbs from Mother Nature's bounty."

And there it was, a tell! She had called him "Mr. Cletus," not "Mr. Cleee-tus," a subtle but important distinction.

Alarm bells began ringing in his head. And just like that, his brain directed his attention to another minor, almost imperceptible difference in Esmereleda's appearance. Her eyes, while still a shimmering green, now contained the slightest flecks of gold. Her chin was still dimpled but a little distant from her lower lip. And when she held her drink, the fingers wrapped under the cup, not around it. He didn't know who this person was, but he was 100% certain it was not Esmerelda. Something began to move underfoot.

"Thank you, Esmerelda," said McHaggis. "I knew the day we met in the bar when you ordered Irish whiskey—we were going to partner in some crime. And the way you and the piano player, who was smitten with you, as was everyone else, fell right in time with you when you began singing, well, I've never seen anything like it!"

"Oh, you are most kind, Mr. Cletus! We always want everyone to feel comfortable like we are one big happy family," she excitedly responded, feeling somehow she had let something slip. "It was fun, as you say, but I think you recall my beverage of choice incorrectly, as I only drink tequila."

"Oh my. Yes, you are quite right. Please forgive me. This tea must be making my brain a little dizzy." His stare wavered for not one second during the exchange. Now that he knew she was someone other than Esmerelda, he wondered exactly what was at play and how he could get himself untangled from it or, better yet, turn it to his advantage.

Desdomena got up and threw a few sticks into the fire, sending sparks floating into the night sky. She then looked down at Cletus with her most devastating gaze. McHaggis stared back at her, not moving. It appeared he no longer required regular breathing; such was his intensity. Finally, after a few minutes, she calmly stepped back behind the wagon to confer with Esmerelda about the plan, leaving Cletus in what she thought was a hallucinogenic stupor.

Esmerelda couldn't hear the entire exchange between Cletus and Desdomena but felt the plan was proceeding satisfactorily. Thinking Cletus was now baked, they decided to have a flirty time with him, just for good measure, and then roll him like a pair of dice.

While they hatched their plan, Cletus never moved a muscle. Even Juan Carlos felt the gringo was beyond offering any resistance to whatever the girls had planned.

"Oh, Mr. Cleee-tus, how willing are you to pursue pleasure now that you're in such a blessed state of peace?" Esmeralda softly asked. Even Satan would have blushed in her presence if his complexion weren't so crimson.

Then as slowly and seductively as a feather on a warm breeze, she floated over and straddled him like she was riding bareback. Cletus just gazed out into infinity while his mind spun like a top. Then, she pushed off his hat, revealing his almost bald head. She always found a bald head erotic. She loved the feel of a naked egg surrounded by a furry fringe. Rising to kiss him repeatedly on top of his head, she gently squeezed his body between her elegant legs and pressed her ample breasts against his face. Settling down to look at his face, she saw only Clete's blank, emotionless gaze. Then, feeling emboldened, she pushed his jacket off his shoulders, revealing his fat wallet in his vest pocket, hanging on a chain tied to his belt. The prize was in sight!

Rocking back on Cletus's lap, she looked him in the eyes, which were still glazed over, and demurely kissed him while simultaneously reaching for his wallet, thinking, "This is almost too easy."

Little did she realize that Cletus's gaze was now quite clear and fixed on her eyes. His left hand firmly grasped her slender wrist, while his right now held a small pistol under her delicate chin. Then, slowly pulling her arm behind her, causing her to feel the slightest pain, he said, "Well, Esmerelda, it appears you see me as just another stooge waiting to be duped and dumped. That is most unfortunate, as we were getting along so well. So where is your partner in crime?"

Seeing what had happened, Desdomena cautiously stepped out from behind the wagon and approached the two. "Please, Mr. Cletus, we are only here to make pleasure for you, not dupe you as you say. Surely there is something we can do to change your mind."

Curiously a scenario occurred to him that would provide pleasure but not be too painful for anyone involved. He would also get to exercise his most potent weapon—his steely gaze—in a new and different way.

Turn About, Fair Play

He told Desdomena, "Go fix us up another couple of rounds of that famous tea we had earlier. And Juan, you join us this next round. We're all going on a long, happy journey, and I'll be your guide. Of course, it will involve getting enthusiastic with each other, but I doubt it's anything you haven't tried before. And when I say we've reached our final destination, I'll bid you a fond farewell and be on my way."

As Cletus released her arm, smiling expectantly, Esmerelda felt she may still regain the upper hand. But once again, to her misfortune, she underestimated Cletus. While they were drinking tea and getting higher than kites, Cletus stared eagerly at them and occasionally would give an order. "Esmerelda, I want you to undress Desdomena and Juan slowly. Then I want you to dance around this fire in your birthday suits so I can inspect you from all sides."

Feeling the full effects of the tea now, they thought this the most fabulous idea conceivable and enthusiastically obliged, dancing and singing around the campfire. Various body parts kept time to their singing while others moved to an offbeat. It was a thing of beauty. Then, of course, the dancing transitioned on its own into other playtime activities, as Cletus knew it would, so he continued to stare as each player fulfilled their wildest fantasies. Kisses moved from top to bottom, one side to the other, and back again. Various items were sucked and licked like carnival treats, an unbridled fantasy come true.

As Cletus watched in rapt attention, he recalled his mother's advice long ago: "Cletus, if you find yourself in a foreign situation of any sort, son, remember: if it's wet and not yours, DON'T TOUCH IT!"

After an hour or so, Cletus had seen plenty. He got up and left the dancers to their own devices with no signs of winding down. He tied his horse to the back of the covered wagon and, climbing on board behind two hitched horses, rolled away into the night.

Looking up, he could see a million stars blinking back at him.

He calmly met their gaze and kept moving into the night.

Gloriah Jellylooloo

Gloriah
Jellylooloo

"Here we go, Little Looloo," whispered the bent-over lady as she tucked the wicker basket under the steps of the carnival wagon. "It's not quite like setting you adrift on the Nile, but hopefully, fate will have a similar purpose for you." She patted the small child lovingly with gloved hands, even though it was the dog days of summer.

"Don't dawdle, woman, or we'll get pinched here sure as the sun comes up this morning," the old man whisper-screamed under his breath. "We've made the decision, and now's the time to go. No turning back!"

Appearing to be a pair of homeless street people, invisible to most, they moved away into the lessening dark, leaving behind an unfolding mystery.

And there, amid the sights and smells of the traveling carnival, Gloriah Jellylooloo fell into the spin of the wheel of time.

No accompanying note explained why she was left behind. And since she was just a tiny thing, not even two years old yet, or so it appeared, she couldn't speak for herself.

As the cocks began crowing, Marissa the Mystical descended the narrow stairs of her wagon. Something stirred as she set foot on the last rung. Spying a basket big enough to hold a small loaf of bread and perhaps a bottle of wine, she thought, "Why, Alli left me a gift. He's so full of surprises." Alli, the Alligator Man, sported skin that looked like an alligator's hide.

"Alli, you old goat you! I see you've left me some nibbles," she yelled back into the half-open wagon door.

Sleepily sticking his head out, Alli replied, "Ha. Looks more like you've got a secret admirer. You know how to work the locals."

Marissa picked up the basket and carefully uncovered little Gloriah, who silently looked up with her moon-beam face. Then, she reached up her tiny hand to touch Marissa's face.

"Lord, there's a baby in this basket! And a cutie, too," she squealed.

After a moment, Marissa set the basket on the ground. Then, sitting on the steps, she stooped over to get a better look. Gloriah grabbed her finger, and at that moment, a memory from Marissa's childhood flew into focus.

It was her fifth birthday, and she was playing under the wagon, like most days. Birthdays weren't celebrated much at the carnival, but on this day, Papa came home with a puppy he found beside the road. He was a runt of a thing, but she loved him dearly at first blush. He licked her face, and she giggled wildly. "Papa, I love him. What should we call him?"

Quickly pulling her finger free, as if she'd been shocked, the memory faded even faster than it had landed. "Why was I remembering Clyde just now? He's long gone to doggie heaven," she thought. "Even my crystal ball and peyote tea couldn't conjure such a spell."

She knelt next to the basket. "This little gal will turn all the boys' heads before you know it," she proclaimed. Then, as Marissa had done earlier, Alli reached in, and Gloriah grabbed his finger.

Suddenly, Alli tumbled into a mirage.

"Please help! My son's in the house and can't get out!" his mother cried.

"Get back, ma'am, or you'll scorch yourself!" the fireman yelled.

"Mama, help me! I'm burning!" Alli screamed.

Jerking his hand back with a dreadful panic, he began frantically trying to put out the fire that had engulfed him as a young boy. He only realized he wasn't on fire after thrashing and rolling around in the dirt; it was just a terrifying memory.

"What the hell was that? I was back years ago in our house that burned, and I couldn't get out. It was so damned hot, and I was on fire! On fire, I tell you! My clothes burned clean off me. God a mighty, that's some unholy shit!" he declared, suddenly frightened of this small child.

Gloriah looked at the two, calm and collected. She had witnessed this kind of behavior countless times in the past, so this was nothing new.

Flashback Gullywashers

Little Gloriah Jellylooloo is what you might call a "memory catalyst." Recording and preserving her own memories—not happening. Recalling dreams of others—absolutely—through simple touch, as in the grab of a finger or nose. Even the briefest touch could stoke a memory, including yet-to-be memories. Moreover, because she had no memory bank of her own, she forgot to age. She may have looked the part of a toddler, but she would be way older—way, way older.

Back at the caravan, a sense of confusion reigned. What strange power does this child hold, and how did she end up here? And of more immediate concern, what would they do with her?

"Okay, so we both had these visions pop up when she touched us. Do you think that will happen again? I'd risk it since my memory was kinda nice," Marissa smiled.

"Are you sure? Next time you might not be so lucky," Alli answered.

"To look so tough, you sure are a wienie," Marissa said. "I'm doing it."

She peered back into the basket, and Gloriah grinned ever so slightly. It was the kind of grin that, if you were a nervous sort, would have put you on edge, but not so with Marissa. She slowly put out her finger, and without hesitation, Gloriah reached up and grabbed it.

"Get the animals out of here! Gather up all the horses before they run away!" screamed the ringmaster as the wind howled overhead. Suddenly the big-top tent disappeared with a roar; pelting rain and hail slashed across Marissa's terrified face. Lightning flashed, and thunder popped all around. It was absolute chaos as a tornado ripped across the prairie, taking anything and everything in its path.

Jerking her hand free, she cried out, "Christ almighty, I've never seen anything like that. We were in the Big Top, animals and all, doing the show the same as always, and a killer storm swept in out of nowhere and wiped us off the map, leaving nothing untouched. What I just experienced cannot be a memory. Surely to goodness, I'd remember that!"

A gentle cooing rose from the basket as Gloriah squirmed. Soon, the carnival sounds began to increase, breaking Alli and Marissa's focus.

"Well, let's just hide her in the wagon for now, and we can deal with whatever she is later," Alli said nervously. "She doesn't seem hungry or in need of any attention on her little backside."

Marissa nodded in agreement, "Okay. But what are we gonna call her? How 'bout 'Marilli?' It's a combination of Alli and Marissa."

So Marilli found herself born into another world filled with sights, sounds, and opportunities. How often has this happened to her before? She couldn't hazard a guess.

After their morning routine of checking on the animals and other carnies, Alli and Marissa returned to their wagon to trouble over circumstances. The basket was exactly as they had left it, and the child seemed totally at peace, not a whimper or wiggle. They began to piece together at least part of the mystery as they took stock of what had transpired that morning. The vivid memories or visions were triggered only when she made physical contact, like grabbing your finger. These memories belonged to whoever was touching her, but she, the baby, was not part of the trances she brought forth.

"Let's try something. Put on your long black gloves, let her grab your finger again, and see what happens," Alli suggested.

Marissa retrieved her gloves from the costume trunk and slipped them on, ensuring there were no holes or tears the baby might touch skin through. Then she hesitantly put her finger out for Gloriah to grab again, which she immediately obliged. Finally, with a slight jerk, more out of fear than response, she said, almost in tears, "Nothing's happening. I just feel her little hand squeezing my finger!" Relieved, she reached in with the other hand and started to tickle Marilli on the chin, causing her to cackle like a hen.

Alli quickly put on his work gloves and repeated the action, and much to his delight, experienced the same outcome. Now at least, they knew what was triggering the memories or visions. They were still clueless about why or how, but sorting that out could wait; they had more significant concerns. For example, what were they going to do with her?

"We'll keep her in here away from prying eyes until we can make a plan," Marissa whispered. "No need to kick up a ruckus when we have no idea what we've got on our hands."

"Agreed," Alli shrugged.

Thus became the new normal for Marissa and Alli, taking care of little Marilli on the sly, stealing bits of food and milk to feed her, keeping her quiet inside their wagon, with only a rare walk out in the open among the stars late at night.

Crystalizing the Past

Eventually, an idea came to Marissa she very much wanted to explore. She wondered if the visions in her crystal ball, little more than shadows swirling in a thick liquid, could be activated with the memories Marilli brought forth. So she built a shelf under the table for the little gal, concealing it with the tablecloth. Then, when the time was right, she'd reach down and let Marilli grab her finger while she worked the ball with her other hand. If things worked as she hoped, a brand new wrinkle would transform her usual show.

For his part, Alli was more than a little dubious. "What makes you think whatever she does when she touches us will work inside some stupid glass ball? The old lion licking your butt would sooner happen."

"Up yours, Alli. You're such a wiener. Where's your sense of adventure?" she taunted back.

She set the newly modified table up in the middle of the wagon and draped it with her most cosmic-looking cloth. Then she settled into her throne, dressed in full regalia, and adjusted the ball to be easily accessed with one hand as she reached under the table for Marilli with the other. Turning the kerosene lantern down as low as it would go, she made her space as dark as possible without it being a black hole. Then, feeling set and ready, she nervously reached up and awakened the crystal ball, causing the dark liquid to swirl. Apprehensively, she reached under the table and felt Marilli grab her finger.

Immediately the ball lit up as if a searchlight switched on. As the imagery settled, she and her mother, Shena, were running for their lives. She recognized this memory, which threw her into a panic.

The threat of fire was always a significant concern for folks working in the carnival. You had fire eaters and twirlers, cannons shooting off, fireworks, open braziers burning, and a dozen other ways things could go up in smoke. Add the fire of racial hatred some townies brought, and you had a recipe for disaster.

Marissa was what folks called a "high yellow." Her mom, one of the high-wire trapeze artists, was white, and her father, a behind-the-scenes laborer who helped put the big tents up and took care of all the workings of the carnival, was a gentle Black giant. They met when Shena joined the show on its way through Chicago. It didn't take long before they were madly in love, even though that was risky business. Marissa was born a little over a year after they met. Shena had long red hair and fair skin, while Abraham was ebony with wavy hair. Seeing the two of them together was not something most people overlooked, but if you were one of the many white supremacists of the time, Klansmen and the like, you were sure to take special notice.

And so it was that the Klan came calling as the carnival passed through a small midwest town. They had all seen or heard the news about Klan activities in the area, so they knew to look for trouble. What they didn't expect was that the local sheriff, whose duty was to "serve and protect," was a Klan leader in the area.

The carnival rolled into town and set up the big tents and sideshows. The sky was clear and bright, and there was excitement in town, as the carnival came only once a year. The sheriff arrived on his "courtesy call" to ensure everything was going okay when he noticed Shena and Abraham together with little Marissa. He mentally noted this disgusting scene and bid the carnies "good day."

That night the show was in full swing, with trapeze artists swinging to and fro, elephants and ponies doing tricks, and clowns clowning. The audience loved the energy, and everybody tumbled into a great time. Then, just as the ringmaster was about to announce the grand finale—a high dive off the trapeze tower into a shallow pool—Abraham came running into the tent screaming, "FIRE! FIRE! THE TENT'S ON FIRE!"

Absolute panic ensued as the crowd, animals, and performers all tried to exit at once. People trampled others underfoot, and the big tent, constructed of heavy canvas coated with rubber, went up in a blaze.

Amid the confusion, several of the sheriff's Klan associates caught Abraham, tackling him from behind and dragging him away. Shena and Marissa got out safely, but their wagon, which was parked next to the big tent, caught fire, and they lost everything except the clothes on their backs. All they could do was watch the fire burn, as the local fire department, whose chief was also in the Klan, was nowhere to be found. Later that night, on the outskirts of town, they found Abraham's body scorched through and through and hanging from a locust tree within eyesight of the leftover rubble.

"Momma, what are we going to do? Where's Ham?" cried Marissa.

Shena was so distraught all she could do was grab her and rock back and forth, "I don't know, baby, I don't know! We'll figure something out."

Marissa visibly shook as she pulled her hand from under the table and slumped back in her chair.

"Oh my God, that was horrendous," she sighed. "I haven't thought of that God-awful day in a long time. I could almost taste the smoke in the air. I could hear the animals crying out!"

Alli could tell she was shaken, far worse than he'd ever seen her, and he didn't know what to say. "Well, at least your thinking about the ball seemed to work. What now?"

"I don't know. I need to catch my breath," she said as she stripped off her cosmic costume and flew the wagon.

Alli pulled Marilli from under the table and gently put her back in the little crib. She gazed up at him as contented as possible, seeming to have no care in the world. He had never encountered anything like this, and the more they lived with her and tried to understand her power, the more unsure he became.

Tug of the Past

As she walked around the carnival, Marissa replayed what had happened in her mind. The memory transfer from Marilli to the ball seemed to work exactly as she had hoped. If anything, it was even more intense. Then, in a thoughtful walkabout, another idea popped into her mind when she saw several men pulling on a rope to erect one of the larger tents. She wondered: What if the memory transfer was like a rope or a chain made of multiple links? And what if the person at the rope's end winds up as the person with the memory? Hmmmm. That could work, she thought.

Climbing back into the wagon, she told Alli about the concept. He seemed skeptical, as always, but was willing to shuffle along to keep the peace. "We'll try it again, only this time you'll sit opposite me and the ball, like a paying customer, and Marilli and I will be in our places like before. I'll devise some mumbo-jumbo to convince the mark to put their hand on the ball since that's not how it's usually done. Shall we give it a go?"

"What's the worst that could happen? We'll see some more awful stuff, so it's pretty much like any other day," Alli surmised.

Marilli was carefully tucked back into her slot, and they took their places. Marissa didn't worry about dimming the lights this time, as what happened inside the ball was as vivid as real life. She put her hand on one side of the ball and asked Alli to put his opposite hand on the other. The gentle swirls started just like before—normal cloudy scenes. Then, Marissa reached under the table, and Gloriah took her finger. In a flash, the ball lit up with a cosmic strangeness.

"It's working! Tell me what you see," she urged.

"We're together at the carnival, watching the crowds stroll by. It's pretty quiet, with nothing much happening. I don't recognize where we are, so maybe this hasn't happened yet," Alli said.

Marissa chimed in, "I see the same thing. This is great! I hear the crowd in the Big Top cheering the elephants on as they do their tricks."

Then they both heard a big bang and a series of smaller charges, like an explosion, but muffled as if far away. The blasts emanated from the town's armory as if being blown to bits and wracked by fires.

Releasing Marilli's connection, Marissa exclaimed, "Oh my God! This is fantastic. It's a whole new show that no one has ever seen before. And the visions are so clear I don't even have to pretend. All I have to do is touch tips with little Marilli, and there you have it."

"Right you are, little lady," Allie chimed in. "Why, word'll spread like wildfire about the scenes you can stir up. We'll need to think on what to call this new thing—these aren't plain ol' fortunes, you know!"

"Yes, that's a thing to ponder for sure," she agreed.

Déjà vu Takes Another Turn

So, this what-cha-ma-call-it inter-spatial phenomenon is not the first time Gloriah found herself at the center of a cosmic loop of disbelief.

Once at a Catholic orphanage, the Sisters learned of her special gift. Feeling that God had delivered Mary (as they so named her) for some divine purpose, they put their faith in the almighty to try and see into the future. Several grabbed hands, forming a tight prayer circle with little Mary in the middle. The visions came to each chain member with similar details. Each found themselves in a small, darkened room with only one window and a single doorway. They sat on the floor in complete silence. Then, a man of indeterminate age and race entered the room and stood before the window. The light behind him seemed to grow in intensity as if the sun itself were moving closer.

"Fear not, sisters. I have come to release you from this world of pain and suffering," said the silhouetted figure. "Your faith has brought you thus far, and you will soon benefit from your many good works." The figure approached each sister and took her head in his hands. The light behind him was so intense they had to close their eyes. Then, filled with overwhelming joy, they began to cry as he shouted, "I release you from this mortal coil!"

At this exclamation, they broke hands, and the vision receded as quickly as it had arrived. Each assured the others they had witnessed some form of rapture, gasping for breath and crying together. Then, they all gathered around Mary, raising her little basket above them, and thanked God for this divine messenger.

Not two days later, their shared vision played out in cold-blooded reality. The sisters were indeed released from their lives of pain and suffering. The room they departed from was like the small room in the vision. But, unfortunately, their victory over death was not the rapture they had visualized, but rather, strangulation at the hands of a madman lunatic who recently escaped the mental clinic.

As she stared out the wagon door, Marissa said, "What if we called it "Mystic Travels–Journeys to the past and future?" Or maybe "Mystic Visions.""

Alli replied, "I like Visions better than Journeys, so go with that."

And so, Marissa the Mystic arrived, ready to introduce the new "Mystic Visions" show at their next stop. She had sorted out new commands for her customers, and the table was set and waiting. Marilli relaxed, quiet, and content in her hidden basket. Shena, who had retired from hi-wire acts after experiencing a near-fatal fall, stood as Marissa's carnival barker. She wore long flowing robes and a red turban, accentuating her flowing red hair.

A small crowd gathered outside the sideshow wagon, curious to hear more about rumors of unexplained magic. Shena noticed a man near the back of the group, looking at her as if he recognized her. To the best of her recollection, she had never seen this man before, and even if she had, he was one of the thousands of such faces to cross her gaze any given year. He was about to move along when Shena called out to him, "You, sir, there in the back with the fine Boss of the Plains hat; clearly, you are curious about what visions could lie in store. Come up, and Marissa the Mystic will open the curtains of time for you."

Rising to the challenge, the mystery man strolled through the crowd and entered the wagon, where Marissa waited. There was a small antechamber where the man stopped and waited, unsure how to proceed. He soon heard Marissa's voice through the curtain, "Please enter, oh curious wanderer, come see what visions await."

Entering the small, dimly lit room, he sat before the crystal ball and studied his surroundings. Long drapes created a cacoon of sorts around the table, focusing attention on the ball in the center of the table.

"Please put your right hand on the side of the crystal ball, and I will place mine on the other side. Doing so will allow us to join hands through the void of time," Marissa quietly commanded. She reached up and put her hand on the ball first, and the man followed suit. Then, grabbing Marissa's other hand, Marilli started the show.

"FIRE! FIRE! THE TENT'S ON FIRE!" The scene was from the horrific fire in her childhood! How could this be? Then the scene changed to pandemonium outside the tent, and the view was that of someone tracking 'Ham as he ran about trying to help people move away from the fire. Then, the man and a couple of others grabbed 'Ham, knocking him out with a sharp blow to the head.

"Now we got you, boy! We'll teach you to be messing with our white women," taunted the man.

Next, the scene jumped to the three men gathered around a tree with a noose hanging down. 'Ham was on his knees, badly beaten about the head and shoulders. He was shaking with rage, trying to scream through the gag in his mouth. "String him up there, and we'll send him straight to hell."

Marissa broke her connection to the ball and released Marilli's grip, quietly shaken. When she looked up and saw the man's evil smile, it was all she could do not to leap across the table at him.

Collecting herself, she said, "That was quite a dark vision. Sometimes the ball shows us things we imagine or things that haven't happened yet. It's sometimes hard to tell which is which."

"That's quite the trick you got there. Much obliged for the look-see," the man calmly said as he stood to leave. But, as he left the wagon, his footsteps seemed to echo menacingly in Marissa's mind.

"What in the living hell was that? I just saw Abraham beaten and hanged right before me," she screamed. "That man was there! He and his henchmen did it!"

Shena could hear yelling inside the wagon but couldn't understand it. When she went inside, Marissa told her all about the vision she had just witnessed. Then Shena recalled the man looking curiously at her before entering the wagon. He HAD recognized her from that time long ago, but she failed to recognize him.

She ran back outside to see which way the man had gone. She spotted him slowly walking toward the big tent, carefully surveying everything in his path as if he was sorting out another plan. Alli was getting ready for his show to start across the way when she frantically waved him over.

Marissa and Shena relayed the story as quickly as they could. The pain both had felt losing Abraham all those years ago flashed fresh as if it had just happened. They vowed this man would pay for his deeds. Alli would track him into town, and when the show was over, he and some other carnies would kidnap him and re-enact Abraham's murder down to the last cinder.

One thing white supremacists share is a false sense of security. Because their actions are so off-the-charts mean, they assume no one would ever be crazy enough to try and harm them. In their minds, they are invincible, and God is on their side. They conveniently forget that God is on all sides.

Tracking this piece of shit was easy for Alli, and he rather enjoyed beating the hell out of him before bringing him back to the carnival. No one has a greater appreciation than Alli for the pain fire can inflict, and he made it clear to the man that he would suffer greatly for what would feel like a very long time.

Shena, Marissa, Alli, and a couple of others dragged him across a nearby field where a lone locust tree stood. They threw a rope over a high branch and let it swing. Then, marking the spot, they created what could only be described as a funeral pyre, made up of branches gathered nearby and doused with kerosene. Finally, they tied the other end of the rope to a horse, which would pull the man above the fire when the time was right.

As the fire started, Shena preached, "Long ago, you took from me a man I loved dearly, and for no other reason than he was a Black man. You warned him about messing with your white women. You beat him to death and then burned him for added measure. And you felt righteous in doing all this. Well, your righteousness is at an end. An 'eye for an eye' is about payment coming due, which will now be collected."

Alli kicked the horse, dragging the man so he had to stand next to the fire. After a moment, his clothes caught fire, and he started screaming, trying to turn and run from the fire, but the rope would only allow him a single step before he began to choke. Once fully engulfed in flames, the horse slowly dragged him directly above the fire. His screams gradually gave way to the sound of his body burning.

Shena and Marissa held each other for a long while before turning away to head back to the carnival. No one said a word.

When they entered the wagon, Marilli looked up at them as if she knew what had happened. Shena spoke, "Lord, I know not how your will is done through this child, but I thank you for sending her to us. We shall be forever grateful to her and ever in your debt, as always."

The next day, Marissa and Alli talked about the previous night's events and decided the time had come to pass Marilli along to her next mission. They could no longer look at her without reliving that terrible vision again, even though that vision had brought them all a sense of peace regarding Abraham's death.

The carnival would depart the following day, so they decided to take her into town. Marilli seemed to understand what was happening. She made noises when they got near a particular bakery and started getting restless. Marissa took this as a sign they were at their destination. They settled on tucking her behind crates of empty milk bottles at the rear of the store.

"Thank you, my little Marilli. I don't know what the future holds for you or me, but I feel it will all work out okay. So bless you, and goodbye," Marissa whispered.

Marilli quieted down in her basket as she patiently waited on the next spin of the wheel of time.

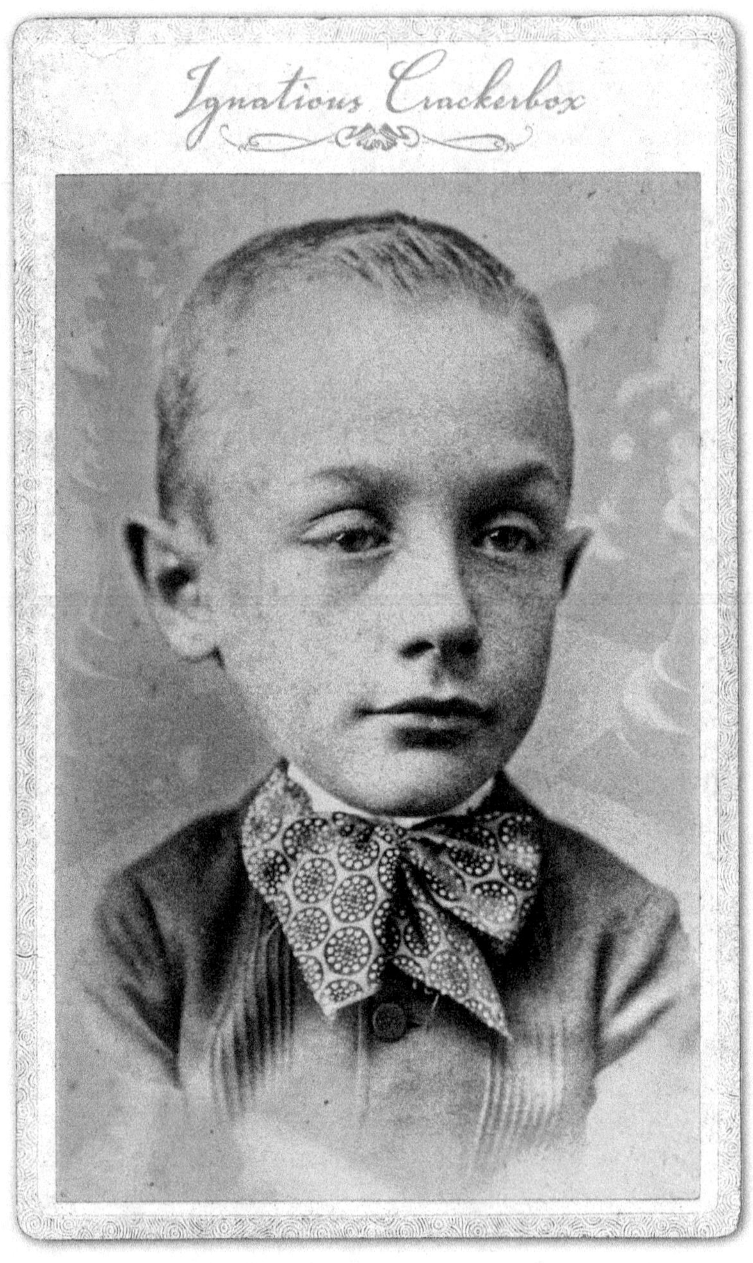
Ignatious Crackerbox

Ignatious Crackerbox

Ignatious' mother, Ethel, grew up on a ramshackle farm in the Southern Appalachian Mountains and had many Cherokee friends. She was petite, barely five feet in height. Many folks thought her shy when, truth be known, she was keenly observant. Unfortunately, fate did not bless her with what individuals around her deemed "common sense." How to care for a home, raise a family, and, most importantly, defer to her husband in ALL things. She was intelligent and self-reliant, quickly learning how to read, write, and do well in math. Because of this, many felt she was too smart for her own good, and all her "book learning" would translate to no man ever marrying her.

Ethel followed the belief, "Better to remain silent and thought a fool than to open one's mouth and remove all doubt." So, even when asked a direct question, she was slow to respond, just in case you meant to ask someone else the question, or after a brief reflection, you might want to rephrase your query. However, when she did respond, it usually caught folks off guard, as she was sly and intuitive, so much so that her Cherokee friends named her "Wa ha ya," Cherokee for fox.

However, Ignatius's father, Jed, was widely known as the town idiot, a world-class ignoramus, and the resultant son of a marriage of necessity. Typically when you hear the term "marriage of necessity," you think, "Uh-oh! He poked fun at her, and she took him seriously," but that was not the case in this instance. Instead, the necessity was that parents of both parties felt their offspring possessed few, if any, attributes in the "common sense" department. It was generally surmised that the limited prospects they did have would be determined by their respective parents.

While Pop was a known idiot, Mom had all the brains anyone could want, even if she was no homemaker. As he grew older, it appeared that Ignatius, in addition to his birth allotment, also picked up all the brains his father had left behind when he was born, as Ignatius was simply brilliant.

The debate over the origin of the Crackerbox name had raged for generations. Most think it was the product of the underactive imagination of an immigration official who assigned this name to Ignatius's Irish immigrant grandparents. Unfortunately, the official was so overworked he took his cue from Native Americans of the past and latched on to the first thing he saw as the couple entered his line. Seeing them, he called out their new name: "Crackerbox."

Ignatius grew up in the town's general store, where his father worked as a "stock boy"–his only job requirements boiling down to heavy lifting, following simple instructions, and staying out of trouble. Mr. Wright, the store owner, was a well-educated and kind-hearted soul who did his best to look out for Pops. So when Ignatius came along, he realized something special in the boy and became his surrogate grandfather, allowing him to play in the back office and read books from his library.

One day, Mr. Wright said, "Nate, it's time you learned how to play chess. I think you'll find it as challenging as crossing a big ol' mountain river in the spring."

Ignatius had read about people playing chess but had never seen a board or any of the various playing pieces. He knew it was a game of "strategy," but he wasn't exactly sure what that meant.

"I'd like that," he said. "You'll have to teach me how each piece moves around the board."

"That's the part I think you'll like most. Each piece is assigned a specific 'role' based on various European religious and political folks. So you have kings and queens, rooks, bishops, knights, and other characters," said Mr. Wright. "The board looks like a plain ol' checkerboard, so you should be familiar with that."

Ignatius listened quietly while Mr. Wright described each piece, their starting positions on the board, moves they could make, how they could be captured, and finally, how you won the game by yelling "checkmate" while capturing the other player's king. He intently absorbed every word and quickly got comfortable playing. Little did he know these lessons would affect the rest of his life.

Queen to Rook Five

Growing up and eventually working in the general store exposed Ignatius to all the people in town. With rare exceptions, everyone came into the store to buy something they critically needed at one time or another. Being a keen observer, he started noticing how different types of people reacted to other types, in his mind, much like pieces on the chess board. He saw how certain people of means looked down on and sometimes even took advantage of those less fortunate. He discovered what "hypocrite" meant as he witnessed so-called Christians being anything but charitable to specific individuals and businesses in town. All these bits and pieces of information formed a complex web in his mind, and after a bit of study, he began to see patterns emerge from which he could predict future behavior. These patterns begged the question, "Why did certain people feel they had the right to abuse others, and others turn a blind eye to the abuse?"

"Nate, I think I've created a monster. You can get me all tied up with just a few moves now," Mr. Wright said with a certain amount of pride. "It's like you know what I'm going to do even before I do it."

"Thank you for teaching me this game. If you look at it a certain way, it's much more than a game and more of a way of dealing with everyday life. I like to think of every person in town as a piece on a huge board. Some players have more power and influence than others, and so can move about more easily," Ignatius replied. "Don't you see it like that?"

Mr. Wright was stunned by such an observation, as Ignatius was only 13 years old. "Why no, Nate, I can't say I have, but now that you've put it to me like that, you're exactly right." He thought for a long moment and then said, "It seems to me there's another idea you might find fascinating, or at least challenging: politics. Do you know anything about politics?"

He thought for a few minutes and then replied, "I've seen 'Vote for Me' posters around town at different times, and I've heard these folks doing what they called 'stump speeches,' but I've never really considered it very much. So what's it all about?"

"Well, like chess, politicians use their connections to various groups, such as all the people you've keenly observed, and leverage these connections to win votes and, ultimately, an election," mused Mr. Wright. "They might be running for mayor or sheriff or some other office. These positions of power affect everyone's daily lives. Most politicians are wealthy and feel gaining an office is a way to remain so or, in some cases, create even more wealth. But some politicians have a wealth of morality instead and seek office to improve circumstances they feel are corrupt or unfair. It's all about seeking advantage."

"Have you ever wanted to be a politician?" Ignatius asked. "I think you'd be great at it. Your store is like the center of town, where people of all sorts drop in when they need to. Everyone trusts and respects you."

Mr. Wright smiled proudly at this and said, "I have thought about it, but the other thing you need to know about politics is how downright dirty and dangerous the practice can be. There's a phrase, 'Absolute power corrupts absolutely.' So let's say you're a governor or mayor with a strong support base with many people willing to follow your lead. If your ideals are beyond reproach, amazing things can happen. Everyone can prosper. But what if your intentions are less than good? That same power can make the lives of certain people challenging while others take unfair advantage. I've heard people say they were turned down for a loan to buy a piece of property for some petty reason, and then that piece of property was purchased by someone else who had inside information and took advantage."

Mr. Wright looked at Nate as he reflected on this information, feeling great pride as if he were his son. But, he thought, "This boy will be a force to reckon with one day. It remains to be seen what the nature of that force will be."

Picking up on the silence, he said, "There's another phrase you may have heard about political candidates called 'slinging mud.' The notion of 'Slinging mud' is when one candidate tells a whopper of a lie, or at best, a gross misinterpretation of the truth, about the other candidate, knowing full well that a specific type of voter will be disgusted or turned away by this information. 'He's a child molester! He's a carpet bagger from the North. He's not even from here.' Unfortunately, people tend to fall into camps with like-minded folks, and these camps can pick up on this language and rage, sometimes to deadly outcomes. Politicians have lost their lives because of lies others told about them."

Ignatius thought back over his brief life and saw how this new information had already influenced the arc of his development. From time to time, he remembered how folks belittled his father for his lack of intelligence, making his life hard. He saw his mother's reaction to events and how she managed to avoid peril through a combination of wit and pluck. Ethel reminded Nate repeatedly, "Remember what I say, son: better sometimes to remain silent and thought a fool than to open your mouth and remove all doubt. Tricksters use all kinds of words and deeds, especially religion, to trap and twist your thinking. So it's always best to pay attention to what people 'do' more than what they 'say.' Talk is cheap, but it can also be deadly."

As Nate matured, he began to add depth and understanding to the patterns he had seen emerging as a young boy. He saw how religious figures played various groups against one another, saying, "God is in our camp, and these others are just plain old 'heathens' not to be trusted." As if God had time to fritter away on such silly matters. He saw how bank owners coddled the rich and sometimes worked in the opposite regard for the poor. "I'd love to give you this loan, but the bank's policy requires a certain amount of collateral, so my hands are tied. Sorry." No argument could overcome the dreaded "bank's policy" roadblock.

Ignatious used his intellect and tenacity to gather information and get to the truth of whatever issue he faced. Then, armed with facts and reason, he devised strategies to get the desired change—with his mother and Mr. Wright sometimes acting as co-conspirators.

Growing into young manhood, Nate decided he would get involved with the weekly newspaper in town. He desired a job that allowed further investigation of some of the stories he heard about in the general store, particularly political dirty tricks. By now, his sense of what constituted fair play was well ingrained. And his ideas on how to deal with those who didn't play fair took on a bit more nuance.

Eyes on the Board

Being a reporter requires the creation of a network of informants that can be relied upon. The best informants are those whose businesses or connections give them access to a wide swath of the population, such as a laundry service, tavern, or diner. The people Nate identified as best connections were those most overlooked or ignored, such as the dishwasher collecting glasses in the bar or a hawker selling papers on the street. You'd be amazed what their ears could pick up just by being nearby—dirty business deals, romantic entrapments, general backstabbing, and occasionally, political dynamite. This network of informants fed a constant stream of grist into Nate's brain, and he connected many a dot, drawing lines this way and that.

Curiously, one of his best sources belonged to his youngest associate. Johnny Lee was ten years old and sold his penny papers all over town. Everyone knew the carrot-topped cyclist with his well-worn paper sack draped over his shoulder. There was no area in town, his town, that he didn't know like the back of his hand. And yet, while he was well known to all, he could also become invisible if he chose to. He had a sixth sense about situations; if he encountered something that got his "tingle" going, he could essentially fade into the background.

"You can't ever let this get back to me that I told you, so you gots to swear it on your mama's soul," Johnny Lee practically begged. "My third cousins, Zacho and Eddie, had a little run-in with the sheriff a while back. He caught them with a carload of bootleg whiskey, but he didn't arrest them. Oh no! Instead, he let them be, blackmailing them for half their take selling to Festus across town. So he has Festus and my cousins in his pocket, right where the rat bastard likes them."

Festus Sumter worked as a bartender at the local tavern and proved to be invaluable in his ability to be a fly on the wall.

Nate and Festus met in grammar school, became lifelong friends, and developed a good working relationship. While Nate excelled in school, Festus struggled mightily. Most of what he learned, which were tough lessons, came from the school of hard knocks. Nevertheless, Nate shared any information he felt might benefit Festus and acted as a big brother, keeping him out of trouble, which was a full-time job. Festus would, in turn, fill Nate's ears with news from whispered conversations and shady meetings that regularly occurred at the tavern. But, on the other hand, he didn't always share everything he knew–it was part of his natural distrust of others, even those he'd call close friends.

"Get those jars of moonshine packed up! Sheriff High Pockets is going to be here any second for his cut of the take, and I want his backstabbing ass out of here ASAP," yelled Zacho.

Eddie replied, "Yeah, he's such a fucking snake. I'd love to yank his head off and crap down the hole."

Sheriff High Pockets earned his name because he wore his pants with his beltline right under his boobs. He made Zacho and Eddie's acquaintance late one night when their moonshine-running Ford found itself half submerged in a ditch on the side of the road, resulting from a little too much aggression with the old gas pedal. The sheriff's shady reputation was known far and wide, so when the boys saw his blue lights come on, they knew they would be in for it.

"Well, it looks like you boys have got yourselves in a bit of a bind here. Whatcha haulin'?" asked Pockets with a heavily chewed toothpick sticking out of his cheek. "That wouldn't be moonshine, now would it?"

"Why no, officer, what makes you think that?" simpered Eddie.

Zacho added, "How would we be hauling moonshine? We don't know the first thing about stillin' and whatnot."

Pockets smiled that "Got yo' ass" smile of his. "Well, that's not what ol'

Festus down at the tavern says. And I'm feelin' if anyone in town knows who's runnin' bootleg liquor, it'd be him. Whatcha think?"

Eddie fumed, "That glass-polishing, bar-wiping shitbag! I knowed we couldn't trust his ass any further that we could throw him."

"Yeah, Festus is a crafty sort, but he might yet be of some help to you boys," Pockets replied as he walked over to their car. "You see, me and Festus have a little arrangement going. I let him sell moonshine under the table, and he gives me half the take. Works out perty fair."

"Half! So I suppose you see a similar deal happening here?" Zacho asked, giving High Pockets the stinkiest eye he could manage.

Pockets turned the figurative knife saying, "Seems only Christian of me since you boys are so blatantly breaking the law and all. Don't you feel I'm being charitable?"

"God damn you! Help us get this piece-of-shit car out the ditch then, and we'll all be on our way," Eddie replied, barely controlling his rage.

Just then, the radio chirped in his patrol car, and High Pockets said, "I'd love to help boys, but it seems I have other urgent business to attend to. So, ya'll be careful now."

It's funny how High Pockets foisted the Christian thing on Zacho and Eddie when a man of the cloth admonished the sheriff for his own transgressions, as Nate would soon discover.

Tithings for the Bishop

"And the Lord sayeth, 'Give as ye have so been given.' We'll now pass the collection plates," announced Reverend Raymond from the pulpit. The taking of tithes and offerings was his favorite part of the Sunday service, seeing all that hard-earned money coming his way. He would make sure to put it to excellent use.

High Pockets was one of the ushers on this particular Sunday, and as he gathered all the collection plates, he discretely slid a few bills off the top into his meaty fist. Then, finally, he bowed his head as if in prayer and carried the collections up to the Reverend. Returning to his seat, he felt mighty proud and self-righteous.

As the Sheriff was about to leave the church after the service, shaking hands with the preacher, Reverend Raymond asked if he could meet privately for a few minutes to discuss some church business.

"Certainly, preacher," he said. Pockets' internal alarm started tingling ever so slightly at this but seeing as he was dealing with a bible thumper, he ignored it.

The Reverend closed the door after they entered his office and proceeded to take off his long robe and vestments. "Thanks for agreeing to meet with me. When I saw you gathering the collection today, I thought, maybe we can do some business together, all for the church's good."

Pockets felt a chill run down his spine but kept his confident smile locked in place. "Well, Reverend, what type of business do you see us doing together? I'm already pretty tied up with the town's law and order, and surely you're not involved in that." He thought to use the universal fear of justice as his first move in this as-yet-unknown game.

"Oh no, I'm not involved in any nefarious activities beyond those of the members of my flock who call on me for guidance. But you, on the other hand, and I use that phrasing literally, have been up to no good. Starting a few months back, I noticed when you manage the collection of tithes and offerings, there's always a little sleight-of-hand action you do as if you're signing the cross over the plate," the Reverend explained. "Then it dawned on me what was happening. As you retrieve the plate at the end of each row, you quickly tidy up the offerings, arranging the more considerable paper money on top of the pile. Then, finally, just as you're handing it off, you perform your little shuffle, and a fair number of those bills follow your hand back into your suit jacket pocket. Pretty clever trick, I must say."

"Well, I suppose this is where I say something like, 'You got me there, Reverend,'" he smiled back as menacingly as possible. "Or, to use your language, 'let he who is without sin cast the first stone.'"

"Well, sheriff, I have no intention of turning you over to any legal authority, nor do I even mind if you continue with your method of religious practice. Oh no. We are all called to do the Lord's work in mysterious ways, and yours is no different, and indeed you are called by the Lord," preached the Reverend.

"And what form might this service to the Lord take?" he asked.

"Well, Mrs. Imogene Wayward called me into service regarding a house of ill repute on the outskirts of town. She claims they have young girls and boys out there doing the most despicable things imaginable. I suspect you know Imogene, and you know what a demanding, self-righteous sort she can be. So, I grabbed my Bible and visited them to see what I might learn," explained the Reverend.

On hearing this, the Sheriff perked up on his chair a bit, "I know the establishment you're speaking of. Lady Anne Marie is the 'curator' there. She has quite the range of 'personal services' for men and women of means."

"Oh yes, indeed she does," the preacher replied enthusiastically. "So I finish my call on the curator, and as I head out of the house, I hear a small voice call out my name. Turning, I see this young girl, a child really, in a pretty little dress. She's calling me to the back of the house as if she wants to show me something important. When I turn the corner, she drops down on her knees and, quicker than the last heartbeat, has my pecker in her mouth. She caught me so unawares I didn't know how to respond, although it wasn't long, a blink really, before the 'little head' took over my thinking, if you know what I mean. Just as my eyes roll back in my head, I hear a tap on the window and look up to see Lady Anne Marie smiling down at me."

Pockets chuckled at this. "Let me guess—you'd like me to call on Lady Anne Marie and put the fear of God, and the law, in her. Does that sum up our business dealings?"

"Thy will be done," replied the good Reverend.

Leaving the church with his new calling, Pockets felt this might all work out for the better. He and Lady Anne Marie were already well acquainted, so keeping her lips sealed on the Reverend would not be a problem. However, they'd have to sort out how to deal with the self-righteous Imogene Wayward and put her in a box.

Pawn Takes Pawn Takes Pawn

Imogene was recently widowed when her wealthy banker husband died unexpectantly of a heart attack at his office. There had been a hint of suspicion around his death. Finally, however, an autopsy showed his heart just let go for some reason.

This heart-stopping stressor was none other than Lady Anne Marie, newly arrived in town and calling on the bank for financing. Lacking collateral in the typical sense, she offered herself as having sufficient value for the loans she sought. Mr. Wayward, true to his name, allowed that, indeed, her "personal assets" would suffice. They agreed to meet the next day to finalize the details, and afterward, Lady Anne Marie would get her money. After a quick lunch at the tavern, the two crossed the street to the inn, where they finalized their business.

"Mr. Wayward, I can't tell you how much I appreciate you seeing me like this. You've been so accommodating in my time of need," she purred as she pulled off her elbow-length gloves, dropping them to the floor. Other garments, designed to quicken the pulse and loosen inhibitions, quickly followed suit as the banker watched in rapt attention.

The banker hadn't seen Imogene naked in years and had never seen a creature as perfect as Lady Anne Marie. "Why you're most welcome, my lady. Glad we could come to satisfactory terms."

With that, Lady Anne Marie laid back on the bed and beckoned him to come over and start putting a valuation on her considerable assets. It's a curious irony that as one particular type of flesh hardens, all others weaken.

All this activity was visible through the peephole the sheriff had drilled right through the eyes of a painting that hung directly over the bed. He silently watched as she led the unsuspecting banker to the slaughter. It was over in a matter of seconds. Just as the banker began his assessment, he fainted dead away, landing his considerable bulk on top of the curator. Then, in a panic, Lady Anne Marie rolled him off, freeing herself. She jumped up and rapped on the wall screaming for the sheriff to come and help her get him back up.

Yelling as he burst through the door, "What in God's name did you do to him? Is he dead?"

Nervously she replied, "I don't think so. We were just about to get happy with it, and he just keeled over. He didn't even have his little pencil pulled out yet."

"Help me get him back to the chair," Pockets exclaimed as he tried to wrestle the big man off the bed. "Check his pockets, put his shirt and tie back on, and I'll get his shoes."

When they finished putting him back together, Mr. Wayward started coming around. But he panicked when he saw the Sheriff and asked what was happening.

"Well, you and Lady Anne Marie were about to conduct a little business when you had a bit of a scare with your ticker. Luckily I was nearby when she called for help," the sheriff replied with his best poker face.

"Yes, yes. We were about to discuss a bank loan after having a wonderful meal. I guess my indigestion must have acted up, so I ended up here," the banker said, trying to regroup.

Then the sheriff looked at the banker with his most sinister eyes, "I'm not sure that's what happened here. You see, Lady Anne Marie and I have a little business venture on the side, and I know you were here under some pretext about a bank loan. Only now, the remaining question isn't about the loan, but what to do about you."

Mr. Wayward broke out in a sweat and started moaning and groaning as his head slumped down on his chest. Eventually, he looked up and said, "Alright, alright, alright! You'll get your money if none of this ever leaks out. You've got to swear it to me on whatever passes for holy within you."

"Done and done," they said in unison. "Nice doing business with you."

When he returned to the bank, he had several messages from his wife.

11:45 a.m.: The first message read, "Your wife stopped by for a surprise visit hoping to go out for lunch. I informed her you were already at lunch with a new client. Imogene thought she knew where you might be and decided to try surprising you there."

1:00 p.m.: The second message read, "Wife called, sounded very upset. Please call ASAP."

Mr. Wayward exclaimed to himself, "Oh shit! Oh shit! Oh shit! Did she see me with that woman at the restaurant? Or later? Oh God, this is so bad. This is not good!" Gathering himself, he got up and closed his office door for privacy. He started feeling severe pain in his chest and decided he better take two of his nitroglycerine pills to calm things down a bit. Unfortunately, he didn't know that the sheriff and Lady Anne Marie had force-fed him two pills earlier to get him on his feet again. After a few minutes, he felt better and decided to face whatever was brewing with his wife. He poured himself a glass of water, picked up the phone, and paged his secretary. "Can you get my wife on the phone, please?"

Letting it ring twice, he picked up, "Hello, Sweetie! I got a message that you dropped by for a surprise visit. I'm so sorry I missed you. I would much rather have had lunch with you than with a new client. Business lunches can be so tedious."

He could hear Imogene breathing loudly on the other end. This type of sound was usual with her, as she was a world-class mouth breather. "Yes, I saw just how tedious spending time with a new client can be for you, you poor thing. The way she practically draped herself over your person, laughing like a drunken hen strutting around a randy rooster. But you were quite a good little soldier, making her feel like she was the only gal at the dance! A real officer and a gentleman!"

Imogene had a habit of closing her eyes when she spoke, which was unsettling if you were talking with her in person. It seemed she used a sort of echolocation to establish where you were seated or standing, like a bat flitting around the backyard, bouncing chirps off bugs. Luckily the phone alleviated that problem.

Then, feeling his chest tighten again, Mr. Wayward responded quietly, "Imogene, darling... I'm not sure what you think you saw, but I assure you my intentions towards Lady Anne Marie are above board. I can't not meet with her just because she's friendly or flirtatious. It can be tough, but somebody from the bank has to do it."

Mr. Wayward could practically hear her eyes slamming shut as she screamed into the phone, "How can you sit there and give me a load of crap like that? So unbelievable! And I suppose that little elevator ride upstairs at the inn was so you could claim your just rewards for a job well done."

At this, his heart started misbehaving as if it had lost all sense of beat and rhythm. It couldn't decide between bossa nova and bebop. Then, the music stopped altogether, and Mr. Wayward slumped over his desk. Imogene continued to scream into the phone for a bit and then hung up in a rage, thinking he had simply walked away from her. It wasn't long before his secretary realized something was wrong when she noticed his phone light was still on with everything in the office quiet.

The next day, news spread that Mr. Wayward had died of a heart attack at his desk at the bank. Festus remembered seeing the banker and a fetching lady having lunch at the tavern. He seemed fine then and wondered if there wasn't some sort of foul play afoot. Just as this thought popped into his mind, Ignatius popped into a seat in front of him.

"Hey, man! How's it going? What's the news on the street?" he asked.

"Well, I'm sure you've heard about Mr. Wayward keeling over at the bank. But, the funny thing is, he seemed perfectly fine when he left here yesterday after lunch. He was wining and dining some pretty young thing, laughing and carrying on like there was more to come if you follow me," Festus confided. "They crossed the street to the hotel together and went inside. The curious thing is, not 15 minutes later; I saw the lady and the sheriff leaving together, looking every which way before quickly strolling away. And another five minutes later, here comes Mr. Banker, looking like he'd been steamrolled or something."

Ignatius pulled out his pocket notebook and quickly took a few notes. "You don't say. What can you tell me about the sheriff? I've always felt there's a fine line between being a criminal and being a lawman. Which side of the line does he land on most often?"

"Nate, nothing gets past you, does it?" Festus laughed. "He's been known to bend the law to his benefit. I hear someone caught him with his hand in the till, though, and is using that information to keep some other unsavory business from flapping ears."

"Well, that explains a little about the call I got this morning from Imogene Wayward, Mr. Banker's newly minted widow. She asked me to come over to her house, that she had some information I might find interesting," Nate responded. "I'm headed there as soon as I leave here."

Festus leaned in, "Be careful out there, Nate. The streets have ears all over the place. I'd hate to see something bad happen to you because of this."

"Thanks, Festus. You take care as well," he said as he rose to leave.

Knight to Queen Four

This conversation left Nate feeling somewhat uncomfortable. He always liked Festus and thought he could trust the information he provided. But he couldn't shake the feeling there was more going on between him and the sheriff, more than he'd let on. Imogene greeted Ignatius at the door and shuffled him through the house filled with well-wishers of every stripe. She was the epitome of the matronly widow, showing little outward emotion regarding her current predicament, dressed in black from head to toe. Following her quietly as she tottered ahead, they entered her study, and she closed the door.

Nate began, "Mrs. Wayward, I'm so sorry for your loss. The suddenness of your husband's death must be devastating."

Imogene closed her eyes for a long moment, and Nate thought she was trying to think of what to say. Then, just as he was about to speak again, she broke in, with her eyes still closed tight, "Thank you, Ignatius. Yes, the suddenness and the situation were very much a shock." She wiped briefly at her nose with her handkerchief and continued, "His heart had been giving him trouble for a while, but his medications seemed to make everything better. So when the doctor said he had died of a heart attack, I couldn't believe it. And when I saw him leaving the restaurant yesterday with that woman, he seemed perfectly fine. Better than fine. Giddy like a schoolboy."

"That woman, you say? Do you know who she is?" Nate asked. "Maybe she can shed some light on what happened to him."

With eyes closed tight and heavy mouth-breathing, Imogene began talking in a low rumble, "Oh, I'm sure she could add all sorts of details to the story! I asked around and learned she's the curator at the new gentlemen's club on the outskirts of town. Curator! Is that what they call it these days? I spoke with the sheriff about her, and he said he would talk with her. But he was quick to add, in his opinion, there didn't seem to be any connections between Mr. Wayward and her. That's why I called you. I've also contacted the preacher to ask his help in talking with this woman."

Nate calmly looked at Imogene and said, "Thank you, Mrs. Wayward, for reaching out to me. I'll do some digging and see what I can learn. But, again, I'm so sorry for your loss," as he stood to go. "I'll see myself out."

Back on the street, his mind saw critical moves on the giant chess board. His instincts told him something was off with the sheriff's quick dismissal of the curator. Trusting his instincts, he felt there was a connection, probably more than one. Sadly, his friend Festus was now another unknown quantity. These connections had to be followed to see where they might lead. He had to check in on his network. And he felt he should run these clues past his Mom and Mr. Wright to gauge their input.

So, it was no surprise that Johnny Lee had information on the curator. He had seen her with the banker at lunch. And a little later, with the sheriff coming out of the hotel. The day before, he had seen the preacher leaving the brothel after meeting with the curator. Ignatius was flabbergasted when he shared that he saw his young girl friend engaged in with the preacher.

"Have you ever spied the preacher and the sheriff meeting? It feels like there's a connection there," Nate said.

Looking around to see if anyone was spying on them, Johnny Lee answered, "The only meeting I heard about was at the church. Of course, everyone with eyes in their head knows the sheriff's been taking money out of the collection plate. But he's the sheriff, so what are you gonna do?" He paused briefly, connecting the series of events, and then added, "Maybe the visit to the curator gave the Reverend Wright a reason to confront the sheriff about his sticky fingers. And he's blackmailing the sheriff to keep the curator in her place."

At the general store, Nate sat down with his Mom and Mr. Wright, shared all the clues he'd gathered, and asked what they felt. Mr. Wright thought quietly for a few minutes, moving various pieces around in his mind, and then responded, "It seems to me that the sheriff is the center of this whole game. His well-known but generally unchecked criminality regarding the church collections ties him to the preacher and vice versa. Moreover, his status as a lawman makes him the logical person to check out someone like the curator. And being someone who operates on the fringe of legality, the curator would instantly recognize someone she might manipulate in the sheriff, and he, likewise. Then there's Festus. He's in a position to see and overhear a great deal standing behind the bar, but I feel there's more to it than that. He somehow has a connection to the sheriff. We don't know what that is yet."

Nate's Mom picked up the thread, "It seems like the common root is money going to the sheriff. He's been openly stealing from the church but goes unchecked because of who he is. The preacher finds himself in a pickle with the curator. So he squeezes the sheriff to intervene on his behalf. The curator, looking to stay on the right side of the law, pays the sheriff to look the other way, and he gladly obliges. Not only that, but she also literally has the preacher by the short and curlies, which gives the sheriff even more leverage. You know, God rest his soul, the poor banker was collateral damage caught up in a bank loan to the curator. The sighting of the curator leaving with the sheriff at the hotel screams foul play. You're right about Festus. But think about it, what role does Festus play that the sheriff could use? Selling bootleg liquor on the take? It wouldn't be the first time something like that's happened."

Ignatius and Mr. Wright looked at her in amazement. Then, finally, she cracked a smile ever so slightly.

Surrounding the King

Nate followed, "The funeral will be tomorrow, and all these players will probably be there, either out of respect or to cover themselves. So I want to watch each of them closely for any tell-tale signs that might be useful. But first, I'll follow up with Johnny Lee and see if he can shed any light on the Festus/sheriff connection. Then we'll see what our next moves are."

Ignatius also considered adding new players to the board, mainly the FBI. If the sheriff were corrupt, which seemed a distinct possibility, he'd need the FBI to help him sort things out.

"You can't never let this get back to me that I told you, so you gots to swear it on your Mama's soul," Johnny Lee begged. "My third cousins, Zacho and Eddie, had a little run-in with the sheriff a while back. He caught them with a carload of bootleg whiskey, but he didn't arrest them. Oh no. Instead, he let them be, blackmailin' them for half their take selling to Festus in town. So he has Festus and my cousins in his pocket, right where the rat bastard likes them."

Suddenly the chessboard got very active. All the pieces were moving, headed toward "Checkmate," but for the moment, more like "Check." He called his contact at the FBI office and shared his research with a field officer, responding to various questions as he went. He was cautious with his information regarding Festus and wondered if perhaps he could be approached in some manner to help entrap the sheriff. The FBI was keenly aware of corruption within law enforcement and moved to root it out wherever it popped up. Finally, the officer thanked Ignatius for the tip and agreed to be present at the funeral service as an extra pair of eyes.

"Mr. Wayward was a pillar of our community, actively involved in almost every aspect of the town's business. He was an alderman, a devout

Christian, and a loving husband. His passion for this community and its welfare will be sorely missed. He leaves behind a loving wife, Imogene, a life-long partner and friend," Reverend Raymond eulogized. These words hit the ears of each suspect a little differently. Their reactions ranged from downward glances to subtle yet sinister smiles, each response matching their connection to the banker and the preacher.

After the graveside service, the crowd departed. The FBI officer trailed the sheriff but also had other officers track the curator and Festus in hopes that one or more clandestine meetings would soon occur. So it was with little surprise that the sheriff turned up at the curator's door only an hour later. A short time later, he left and returned to the church to check in on the preacher. When he departed this meeting, both left the church simultaneously. The preacher looked a little preoccupied, and the officer felt the banker's service was not the source of anxiety. Finally, the sheriff returned to the tavern and checked in with Festus.

Earlier that morning, the FBI officer had interviewed Festus, confronting him with Nate's information. He folded like a house of cards and practically begged the officer to help him. "Hell man, he's the sheriff! How am I not going to do what he wants me to do? Answer me that."

While the lead officer questioned Festus, other officers did the same with the preacher and the curator. Each player was more than accommodating when ratting on the sheriff seemed the best way out of trouble.

"Barkeep, I'll have a branch and a bourbon, please. It's been a hell of a day," the sheriff said. "Better yet, make that a house special."

"One 'house special' coming up," Festus crooned. The sheriff called the 'house special' his ill-gotten, illegally sold bootleg whiskey, courtesy of Zacho and Eddie. Festus had told the FBI officer about this arrangement, so when the order rang out, the FBI officer took notice and slowly approached the sheriff, asking about the special drink.

Caught off guard by the stranger's sudden appearance, he did a quick character appraisal and regained his footing, "Oh, it's just a local concoction Festus here serves exclusively. An acquired taste. Here my friend, let me get you one."

The officer started compiling a long mental list with his drink in hand. He chatted with the sheriff about this and that and the other to avoid raising any alarm bells. Later, he would regroup with his officers and formulate a plan heading toward Checkmate.

Ignatius followed all the FBI surveillance with his team, including Johnny Lee, Mr. Wright, and his Mom. He rightly felt the officers would not share their plans with him until they were a done deal. So, he watched and waited. His wait was not long.

The next day, the lead FBI officer arrived at the police station with a warrant for the sheriff's arrest, citing several corruption schemes, each having reliable testimony from the affected parties. The curator was also questioned but not charged regarding the banker's death. Reverend Raymond was relieved that his actions with the sheriff were not criminal. Unsavory, yes. Criminal, no. Festus was not charged for his part as he was now considered a government informant. His cousins, however, were not so lucky, as the FBI made a criminal referral to the local revenuers.

Game Over

"Checkmate!" exclaimed Ignatius when he heard the news. He ran to share the good word with Mr. Wright and his Mom, who were incredibly proud of their collective work.

Mr. Wright said, "Nate, I must commend you for your vision and tenacity in this real-life chess match. Your ability to unwind all the various plots was a boon to the FBI. They could not have done it without you. They would never have known about this if not for you. I could not be more proud."

"Thank you, Mr. Wright," Nate responded. "I followed Mom's lifelong rule of being quiet and thought a fool. What I learned is you can never underestimate another person's ability to underestimate you."

Ethela Oregard

Ethela Oregard

"No, no, no, no! This simply won't do. You can't succeed at this unless you EXCEED! I want more. I NEED more!" Ethela said emphatically as she viewed herself in the hairdresser's mirror. "It should feel more architectural, more constructed. Not just twirled, piled on top, and capped with a pretty bow."

Rolling her eyes, the hairdresser began deconstructing what she had just spent 45 minutes creating, then said, "I'm not sure you have enough hair to get the look you're after. We might need to add some extensions. Are you okay with that?"

Ethela responded, somewhat irritated, "When the French built Notre Dame Cathedral, do you think they stopped when they first ran out of stone? No! They got more stone. And more of whatever else they ran out of until they achieved EXACTLY what they were after. Perfection! Of course, I'm fine with adding extensions. That's what they were created for, isn't it?"

"Well, I don't have any of those on hand right now, so we'll have to make another appointment. Sorry," the hairdresser said, hopeful she could finally move Ethela out of her chair.

Exasperated, Ethela said, "Very well then. Put my hair back in a simple French, fishtail, English, and Dutch braid combination."

Dropping her chin in absolute defeat, the hairdresser started braiding her hair in a "simple braid" (which would easily take another 30 minutes).

When in Question, More

Ethela Oregarde approached her beauty regimen much like an architect, and a Victorian architect at that. The more decorated and adorned the fashion piece, whatever it might be, the better. She felt flying buttresses were an excellent way to gather up twirls of long hair and pile them ever skyward, elongating the face and producing creative, unique silhouettes. Makeup application was akin to using French plaster. It had to be, at once, generous and measured. You weren't covering up some perceived flaw. No, you were developing texture and drama. So what if the plaster occasionally cracked and fell away, like an old building? That provided even more character and interest. Fragrances were another field of fascination. But rather than thinking of smells as a singular experience, such as vanilla or citrus-based perfumes, she approached them more as a winemaker, creating an aromatic "Meritage" from various, often quite different smells. While some thought these combinations bordered on smelling rancid, she preferred to think of them as "complex." Fashionwear was, of course, her raison d'être. If two buttons were adequate, surely a dozen would be even more fabulous. The more volume she could create using frills, shoulder pads, and layers, the better. Mixing patterns like stripes and plaids, while tricky even for her, could prove interesting. She was all about MORE! And MORE! And her use of found objects was second to none.

ANYTHING could be used to create something unique. Serendipity was her muse and constant companion.

Her perch behind the makeup counter at the local department store offered her a steady stream of customers for critique and closer study. As she saw a customer crossing the store, she thought, "What did she see before she walked out of the house today wearing that assembled garb? Clearly, she doesn't own a mirror. The blouse, skirt, and shoes can't ALL be in the same color family. You must have variety. Contrast. Shock!"

Suddenly, a customer from the opposite side of her counter called out, "Excuse me, I'd like your recommendation, please, on which lipstick goes best with my complexion."

"Of course. Which shade are you thinking of?" Ethela asked.

"Well, I've been told I have a "winter" complexion, so something that will accentuate that."

Ethela thought to herself, "Oh my god! Another seasonal complexion analogy. "I'm a winter." No, you are not a season! Your complexion is not defined by the tilt of Earth's axis!" She thought a moment and said, "I think this chartreuse shade will accentuate your pale complexion and make your auburn hair glow. Here, let's try it."

The customer looked at her, very baffled by this recommendation, yet found herself surrendering her lips for application. "Oh! Okay?!"

Ethela applied a most generous coating, first on the lower lip, then the upper. Then, she asked the customer to roll her lips together to help smooth out the color, only to have it coat her upper teeth. Oh well. Poor thing.

Holding a mirror for the customer to gaze into, she said, "Look at that transformation! Amazing! What do you think?"

The customer gasped in shock and quickly started wiping away the day-glow green smear on her face. Her surprise was so deep and complete that she couldn't form words. Instead, she ran away as fast as her "smart shoes," as Ethela called them, would carry her.

Nonplussed, she returned to her observations from behind the counter. One day, she would break out of this forced servitude to mediocrity and launch her own makeup line, forever changing the world's view of fashion. The fashionistas wouldn't know what hit them. And makeup would be just the underpinning of an empire. She would leave no creative sector unruffled.

As the clock approached 9 p.m., time for the store to close, she hoped no one else would ask her for assistance. She had important work waiting to be captured in her ubiquitous sketchbook at home. Over the years, her sketchbooks had clustered together the brunt of her wild stabbings at design, documenting them for some distant film. Maybe the current chapter would be entitled "Early Musings" or "In the Beginning..."

Finally, the announcer's voice came over the loudspeakers and said, "Attention shoppers: the store is closing. Please take any purchases you wish to make to checkout now. We will reopen at 10:00 a.m. tomorrow. Good night." Ethela closed the glass doors of the lipstick cabinet, locked up her counter, and turned off the makeup lights next to the mirrors. Another day down, another day closer to the dawn of her empire.

Another Man's Trash

She always enjoyed making her way home to her fifth-floor walk-up apartment. It gave her time to clear out the detritus of the day, the garbage of dealing with customers who were all by and large absolute morons in terms of fashion. A purge was needed so she could approach her current sketchbook with a fresh mind and work up her latest inspirations.

For example, she had the brilliant idea to create a veil covered with silver and gold sequins. (Forget that you can't see through sequins. It's not the looking out that's important; it's the gaze that's gathered in.) The piece would be part of an elaborate hat featuring a one-of-a-kind combination of turkey feathers and metal machine turnings she found quite by accident at a local machine shop. The metal spirals were a by-product of large holes being drilled in thick metal plates. They fascinated her. And when she asked the drill operator if she might help herself to some of these fabulous twizzles, he flipped his protective face shield up, looked at her, looked at the turnings all over his shop floor, and said blankly, "Sure. Why not?"

Overjoyed, Ethela exclaimed, "Thank you so much. These will be a great addition to my latest haberdashery. By the way, where did you get that sporty face mask?"

Sensing he had made a mistake by entering into a conversation with this person, he quickly said, "Hardware store. Look, lady, I got stuff to do here, so help yourself."

She quickly gathered a generous amount of metal turnings in a bag and scurried away as if she had won the lottery, thinking, "What a fabulous find. I'm stunned that no one has ever considered using these materials as fashion accessories. But then again, I really shouldn't be surprised. People are so provincial and dull. Where's the drama?"

Back in her apartment, she separated the turnings into piles, from large to small, and now she noticed various metals. Wonderful! Some were brass colored, while some were shiny like steel. She also quickly discovered they were very sharp, cutting her tender fingers deeply when she mistakenly tried to straighten one out. "Ouch! Didn't see that happening. Oh my, now I'm bleeding all over everything! The things we must endure for the sake of art."

After she cleaned and bandaged her fingers, she started thinking about the veil part of the design. "That flip-up mask thingie the worker wore might be the perfect platform for my veil idea. Maybe I could incorporate it into the design. Instead of sewing each sequin to a traditional veil, which is very time-consuming and SO pedestrian, I could use glue and stick each one to the mask. Much quicker and less chance of gouging myself with that infernal needle again."

She planned on popping into the hardware store on her way to work. Who knows what other creative gems she might uncover there?

In her bed-chamber, as she liked to refer to it, she turned on her small lamp, which featured a one-of-a-kind shade made out of linguine noodles and scallop shells. Not long ago, the old shade's fabric had rotted away, revealing the wire frame. In a flash of what can only be called serendipitous brilliance while cooking noodles one night, she threw one of them toward the wall knowing that if it stuck, dinner was done. Fortunately, she missed the wall and the noodle wrapped around the upper and lower wire sections of the shade she had left disassembled on the kitchen table. Seeing this, she thought, "News flash! Linguine can also be used to make lampshades!" She drained the noodles in the sink, dried them on a towel, then wrapped each carefully around the wire armature. Next, she rimmed the bottom and top edges of the shade with small pasta shells, adding a break line in the wobbly linearity of her design. Another unexpected benefit occurred when she turned the completed lamp on for the first time. As the tiny bulb heated up the noodles, the air filled with the smells of freshly made pasta. Yum!

Changing out of her work clothes, she opened the closet and pulled out her favorite nightgown. This was another creation or her own design with a genesis equal to that of the linguine lampshade.

As she watched an associate struggling to put stockings onto a store mannequin one afternoon, stretching and pulling and eventually creating a giant run down the leg, Ethela thought how fabulous it would be to have an entire suit that wrapped itself snuggly around her body like that. So she approached the associate and asked what she was going to do with the damaged articles, of which, she noticed, there was quite a pile growing. "You want them; they're yours. They'll just end up in the trash otherwise."

Etehla gasped, "Trash! Absolutely not. I'll take all you have, please."

The associate said, "There's more in the stock room. Follow me." They headed to the rear of the store, an area Ethela had never visited before. She was amazed at all the boxes, pallets, and racks of everything. It was like walking through a giant candy store but better. "Here we go. Anything that gets damaged in the store ends up here. As you can see, there's no telling what you might find. You just have to be willing to dig through all this junk." There were several large baskets on wheels, each stuffed to overflowing.

Ethela thought to herself, "Junk? Junk! Are you kidding me? This is better than finding King Tut's tomb. Look at all this treasure, and it's mine for the taking." She said, "Thank you very much. I'll stop by before my shift starts tomorrow and go through everything. I'm so excited!"

The associate gave her two thumbs up, turned, and left without a word.

So, Ethela took several of these stockings, cut them apart into various artfully inspired shapes-chevrons, triangles, squares, and circles–pinned them one to the other, using her body as a form, and eventually stitched them together with dental floss, which she got FOR FREE from her dentist each visit. Then, she used one of the plus-plus size units she found, quite by accident, to create the collar. The armholes were fashioned from the children's hose, which she found in a striking red and white stripe. They fit around her slender arms perfectly.

When she slipped into the full-body stocking for the first time, she noticed just how sheer the materials were. She could clearly see her nipples and underwear. Provocative! It fit her quite snugly, and the effect was like being hugged tightly all over, creating a fantastic sense of calm. The only calamity she encountered was when she visited the toilet at night. Pulling the hose up so she could sit proved quite challenging, but after a few minutes, she was successful. Note to self: add time to bathroom breaks.

Punching Things Up

The weekends were Ethela's favorite time to seek inspiration for her next project. First, she'd scour the flea markets, taking particular interest in things others viewed as trash. The crinkled kraft paper a vendor might have used to wrap an oriental rug or a knocked-together crate made from paint sticks, complete with various paint colors. While not beautiful to most eyes and not inherently handsome even to Ethela, these things still had an underlying character she found attractive. Her task was to pull out the buried beauty, using all her creative abilities.

As she was crossing the park heading towards the large fountains, she noticed a photographer was working with a model. The model was dressed, if you could call it that, in the most bazaar outfit. It looked like she had simply been rolled up in tin foil, exposing certain provocative areas and barely covering others. Her hair had been colored silver to match, and her skin was also painted. As a result, she sparkled in the bright sunlight.

The photographer wore what appeared to be an equestrian riding outfit with a scarlet cape draped around her shoulders and a black beret. She barked orders to several assistants holding up large whiteboards that reflected the sun back towards the model, filling shadows with soft light. "No, no, no! I need more light on her midsection, not her face. You're blinding her with the reflections."

Ethela watched as the model and assistants tried to execute whatever the photographer saw. Then, she thought, "I know what she's trying to capture, but she needs something else. Her silver tone was too close to that of the water sparkling behind her. I know! She must hold her red cape high like a flag." She looked around her and spotted a long pole that could be fashioned into a flagpole for the model. Then, she approached the photographer, who had poked her head under a black drape covering the back of the camera.

"Excuse me, ma'am. Excuse me!" Ethela shouted, trying to capture her attention.

The assistants looked at her like she was on fire. How dare she speak to the photographer! Did she not know who this was?

Throwing the drape off her head and shoulders, the photographer looked around, irritated, to see who was shouting at her. "Who are you, and WHAT do you want? Can't you see I'm busy creating here?"

Ethela surged forward, oblivious to her bluster, and said, "I can see that you are creating here, and I am excited about what you are trying to capture. But, if I might suggest, you need a bold something to shock the rest of the color palette into shape. Something like the red cape you're wearing as a flag, waving back and forth over the model's head."

The assistants were aghast! This complete stranger, clearly an imbecile, dared to make a creative suggestion. To her! What is happening?

The photographer was so taken aback by this intrusion that she could hardly speak. But as she gathered her anger and was about to torch Ethela's ears, her brain evaluated the concept she had proposed and whispered, "You know, she has a good idea there. Check it out."

"You... red... what... flag... what! Wait. I see it! Yes, let's do that," the photographer stuttered and embraced Ethela's idea, barking new orders to the assistants, who panicked, and the model looked dazed. Moments later, the red cape flag was in place, and the model waved it back and forth like a silver band majorette. "That's it, wave it back and forth just like that. Try and get it to flare out more! Yes, that's it." She ducked back under the drape and started snapping photos, exchanging the large negative plates between each exposure.

Ethela stepped back and watched with fascination. She had no idea what these pictures would be used for, but she knew creating them and being a part of whatever this situation was would become her new mission in life.

When the photographer ran out of film, she yelled, "That's a wrap. Break everything down and pack it up." She saw Ethela still standing nearby and approached her. "I'd like very much to thank you for your excellent idea. I struggled with what was missing in the shot, and you came along and put your finger directly on the problem. Jamie McFadden, at your service," she said, holding out her card.

Ethela replied, "Why, thank you Jamie. My name's Ethela Oregard. I'd love to learn more. I'm fascinated with the creative process, and seeing your performance today really opened my eyes."

"Let's grab a coffee soon. Do you live nearby?" Jamie asked.

"Yes, just a couple of blocks away. I don't have a phone, but you can stop by the makeup counter at Bright's Department Store, and you'll find me there. It's not my ideal job, but it keeps me off the street. And, good grief, what a great place for raw materials."

Jamie followed, "Good then. I'll plan to see you tomorrow afternoon, and we'll go from there."

Ethela replied, "That would be great. Thank you again."

That night, as Ethela thumbed through some of her favorite fashion magazines, she now saw the images differently. These things didn't just happen. Someone made them happen. Someone directed the whole scene and made every little decision, what stayed in and what came out. There were so many variables to deal with. Models. Light. Cameras. You had to be part circus ring leader, part magician.

The more she studied the images, the more excited she became. Yet, at the same time, she could feel herself getting bored with these images. While they were beautiful and perfectly crafted, she thought they all fit into the same basket. There was no shock. No drama. No surprises! Nobody would look at these and say, "Wow, I never thought to wrap a model in a cape made from used wine corks and put a crown of corkscrews on her head. Unexpectedly brilliant!"

Ethela pulled out some of her old sketchbooks and revisited them, looking at them again with fresh eyes. She saw her cape made from used wine corks and synthetic grape leaves–Cabs, Pinots, and Zins. Knee-length boots covered in flattened beer bottle caps. A long and skinny handbag made from an old car tire inner tube. The blouse covered in dried hydrangea blossoms, looking like a walking floral display. A smart belt fashioned out of braided bubble gum wrappers, all the same flavor. And one of her favorite designs-an origami turban created using old Christmas cards, spiraling ever higher and topped with a twinkling star. "I'm going to share these with Jamie. If anyone can see the brilliance captured herein, it's her," she thought.

Shock Value

Jamie carefully reviewed the contact sheets from the shoot in the dim red glow of her darkroom. She loved the motion and drama seen through her loupe. Thanks to the relatively long exposures and the large movements the model performed with the flag, certain parts of the image were sharp and crisp, while others seemed to move and vibrate on the surface. Very avant-garde. And when they were enlarged to life-size prints, they would be genuinely spectacular.

She walked out of the darkroom and met her assistants. "I've reviewed yesterday's shoot—great stuff. There's motion and there's drama, but then there's high fashion going on too. Great work, especially considering a lot of it was inspired by our drop-in art director, Ethela Oregard."

As always, the assistants fawned over Jamie, "Fabulous! Wonderful! Visionary!" At the same time, they thought, "Who is this Oregard person? She looked like a bag lady."

Jamie added, "I'm going to meet with Ethela today and see how we might collaborate. There's something intriguing about her. She doesn't understand enough about photography and design to know why certain things aren't done. We know too much while she knows too little. You know, maybe, there's something great in all of that."

Fashion photography depends greatly on the concept behind the image—the act of creating, the "how," becoming more important than the "what." Artists expected their audiences to invest in the creative process. If they didn't capture the majesty of the creation, the blame lay on them, not the artist. It didn't matter if you were catching an "impression" or "abstracting" a political perspective or flinging paint randomly onto a canvas. There could be no art without a story. Sadly though, there were instances where the "story" took over the art, creating cynicism towards traditional composition and execution.

These thoughts, and many others, ran through Jamie's mind as she went to the department store to meet with Ethela. Curiously, she found herself excited to be seeing her again. Perhaps her naiveté could rub off on Jamie and allow her to see things as a layperson might, a gift she had long ago lost.

As she stepped out of the revolving doors into the store, she started scanning the internal horizon for the makeup counter. After a quick sweep, she saw it near the store's center, situated like an island in the stream. As customers made their way from one part of the store to the other, they invariably had to pass the counter. Pretty smart.

Ethela saw Jamie approaching and jumped, dancing with excitement. "Hey! I was hoping you'd stop by today! It's great to see you again."

Jamie hugged her and replied, "You, too. Wow! This is quite the perch you have here. I'll bet you see all kinds of people passing by."

Ethela said, "Indeed! Mostly, I'm just wallpaper, like the racks of makeup bottles, but occasionally someone will stop by and ask for advice. That's when I have a chance to be creative. Sometimes it works, but mostly, people just can't see the same vision I see. It can get frustrating, but I keep at it."

"I know what you mean," Jamie responded knowingly. "Even in my world, where fashion designers reign supreme. They want to see something 'new and exciting,' but when you try and do that, it doesn't match what they have in mind, and you run into the 'I'm just not feeling it' brick wall.

You'd think they would be more open-minded and experimental, but they have their own demons to deal with from manufacturers and store owners."

Ethela replied, "I never thought about that before. How do you get over those brick walls?"

Jamie explained, "I invest a lot of my time and energy creating things designers just can't see. Sometimes it works out, and my investment pays off. But other times, it doesn't pan out, like you with your makeup customers."

"I'd love to help you with these investment projects! I've created many of my own ideas that way, using found materials from the store or other sources. And I have sketchbooks full of ideas," Ethela eagerly replied.

Jamie was intrigued. "Can I see some of your projects?"

"Sure. Can you pop by my place tonight? I don't get off work until 9:00, but I could meet you there at 9:15 or so. Would that work?" Ethela asked.

Jamie agreed, "Yes. Give me your address, and I'll see you then."

Ethela asked meekly, "Would you have time today, before we meet, to look over some of my sketches? I brought some of my favorites for you to see, and I could let you take them to your studio. Then, you could return them tonight."

"Perfect! Hand them over," Jamie said.

Nervously, Ethela pulled out the small folio she had the drawings tucked into and handed it to her. "I know these will seem very rough and odd compared to what you usually work with, but I hope they spark some thought. I look forward to seeing you later tonight."

Taking the folio in hand, Jamie replied, "I always try and approach things with an open mind. That way, new ideas have someplace to land and take root. See you later."

Spinning back through the revolving doors, Jamie made a beeline to her favorite diner for a coffee and scone. She was excited to see what Ethela might have in the sketchbooks but waited until she was seated in her favorite booth before taking a look. Then, with hot coffee and a warm scone in place, she opened the folio.

An Uncorked World of Quirk

The first item she saw was the cape made from wine bottle corks. It was meticulously drawn, and the captions she included to describe what she was trying to achieve were perfect. "The corks should be sawn in half down their length, so one side is rounded and the other flat. Then, a small hole must be drilled in each end so the pieces can be sewn together. Dental floss works great for this, as the waxy nature of the string allows it to easily pass through the small holes. The bright white of the stitching looks excellent with the various shades of tan, each capped with a unique shade of wine color. Artificial grape leaves can be added to create drama. The corks can be sewn together in many popular patterns, like small subway tiles. Herringbone, running bond. Straight stacked. Bacchus would love this!"

Jamie thought, "Wow! What an idea. These are totally unorthodox materials. But I can see how it could work."

Next was a knee-high pair of boots covered with beer bottle caps. The caption reads, "Found a great pair of rugged knee-high boots at work. Unfortunately, the relatively high heels were broken off both, which is probably why they were thrown out. I will replace these with two broken tap handles my bartender friend gave me. Guinness will love it! Then, I'll glue various beer bottle caps over the entire surface. These must be hammered flat first to make good contact with the old leather. Finally, I'll add the handle from a pewter stein to the back of each boot, creating a large boot stein out of the whole affair. Cheers!"

As Jamie made her way through the rest of the folio, she was blown away by Ethela's seemingly random pairing of materials. And yet, somehow it worked: fashion becoming art. Utility took second place to design, but there was plenty of utility too.

Jamie thought, "I can't wait to see what she's made from these and her other sketches."

Ethela watched the clock approaching 9, ready to bolt out the door as soon as the night's closing announcement was made. All day she had wondered what Jamie might think of her ideas. Would she believe her insane? A genius? An insane genius?

Taking the stairs two at a time, she burst through the apartment door and immediately started straightening up for company. Of course, since her apartment was so small, this took no time at all. Looking in her small cooler, she was happily surprised to find two beers.

She thought, "Okay, I think I'm good. I don't want to freak her out with my enthusiasm, provided she even shows."

At that moment, she heard a knock at her door, "Shave and a Haircut." She took a deep breath and opened the door. "Hey there! Did you find me okay? I'm so glad you're here."

Jamie stepped in and replied, "No problems. Thank you so much for having me over. I had a fantastic afternoon going over your sketches. Your ideas are so different, so unique. I kept hearing my inner voice say, 'That could never work,' but then I would counter with, 'Why not?' and I could see things happening. It kinda made my head hurt—but in a good way."

Ethela threw her arms around Jamie and hugged her tightly, catching her completely off guard. After a brief pause, Jamie hugged her back. Then, pulling away, Ethela said, "You have no idea how long I've waited to hear someone say something like that. Thank you, thank you, thank you!"

They made their way to Ethela's small sofa, where she had already put the two beers on the small coffee table. "Come, sit."

Taking a sip from the beer, Jamie said, "You mentioned you have put together some of your ideas. Can I see them?"

Ethela was very nervous but quickly doused her fear with a sip of cold beer. "Yes, wait right here." She entered her bedroom, brought out the small lamp with the linguine shade, and plugged it in. At first, Jamie thought it was just another lamp, but then she noticed the different materials and almost simultaneously smelled them.

"Oh my god. That is amazing! How did you ever come up with that?" Jamie asked.

Ethela quickly took her through her cooking dilemma, which turned magical, as Jamie listened. Finally, Jamie said, "Now that is keeping your eyes and mind wide open!"

Next, Ethela shared her stocking nightgown. "This doesn't look like much on the hanger, so I may need to put it on. I'll be right back." She nervously left and went into her bedroom, where she shimmied into the stocking nightgown. She thought, "This is the moment of truth. She'll either love it, and we'll become lifelong collaborators, or she'll be shocked and quickly leave."

Upon entering the room, Jamie's eyes lit up. Ethela's body was essentially naked but with a veil of secrecy intact. The garment hugged her body like skin. A wildly variegated and patterned skin. The hint of her wine-colored nipples and plain cotton panties showed through.

Jamie whispered, "That is breathtaking. What is it?"

Ethela squirmed bashfully and said, "I made it out of torn pantyhose, sewing the various shapes together like a quilt. Something about the tight fit over my whole body is strangely comforting. It's like a full-body hug."

"Spin around so I can see you from all sides! This is terrific," Jamie said excitedly. "We've got to do something with this. I don't know what exactly, but this must get out there."

Ethela started crying, tears of joy running down her face, "I was so nervous you might not like it. Thank you kindly. Let me get back in my other clothes, and we can chat some more."

Jamie said, "Yes, by all means, let's continue." And so they spent the rest of the night and into the early morning light talking about the various ideas Ethela shared from her many sketchbooks. The energy they fed each other was like a perpetual engine on over-drive, ever increasing in power.

Artistic collaboration is a thing of beauty. Each partner brings their ideas to the sandbox and freely shares with the others, and feedback, good or bad, is received with the best of intentions. Balance is achieved when the others fill in strengths and weaknesses. Openness is the high-octane fuel that makes the engine run. But, as with any engine, everything grinds to a halt if the fuel is compromised. If one party begins to assume too much credit for the success of the collaboration, such a lop-sided affair foments distrust and betrayal, and all spark is lost. So, it is a rare team that makes this magic happen long-term.

There is also something about an artistic collaboration among women. When their creation rises above a sexual or power dynamic, women can work together in seamless strength and in a union defined by the end goal.

And so it was with Jamie and Ethela.

As Jamie had surmised, she and her team knew too much about art and design and had lost the ability to see things as everyday people saw them. They assumed their audience was in on the trick and could understand what they were trying to communicate artistically. But at times, the general public was genuinely clueless about what was being said with an image or design and turned away in confusion.

Ethela felt most people had an excellent appreciation for whimsy and found joy in seeing something they were intimately familiar with used in a new and exciting way. Her challenge was to sort out how to make the most of this familial connection, gently widening the creative opening without shooting over her audience's head. And like any muscle, the more the creative mind is exercised, the stronger and more resilient it becomes. Risks are easier to accept and understand. Understanding expands.

Rejoining her team, Jamie announced, "I had a great meeting last night with Ethela Oregard, our mystery art director from the shoot the other day. She is a unique individual, totally open to "happy accidents" as she calls them, and we've briefly discussed joining up on some wildly different projects. So I'd like her to meet us here to see how our operation works and speak with each of you. I hope you'll make her feel at home."

A low-grade buy-in filled the room: "Oh, sure. Look forward to hearing what Ethela has in mind. Sounds like fun." But internally, the crew sang a different chorus. "What the hell! This bimbo comes out of nowhere, and she's suddenly a shining star! What about all the years of ass-kissing and sucking up? "Oh Jamie, you're SO talented. Everything you touch turns to gold." Does that not count for anything? WTF?!"

The girl was going down, and not in a good way.

Ethela was doing her best to stay busy behind the makeup counter, but her mind couldn't help thinking about last night's meeting with Jamie. They had clicked so perfectly! There was no judgment, no awkward silences, which Ethela would silently fill in with, "What in the heck was she thinking with that idea? Totally absurd." Jamie listened intently and seemed beyond interested in whatever Ethela was showing her. She couldn't think how the evening could have gone any better. So, it wasn't surprising that she felt nervous about seeing Jamie the next go-around. Things were just too good.

Jamie welcomed Ethela to the studio and showed her around. The shooting bay had this unique area with what they called a "cyc wall," which is shorthand for "cyclorama." They had all kinds of colored films to attach to the bright lights to create different moods. Giant rolls of colored paper were used as backdrops for various settings. They even processed their own film. And cameras. Holy cow, did Jamie have cameras! Some were small, like the box cameras you see in stores, but others were huge, shooting 8 x 10 sheets of film. These contraptions were mounted atop long spider-like tripod legs, and you had to wear a cape and learn to view things upside down. So much to learn.

"Well, that's a quick tour through the fun factory. What do you think?" Jamie asked.

Ethela responded with eager enthusiasm, "This place is incredible. You have so much stuff to create whatever you imagine. I scarcely understand how it works, but my brain is already running a million miles an hour trying to figure it out. The film processing seems like absolute magic to me. I can't wait to see how that's done."

Jamie laughed and said, "That will all come in time. It took us years of trial and error and experimentation to master what we can create today. I think the best way to start is to have you shadow us as we go about our work. You can ask questions anytime, and we'll explain what we're doing. And, if an idea pops into your mind about what we're shooting, please go ahead and share it. You can see things we can't."

The assistants silently took in this exchange between Jamie and Ethela, and each developed a strategy for sabotaging the collaboration. How dare Jamie defer to this know-nothing, never-been-anything neophyte. They'd all forgotten more about fashion and photography than this rube would ever know.

It Ain't Easy Being Green

As luck would have it, Jamie had her most demanding client in the studio that week. They were getting ready for the upcoming fashion show and needed a library of all their latest designs. The models had to fit within exacting but hard-to-define criteria. Not too thin, but definitely not average or regular. Think healthy but gaunt. They had to possess a flawed beauty. Perfect skin was looked down upon. A gap-toothed smile, whenever encountered, was excellent. And most importantly, their overall demeanor should say, "It's so hard being a beautiful creature. Buy these clothes, and you can be pathetically beautiful, too."

Oh, and the colors had to be spot on. If the reds were off in any way, the world would simply come crashing down. And not just reds. ANY color! This required Jamie to be exceedingly careful with lighting, exposures, and, most importantly, film processing. A lapse in any of these steps could lead to disaster. And that's just the technical stuff. Forget working with the moody meat puppets in front of the cameras.

"Okay, let's get the first gal out here," the fashion director yelled. The model sauntered onto the set with that well-practiced runway stride. She had long, flowing platinum-blonde hair and wore what looked like a giant emerald-green tent with armholes. The garment draped formlessly down to her boney knees. The overall effect was like looking at a snow-capped Christmas tree on legs.

The assistants, sensing an opening to suck up to the director, said in unison, "Lovely, lovely, lovely! So elegant! What a statement."

The director turned and gave them all a withering look and then said, "Let's get a fan over here and have it blow towards the model. This piece only works when the fabric is pressed loosely against the model's body. Otherwise, she's just a walking green sack."

So Jamie started working with the model, adjusting the speed and direction of the fan, making sure she had a suitable drape against the slender wraith's body. Her hair blew ever so slightly behind her as she stared into the distance.

"Okay, let's do some test shots and run them through the soup," Jamie said. She ducked under the black drape and checked the focus, then began the tedious process of bracketing a series of shots. Bracketing is where the photographer starts with what should be a primary exposure and then shoots several variations, lighter and darker than the primary exposure, using shutter speeds or f-stops to achieve the various steps. Like Goldilocks and the three bears, one of the half-dozen shots will be just right.

When Jamie finished, she handed the film sheets to one of the assistants to process. They'd have their first look at the setup in an hour or so. From there, adjustments could be made.

The assistant asked Ethela if she'd like to help with the processing.

"Yes, yes! I'd love to see how you do that," Ethela responded.

The assistant gathered up the film and said, "Follow me." She had followed the routine enough times to know that Jamie had exactly what she wanted on the film, so there would be no great revelations coming. Nor would there be any need for adjustments. And with that knowledge, she moved forward on a plan to put Ethela in the middle of a colossal catastrophe.

Jamie popped into the darkroom, looked at the proofs, and said, "Okay, it looks like we have exactly what we want as a starting point. Load some more film, and we'll get started on the real shoot."

The assistant asked Ethela if she'd like to help load the film. "Of course, but you'll need to show me what to do."

"It's easy. The trick is to remember which side has the emulsion on it and put that side so it faces out in each holder. They are loaded into the boxes emulsion side up, so just keep that in mind as you load them," the assistant dictated. What she didn't tell Ethela was that she had flipped the film sheets she handed her so the emulsion side would be facing down, an accidental process called "Redscale," making every exposure wildly off from their test shots. This mistake would not be evident until after they had reviewed the entire shoot sequence and reviewed what they had captured.

So, the fashion director settled into her chair, and Jamie started her sequence, asking the model to try certain poses and expressions. Lights flashed, the fans blew, and the model twisted and smiled. It was all very tedious and time-consuming, and they shot dozens and dozens of shots hoping to get the perfect one. Finally, Jamie said, "I think we've got that one. Let's break and run these through the darkroom.

The assistant immediately said, "Right away, Jamie," grabbing up the stacks of exposed film and ducking into the dark room to uncover the awaiting catastrophe. She ran the sheets through the process, same as always, only this time, the results were very different, as she knew they would be. She smiled knowingly, worked up her best "I can't explain what just happened" expression, and walked back into the studio.

"Um... Jamie... can I talk to you in private, please?" the assistant whispered.

Jamie followed her into the darkroom, where the drama would unfold. "What's wrong? You look like you've seen a ghost or something."

The assistant replied, "The shots are all wildly off from what we had when we ran the tests. The colors are all reddish and golden, not natural at all. And they're dark. Very dark. And moody. I can't explain what happened," which was very much a lie.

Jamie gasped, "What! How can that be? Let me see them."

The assistant laid out all the proofs for her, knowing the fashion director would be incensed when she saw them. At that moment, Ethela popped into the darkroom to see what was happening. Jamie was speechless as she looked at the proofs, trying to figure out how she would handle this with the fashion director.

Ethela said nervously, "What's going on? Can I take a look?" Jamie stepped aside, shell-shocked, and motioned for her to take a look. "Wow! These are incredible! I've never seen colors like this before. The overall effect is so dramatic. I had no idea that's what we'd get after seeing the tests earlier. You're a genius, Jamie!"

When she heard Ethela's response, Jamie jumped back to attention and looked at Ethela like she had scorpions climbing out of her eyes. "No, no, no! This is NOT good. The client is going to freak out. No doubt about that. Freak! Out! Now!"

Ethela shrank back from Jamie and, after a moment, replied with growing excitement, "How can you say that? These are fabulous. They're not what you expected, but isn't that what fashion design is about? Achieving and celebrating the unexpected! I view this as a breakthrough. A triumph! The only problem I see is how we replicate this look again, as you clearly weren't expecting this when you shot them."

Jamie thought about what Ethela said, then replied, "Well, it's one thing for you to see this as a significant breakthrough, but how do we get the client to see that? I'm telling you, she is going to freak out."

Ethela considered this. She knew nothing about this woman and certainly didn't know how she might react. But if there was one thing she did know, it was that this client had an ego as big as the city she lived in. All she had to do was convince her of her genius for recognizing the inherent drama laid before her. If it worked as she hoped, they would all be stars. And if it failed, well, nothing ventured, nothing gained.

"Let me try something with her. As you've stated, I appreciate things more like a regular person, in this case, a typical fashion consumer. You know, if I can show her the excitement these images create within me for this garment, maybe she'll come around. What's that expression–the customer is always right. So maybe it's time we test that. She just might surprise you," Ethela said, spinning hope.

The group gathered several of the best proofs and left the darkroom to face the music with the fashion director. She was busy going over some details for the next shoot when Jamie spoke, trying to muster as much confidence as she could, "Well, we have the proofs back from the first shoot, and I must say they are extraordinary, unexpectedly so. I can guarantee you've never seen anything like them."

The fashion director looked over her glasses at Jamie and then hopped down to see the proofs on the table. The shock of seeing what was clearly a train wreck registered immediately on her face, but she didn't utter a word. She just stared. And stared some more. Then said quietly, "It seems we have entered the realm of the surreal. You are quite right. I've never seen anything like this. I'd wager no one has ever seen anything like this. Part of me is terrified by that possibility, but the other part finds it incredibly seductive."

Sensing an opening, Ethela offered up, "They are truly unique images. They reveal the drama contained within the garment like nothing else could. The whole thing registers as a wearable combination of theater and art."

"Yes, I like that! Of course, we usually try and maintain strict color controls to represent the garments as they are, but this technique allows us to present them as more than they are: as artistic expressions. In stores, the garments are always displayed with their own photographic images. So why show the customer what they already see before them? Instead, we should attempt to show them more. These images are like being seen from the other side of the mirror, not as we are, but as we imagine ourselves to be. I like it!"

Jamie was stunned. And suddenly very nervous, as she had no idea how they had achieved this new look, which was a much bigger problem. Then she said, "Fabulous. I knew you'd see the benefit of the approach. We should break early for lunch and celebrate our new direction. Shall we?"

The fashion director agreed, "Let's. My treat."

Hearing all this, the devious assistant who had tried to sabotage Ethela thought to herself, "What in the hell just happened? She was supposed to blow up when she saw this goat rodeo, but NO, she had to go and be all "I love it. It's so artistic. What the hey!?"

A Bullet, Caught Between the Teeth

After lunch, the fashion director had to step away to make some calls, and Jamie saw her opening to gather everyone together and sort out what had happened. She pulled everyone into the darkroom, "Okay, we dodged a major bullet. But now we have an even bigger problem because I don't know how exactly we achieved what we achieved. I'm hoping and praying one of you can lighten my load here. Did something accidentally get switched around? Bad chemicals? What?"

The assistant nervously began, "I think I might know what happened. I had Ethela help me load the film this morning. I dropped the box in the dark and didn't notice, but maybe it was upside down when I handed it to her to start loading the film holders. We can check some of the unprocessed holders to determine what happened."

Hearing this, Jamie felt something was off with her story. Her assistant had loaded tens of thousands of film holders and had never made such a mistake. Even if Ethela was added to the equation, she was too anal-retentive to make such a simple blunder. Unless, of course, there was more to it. Jamie said, "By all means, let's check the undeveloped holders ASAP. If that's what happened, we'll be golden."

The assistant quickly began her work and, within minutes, said, "Bingo! Looks like that's what happened. All the remaining holders are loaded backward."

Ethela was shocked, "I'm SO sorry. I didn't know."

Jamie responded quickly, "No, no, no. It's not your fault. You've never loaded film before, so she should have checked behind you and caught this. At least now we know how to replicate the new look. Let's load up some more holders and work out the next shot."

And so they began again. Jamie kept her eye on the assistant, who could feel her laser focus practically burning through her skin. Ethela was as eager as ever about what they were doing, nonplussed by the morning's events. The fashion director was genuinely excited about the new campaign. All in all, a great day.

Ethela sat behind her makeup counter, feeling like a battery that had been overcharged. She was excited about what she'd seen and learned watching Jamie in her studio the last several weeks. But, unfortunately, her brain was cycling through ideas faster than she could grab them and get them down in notes. She had to figure out how to harness all this creative energy before it dissolved into nothingness.

Then she noticed a new fashion display being installed across the store. As she left her station and approached the presentation, she could see it was from the shoot she had been involved with at Jamie's! There were larger-than-life prints of the dark and moody shots, bold fields of color and texture, and the garments were hung on the most elegant hardware she had ever seen. It was as if a small fashion meteorite had landed in the store, obliterating everything around it.

"What do you think?" Ethela heard behind her as Jamie approached, beaming. "This is the first installation of the new campaign. I wanted you to be among the first to see it."

Ethela turned and was overjoyed at seeing Jamie and hugged her tightly. Then, pulling away, she had trouble responding, "I can't really say. It's like nothing I've ever seen before. And when you see the competing displays next to it... It's simply mind-blowing."

"The fashion director is ecstatic and wants to expand the campaign far beyond anything we've done before, going international," Jamie said, clutching both of Ethela's hands as she talked. "We did this! You and me. If you hadn't been there to challenge the client and me with this happy accident, we would have never presented this work as a new direction. In fact, we could very well have lost the business. So, thank you very much."

Hearing these words brought waterworks to Ethela's eyes. She hugged Jamie again and buried her head in Jamie's hair. She had never been so happy in her life. "Thank you, Jamie. I am so incredibly happy for you. Truly."

Then Jamie said, "It's not just me. It's us. I want you to join us full-time and be my new assistant. I can teach you all the technical skills you lack, but I can't teach the creative understanding you were born with. You have a gift, and I want us to share that gift with as many people as possible. What do you think? Are you up for it?"

"Of course! Yes! Oh my god, yes! Let me settle my affairs here, which will take no time, and I'll come right over to the studio," Ethela said.

And so began the serendipitous relationship of Ethela Oregard with the unsuspecting fashion world.

Of course, it wasn't always a swimming success, as the full-body stocking tended to lose its grip. But by and large, things held together in an exceptional manner. Excessively so, to Ethela's way of thinking.

Smabdolem Ik

Smabdolem
Ik

Smab came rolling out of the darkness of his perch in the corner of the bar with the fury and fireworks of a straight-line thunderstorm. A moment earlier, he had gotten "the nod" from Paulette, the sole bartender working behind the counter. This subtle directional nod was his signal to take care of a particularly worthless bar-mate in any manner he saw fit. For Smabdolem Ik, it was with extreme prejudice and dispatch.

Grabbing the cretin by the collar, he dragged him, kicking and screaming, out the side door into his office—the darkest of alleys. Smab spoke straight-forwardly to his charge, beating him about the head and shoulders in rhythm as he spoke, "The barkeep in there–told you to settle down–but you chose to ignore her sound advice–Paulette's a sweet girl– and gives lowlifes like you–the benefit of the doubt–way beyond what my temperament would allow–so when she gave me the nod–I knew you had crossed all the lines–and needed some correction."

Now that he had the misfit's undivided attention, Smab added, "So here's my proposition. You promise never to return here again, and I won't cut your ears off. But if I so much as eyeball you around here, your ears will be just the start of my trimming on your worthless carcass. You got me?"

Trying to talk through his busted mouth, the drunk sputtered, "Yeth, Smab, yeth! Pleath don't cut on me! Pleath!"

Smab threw him down as hard as his five-foot-five-inch fire-plug frame could muster. "Then get out of here before I lose my temper."

The drunk babbled, "Yeth sir, yeth sir!" and ran away as fast as his bruised body could carry him.

As footsteps receded into the darkness, Smab looked around the alley and spied his on-again-off-again pet cat, Lucky, prowling around, looking for a rat to dine on. Even though he had only three legs, Lucky was a skilled hunter and, being a Tom to boot, quite the ladies' man.

"What are you looking at, huh? You think I have a little treat for you?" Smab said affectionately.

"Mewowow," Lucky replied.

Smab walked over to Lucky, who calmly sat atop a stack of palettes, cleaning his fur and flicking his tail. Then, as Smab got closer, Lucky gracefully jumped down, sticking a three-leg landing, and nuzzled his head against Smab's legs. But when Smab reached down to pet Lucky, he scampered away, stopping only to meow at him.

Smab chuckled, "Oh, still not sure of me even after all we've been through? Well, off with you then." And being a faithful feline, Lucky obliged, quickly swishing his tail as a parting wave.

Trenches, Docks, and Hard Knocks

Smabdolem Ik grew up on a dirt road in the middle of nowhere. It was one of those areas of the country that didn't show up much on a map and, as such, didn't offer much in the way of opportunity. Some folks tried to scratch out a living farming, growing row crops and tending a few desultory livestock. Others, like Smab, when they came of age, were drawn to the bright lights of the big city, which was more than 60 miles away, taking the worst of jobs: unloading freighters at night down at the harbor. You needed a strong back for the work and a mean disposition towards your fellow man. Friends on the docks were few and far between.

As his luck would have it, Smab got drafted into the army after a couple of months of leaving home. He was shipped off to basic training for a short three months in hell and then overseas to the front lines for a more extended stay. The war would later be called World War I, but as far as Smab was concerned, it was just another series of lessons in his graduate studies at the school of hard knocks. He didn't understand all the ins and outs of who was fighting who, but he knew you could get killed if you didn't keep your wits about you. And he quickly learned the enemy wasn't always across no man's land. He could just as easily be at arm's length in your very own trench.

Sarge yelled at him, "Ik, stick your head up there and tell me what you see across the way. We're getting our asses handed to us just sitting here in this hole."

Smab replied, "Sarge, don't nobody need to stick their stupid head up for a look-see. Those fucking bullets flying at us tell us all we need to know."

"God damn it, Ik, get your ass up there, or I'll blow your head off," the Sarge screamed.

Then, like a fuse that burns out when overloaded by too many demands, Smab snapped. He dropped his rifle, charged Sarge in the trench, and commenced beating on him, the likes of which few had ever seen. Profanity of the most original form spewed forth like molten lava, almost scalding the ears off those nearby. Then, not content to beat him senseless, he shoved Sarge up to the edge of the trench and yelled, "Look over there motherfucker and tell me what you see!" It wasn't long before Smab got his answer as the back of the Sarge's head blew open in a barrage of bullets. Smab, now covered in blood and brains, let go of his limp body, and it slid slowly back down into the trench. The other soldiers looked at him in terror but were too afraid to move for fear they might be next.

Looking around the trench, he realized what had transpired and laughed hysterically. His eyes were wild with rage, and the terror among his fellow soldiers reached even higher levels.

Smab yelled, "Well, it looks like we know what the fuck is out there. It's a shame some people can't figure that shit out for themselves." He then picked up his gun and walked along the trench, looking for a place to rest and gather his thoughts.

Curiously, his mood was lighter now that he had handled the Sarge situation. Even more curious was that no one ever said anything about what happened in the trench. The story was Sarge had simply put himself in harm's way and became one of an endless list of casualties.

Eventually, they would dig and shoot their way out of the trench, and the battle would move on to other areas. Smab was put in charge of the tail gun in one of the newfangled airplanes, and it was here that he felt most at ease. He felt untouchable, flying high above the fray below, shooting down at the enemy as they receded from view.

Smab's immortality was short-lived, though. As they made a low pass over the enemy lines, a former high-school discus star threw a grenade at the plane from his vantage point at the top of a nearby tree. The ensuing explosion ripped all the fabric off one of the wings, causing the plane to crash not far away. Nevertheless, the pilot got them down in one piece, and they evaded capture, but not before some brutal hand-to-hand combat. In the end, those nights working at the docks had taught Smab how to care of himself.

He gave Paulette a nod that said, "problem under control," as he entered the bar and resumed his watchful place near the back wall.

The club wasn't typical—no band or dinner theater as the main draw. Instead, it was a consignment venue where, for a nominal fee, people could bring in acts of any kind and put on a show. The entertainment ranged from stand-up comedians to trained dog acts to run-of-the-mill burlesque fare. No one knew what would happen from one night to the next, and members liked the randomness.

The club's owner, Corene, was a petite Black lady, soft-spoken and kind, with a keen eye for unconventional talent. She smoked various "non-traditional products," from hand-made pipes to two-fingers-fat rolled Cubans. She saw in Smabdolem Ik the best possible traits for a bouncer in her establishment. He was quiet most of the time and didn't drink a drop, and when he felt good, he felt REALLY good. Likewise, he went into a truly dark cosmos when he was down or chewing on something. His darker moods usually involved a customer being less than compliant with young Paulette, someone Smab considered the daughter he never had. Corene liked Smab's protective hovering and let him go about his work as he saw fit, regardless of what that might look like.

Smabdolem had also seen something in Corene he admired. Even her name smoothed out his ruffles.

Cora's World

As a small boy, Smab had what he called his "Black grandmammy," a lovely lady named Cora. She was barely four and a half feet tall but loomed large in his eyes. She always packed her hand-made corncob pipe tight with her George Washington tobacco. Her recurring joke was, "Hey, you got George Washington in a can? If so, you better let him out." A belly-shaking cackle always followed this joke. Her glasses were overly large, covering most of her face, which explains why nothing ever got past her. Many times, Smab thought she could see out the back of her head as well. Her scrambled eggs and bacon were legendary. Even though she used the same pan and stove as his mother, when Cora's hand was scrambling, everything tasted better. Lighter, more fortifying, served with love. When Smab would come down with the "Croup," which seemed like a weekly event, she would rub his chest with Vicks Vapor Rub, take his temperature, and generally nurse him back to tip-top dirt-road health. She always wore an apron and knee-high stockings that sagged like wax dripping off a candle. To Smab, she was an absolute angel.

Smab's father, Raymond, ran a farm with several Black families living and working on the property. He referred to these families as "hands," as in helping hands. The families were provided shelter (of a sort) and were paid cash-money every Friday night for their week's labor. That labor took on many forms, from driving farm equipment ranging from cotton pickers and tractors to sawing and planing rough lumber from logs felled on surrounding farms to repairing all manner of vehicles. He was the original "Jack of all trades, master of none," irreplaceable in the community. Everyone knew who Raymond was, and if they had an idea for something that didn't exist, chances were good he could help them create it or at least build a working approximation. Many referred to his efforts as Afro-Engineering as if that was derogatory in some manner. It didn't matter what people called it, for he always felt great pride when creating something that didn't exist before.

On Saturdays, Raymond liked to tinker with his own projects. These might range from repairing a hole in the side of an engine block, where a rod and piston had decided to come crashing through. Or building a mini-sawmill, complete with an open 48" blade mounted to the front of a tractor and driven by a 10-inch-wide leather belt coming off the power take-off. A real man-killer if you weren't careful around it. The old tube AM radio was his only companion besides Smab.

One Saturday, one of the hands, a barrel-chested, bald-headed beast named Douglas, drunkenly approached his father and started pestering him for "Fi-dollars." (Smab liked to think these visits were rare, but in reality, they were a weekly event, sometimes played out multiple times over a Saturday.) He had paid this man a week's wages the evening prior, but that money was already gone, turned into liquid overnight. Douglas had entered what Smab called "the fifth dimension," a state of significant intoxication reached by consuming a fifth of rot-gut liquor, maybe two or three.

Raymond would ask knowingly, "Didn't I just pay you last night?"

Douglas slurred back, "Yeah, yeah, I mean, but you know, I needs a little more to get me through the weekend—just fi-dollars. Come on. I know you got it. Gimme fi-dollars."

This exchange had been played out so many times by his father and any number of hands that he had the conversation down to a minimal number of back-and-forths. Usually, this "call and response" would go on for 15-20 minutes, and the drunken hand would leave unaccommodated, cursing under his breath as he staggered away. Sadly, come Monday morning, Douglas never remembered being there—just one of the many side effects of entering the "fifth dimension" portal.

But on this Saturday, though, Douglas changed the script. Smab's father grew very irritated as he continued to rant and beg beyond the regular exchange limits. He tried walking away from Douglas, hoping he would trail out, but to no avail. Wherever he went, Douglas followed, constantly nagging for "fi-dollars."

Finally, having had enough, Raymond yelled at him, "I am not giving you any more money to drink up, so you might as well go back to where you came from!"

Then, Douglas made what could have been a fatal error in judgment and pulled a piece-of-shit Barlow knife on Raymond. He yelled, "You won't give me the money? I'll guess I'll have to cut you up then."

In a blink, Raymond cold-cocked Douglas with a right cross, hitting him square in the eye and knocking him to the ground. With one eye closed now, he still hadn't received the message and proceeded to try and wrestle Smab's father to the ground. The pounding only intensified, reinforced by a torrent of profanity that created its own weather system.

Breathing quickly now, Raymond screamed, "Don't you ever pull a fucking knife on me again, or losing your eye will be the least of it! Now get the hell out of here before I really get pissed!"

Douglas crawled to his feet, well-dusted and even rockier now that his brains had been rattled, and staggered back up the dirt road to his home. Back at work on Monday, he couldn't tell anyone why his eye had swollen shut. But somehow, the message had made it through his overly thick skull, as Douglas NEVER asked Raymond for money again.

A week later, Smab asked Cora what she had heard about the altercation.

Cora replied, "Well, your Daddy did what he shoulda done. Dat boy knows better than to come up here asking for money. And pullin' a knife! He damn lucky yo' Daddy didn't kill him wid a pipe or something instead of jest beatin' the tar out of him. I'm sorry you had to see all that. What did you think was gonna happen?"

Smab thought a moment and then replied, "Well, truth be told, it scared the shit out of me. First, I thought Douglas would hurt Daddy with that knife. But then, I got even more terrified when Daddy started pounding him. I thought he would beat him to death right there in front of the shop. I've seen these guys come up and ask for money all the time, but I'd never seen anything like that before. It was scary."

Cora closed her eyes and said, "My, my, Lord, hep us. Dem boys just drinks up dey paycheck as fast as dey get it. Thank the Lord yo Daddy didn't kill him, cause he show coulda. Dat woulda been real bad."

When Smab reached the age he could decide his future, his father asked if he would stay on the farm and take it over after he was gone. Emotionally, Smad had to tell him, "I can see why you'd like me to do that, and I appreciate all you've done for me growing up, but I need to see if there's something else out there. I may be back begging you to take me in in no time, but I want to see how things play out."

Smab found a niche at the docks, unloading cargo ships at night alongside some of the roughest guys he could imagine. He never forgot that fateful day with Douglas and his father, though. He had seen what alcohol could do and swore never to touch the stuff, a promise he kept.

Cruising the Fifth Dimension

Smab's interest in the "fifth dimension" was a lifelong affair. He had been around enough guys of all stripes, whether in the military or down at the docks, to predict when someone might get to the trouble stage. Some got really happy the more they drank and just liked to sing and dance until they collapsed into a harmless pile. Others would come into the bar angry, and the alcohol was like high-octane fuel, blazing them into a full-on rage, where the only stop-gap was a bar-room brawl. These were the guys Smab disliked the most and took an interest in dealing with, especially if they had been rude to Paulette or Corene.

Smabdolem knew there was a delicate balance to be maintained running a bar. Alcohol was the social lubricant that kept customers returning: that and the never-ending stream of random stage acts. He saw himself as the scales of justice in this balancing act, taking care of those patrons who chose to disregard social norms and upholding a sense of relative safety and joy in the bar. He didn't want to hear word on the street that his bar was rough or low-brow, not that there was anything particularly wrong with being rough or low-brow, just not in his bar. As long as people stayed in their lanes, everything ran smoothly.

Now and again, Smab would encounter a patron who was neither happy nor belligerent but just quiet and, eventually, comatose. Such a person would pass out in the booth with their head face down on the table, oblivious to the world, a reminder of other "fifth dimension" altercations he'd seen growing up.

It was at least 100º in the shade. Looking down the dirt road, the ground shimmered. It was lunchtime, and Raymond was taking his noonday nap from 12:30-1:30. Smab liked to use this free time to walk around and gather his thoughts. These thoughts were deep, like if two superheroes were to get into a fight, who would win? Or, if a tree fell in the woods and no one was there to hear it, would they be sawing it up into lumber soon? He truly hated that sawmill and prayed many times that the engine wouldn't start, but it ALWAYS did.

As he walked down the road, passing by waist-high cotton planted in the field, he noticed a pair of feet lying between the rows, just off the shoulder created by the road scraper. They were deathly still, and Smab thought that maybe whoever it was had crawled in there and died. Of course, it was hot as hell's attic space, especially in the cotton field, and dying from a heat stroke was well within reason.

Smab made his way into the field to see who it was. When he got closer and saw the face, he immediately recognized Demus, one of the hands who lived farthest away on the property. He was sweating profusely and soaked through his clothes from head to waist; the smell of liquor coming off him was almost overpowering. Gnats and flies were buzzing around his face, which would have driven Smab crazy, but Demus was so out of it that he never flinched a muscle. If and when he ever came to, his head would no doubt feel like someone had put it in a vise.

Smabdolem backed out of the field and continued down the road, thinking about how all these guys, almost without fail, drank themselves into a stupor every weekend. He knew firsthand that working on the farm as they did was tedious in the extreme. A strong back and a weak mind were all they needed, although Raymond would have liked their minds to be a little stronger as well.

The more he thought about the condition of things, the more he realized that liquor was an escape from the everyday world for these guys, where their biggest opportunity boiled down to getting a chance at some tight nookie and maybe a four-corner cheese nab. When they had a bottle, they knew things were going to change. They would be better at everything, from scrumping to singing and dancing, and if you didn't believe them, you simply had to ask, and they'd confirm it. But man, that return trip was rough.

Sometimes, consequences crossed over from the parallel world. One such time involved Charles, a strong young buck, and Joe, an older hand who should have known better.

From what Smab could discern from the chatter on the farm, Charles' wife, Loretta, and Joe had gotten together and had themselves a bit of a romp under the shade of an old oak tree.

So here's the reentry pattern from this particular "fifth dimension" episode. First, Charles finds out that his wife had this get-together with Joe, his one-time best friend, and he beats her within an inch of her life with a belt. Then, he visits Joe at his house, confronts him in front of his wife, and proceeds to pummel him mercilessly. When he's finished, Janie,

Joe's 400-pound angry-Black-woman-of-a-wife, takes over, throwing cast-iron cookware and flowerpots at him as he runs out of the house, bloodied about the head and shoulders. It was many months before this affair settled into any semblance of normalcy. Thank God Joe didn't get Charles' wife pregnant, as that would have been a bridge too far.

Docking at Corene's

Smabdolem met Corene at a local breakfast joint one morning as he was coming off his night shift. They met at the door, and Smab acted the part of a gentleman and held the door for her, an act she much appreciated, as this was not the norm in those parts.

Corene said, "Thank you kindly, sir. I appreciate it."

Smab replied, "You're most welcome." There was something strangely familiar about her voice and overall demeanor, which attracted Smab. "I'm Smabdolem Ik. It's good to meet you."

Corene replied eagerly, "Likewise, Mr. Ik. I'm Corene Fogle."

Smab was shocked, as his Black grandmammy's last name was Fogle. He didn't pretend to know all her relatives, so he asked blindly, "You wouldn't be related somehow to Cora Fogle? I would guess she would be your grandmother or a great-aunt."

Corene's eyes lit up, "For sure, she's my grandmother, although we haven't seen each other for some time. How do you know her?"

"She practically raised me down on the farm where I grew up. She was my Black grandmammy, and I loved her," Smab said, holding Corene's hands as he spoke.

Corene smiled and said, "Would you join me then for breakfast? I'd love to ask after her and get to know you better."

Smab smiled and said, "Right this way, then, to my favorite table."

They spent the next several hours going over who knew who, asking about whatever happened to so-and-so, filling in information on a cast of until then unrelated acquaintances. As time passed, they formed an unbreakable bond. Smabdolem felt this was one of the best days of his life as she filled an emotional void he didn't even realize he had.

As they finished breakfast and the conversation reached a quiet patch, Corene asked, "Would you consider working for me in my establishment? It's a theater/bar kind of thing, and I could use someone I trust in a bouncer/security position. I understand if you wouldn't want to, but you seem like someone who can take care of themselves pretty well."

Smab took his time answering, thinking back over all the twists and turns his life had taken to lead to this moment. His time on the farm, the various "fifth dimension" episodes he'd witnessed, his time in the army, and the job at the docks. It seemed all these paths converged with this particular relative of his beloved Cora.

Then he replied as earnestly as possible, "Corene, I'd consider it an honor to help you out. Give me some time to take care of my affairs at the docks, and I'll come to see you. Thank you kindly for the opportunity."

As he and Corene left the diner, Smab noticed a three-legged cat preening himself across the street. As if on cue, the cat looked up, stared straight at Smab, offered a formal "Meow-ow-ow" greeting, and after a moment's reflection, returned to cleaning himself. Smab wasn't much into religion, but he did believe in karma. Cora had always told him to do what was right, even if he knew the right thing would be challenging, and to treat people and all God's creatures with due respect. He wasn't sure why but Smab felt this cat was a sign of sorts, maybe sent by Cora's spirit, and called him "Lucky." And like two train tracks, running together but apart, Smabdolem Ik and Lucky rolled on through the years, each keeping a distant but watchful eye on the other.

It was a slow night at the bar, and only one act had signed up to perform, so Corene had to do some time-filling on the stage, something she and her backup singers—The Corenets—did quite well. Her favorite thing was to take an old gospel song, change the tempo, and jazz it up. Now and then, when she had a crowd that was "with her," as she liked to say, when things were jumping, she'd break out an original tune. These were usually torch songs, where some love of hers had done her wrong. You could feel the pain in her voice, and it never failed to satisfy the regulars.

Just before Corene finished her last number, the bar door opened, and every head turned to see what was coming through. Smabdolem couldn't see anything from where he sat as the bar blocked his view, but he could tell from the expressions on the faces he could see this was something out of the ordinary. Then, the procession passed beyond the end of the bar, and he saw the spectacle himself.

All he knew from Corene was the show was a dance group, like dozens they had seen come through before. But this group was extraordinary in at least one critical way: every member was a dwarf. And not just any dwarves; these women were gorgeous in every detail, only in miniature. Some might have described them as devastatingly beautiful—honest to God pixie princesses. The group leader, whose brunette hair and sequined dress shimmered under the spotlight, turned and looked straight at Smabdolem for just a second, and he thought his heart would stop. Their eyes locked, and it was as if every thought he might ever have from that moment onward belonged entirely to her. He was hers, and he was powerless to resist.

A hush fell over the bar as Corene introduced them to the audience. "Ladies and gentlemen, we have a real treat for you tonight. Joining us tonight all the way from the great Mythic Woods of Otherland, please welcome "The Itty-Bitty-Titty-Review!" There was a moment of complete silence, and as the lights came up and the dancers started their routine, it was clear this was a burlesque like no one had ever seen. These miniature beauties looked all the world like children, but once the garments started flying and revealing their perfectly shaped bodies, the crowd went wild. Tessa was the leader, the brunette beauty who had slain Smabdolem with a glance earlier. She sauntered about, singing a well-worn bawdy ballad, enticing the audience to throw money onto the stage, and engaging their fantasies with practiced perfection.

A Tiny Whiff of Trouble

As he watched the performance, Smab felt something he'd never experienced before: he was terribly conflicted. Oh, he had seen many a stripper act waltz through the door, as that was the second oldest game in the book, after prostitution. But the fact that these strippers were so diminutive and childlike in his eyes left him deeply troubled. He had an overwhelming desire to rush the stage and protect them from the lurid stares they so easily and systematically provoked. And none did he want to rescue more than the lovely and devastating Tessa.

Tessa was nearing the end of the routine when she caught Smab's eye, and in that instant, she saw his desire to save and protect her and, with the subtlest of actions, engaged him to act accordingly. It was a look that probably no one else in the bar had seen, but it spoke to Smab as if she held up a bullhorn. She assumed her position behind the microphone, surrounded by her fellow dancers, and bid the audience farewell. Applause washed over the bar as they went off stage to the pitiful excuse of a dressing room.

Moving as if the good Lord had called him to action, Smabdolem followed them close behind. He had no idea what he would say or do, but that didn't matter; he had to get close to Tessa. The rest would play out from there.

The girls were celebrating what they felt was a successful night. The audience had been enthusiastic and generous, and Tessa had a large roll of folding money to prove it. She saw Smabdolem enter the view in the darkened hallway and immediately got up to go and meet him. Like Smab, she didn't know what she would say, but she felt compelled to make contact.

Smab stammered, "Lady Tessa, it is an honor to stand before you. Corene failed utterly in describing your show, as you and your girls were spectacular. I'm Smabdolem Ik, Corene's humble bouncer. If there's anything you need, just ask."

Tessa replied earnestly, "My dear Smabdolem, I know a real gentleman when I see one, and you, my friend, are that through and through. I knew this was so the moment I saw you."

This response was NOT what Smab expected, and he was caught totally off guard. Sensing she had caused him some distress, Tessa quickly added, "I'd like to ask you to accompany my group to our hotel and ensure some overzealous patron does not molest us. Unfortunately, some men assume that because we are petite, they can take advantage of us if you understand me. We can wait until your shift ends and leave then. Can you do that for me?"

Smabdolem replied immediately, "Yes, indeed I can, and it would be my pleasure. Let me check in with Corene, and I'll be right back."

He found Corene behind the bar. She had seen him talking with Tessa and her group and was surprised as much by his actions as he was. He had never shown any interest in any person, man or woman, before. Something was up, and she felt she would soon find out.

Corene said coyly, "Smab, what are you doing back there? It's not like you to get all googly-eyed over a stage act, especially one like those gals."

Smab replied, already in protection mode, "Don't talk about Tessa and her gals like that. She asked if I could accompany them to their hotel to keep them safe from harm, and I told her I would. Unfortunately, they can't wait until closing to leave, so I'm checking with you to see if that's okay."

Corene felt a warmth trickle through her soul. But then, she thought, "I do believe Smab is in love! Well, I never."

She looked around the bar, which was pretty quiet and getting more so by the minute; then, she turned to Smab and said, "I'm sorry, Smab. I didn't mean to upset you. I appreciate you feeling like you need to check in with me, but you don't have to do that. You know when things are okay and when you need to be around. Why don't you accompany your friends to the hotel now? Paulette and I can close out from here."

Smab said, "Thank you very much, Corene. I appreciate the trust. I'll see you tomorrow."

So Tessa and her group, accompanied by Smabdolem, headed for the hotel. Little did he know what lay in store just a few blocks ahead.

Tessa reached for Smabdolem's hand and looked up at him as if he were her mighty protector, "Thank you kindly, Mr. Ik. I truly appreciate you looking out for us. Unfortunately, the world is full of unkind souls ready to take advantage, especially of those like us. They view us as an oddity to be played with as they see fit rather than living beings with full lives of our own. I could break your heart with the calamities we've encountered."

As he looked down into her sweet, beautiful face, Smab's conflict arose anew. She was a woman in full, as complete as any he had ever considered, but she was also very much like a child who needed protection, and she had singled him out for that purpose. He said, "Yes, the world can be a dark place, but as a good friend once said, 'if you encounter a dark place, you should go there and shine a light.' I didn't understand exactly what he was talking about when I first heard that, as I was only a stupid little snot. But as I've gotten older, the meaning has gotten clear."

Tessa squeezed Smab's hand tightly and then released her grip, sending an unspoken "thank you" up his arm. They walked in silence the remaining blocks to the hotel. When they reached the entrance, Tessa mounted a couple of steps so she could look Smab in the eye and said, "Would you like to come inside for a nightcap?"

Smab responded quickly, "I'd like that very much, but I'll pass on the nightcap. I've seen what happens when folks enter the 'fifth dimension.'"

Tessa laughed and pulled his arm to go inside, "Well, let's go inside. What is the 'fifth dimension?' I've never heard such a thing."

Once they had settled in her room, Smab told her his thinking about alcohol, and she listened intently, nodding at many points in the telling as if to confirm that what he was saying was true. As she stared into his eyes, he could feel his willpower draining away, and he knew that if she made any advances toward him, he would be powerless to stop her. Truth be told, he very much wanted her to make a move, which only added to his being conflicted. The childlike quality of her body with the adult allure of a mature woman was driving him mad.

She turned away and took off her dress as if on queue, revealing her miniature perfection. Then, she turned and strolled towards Smab, who was seated in the chair beside the bed. She reached up for his hand, which he instinctively extended, and then pulled herself onto his lap, straddling him like a pony.

Smab tried his best, "Tessa, sweet Jesus! You are something to behold, and trust me when I tell you, part of me wants you worse than bad, but I'm not sure this is a good idea."

Tessa reached up and put her fingers on his lips to quiet him. "Shush now. We're both grown adults here, and clearly, I'm in a consenting mood, and to use your expression, trust me when I tell you, I want this."

Then quick as Lucky the cat, she slid off his lap and stood between his legs. Slowly undoing his zipper, she grabbed Smab's now fully awake member with her little hands and slowly began to blow his mind and, finally, his wad. Smab's head rocked back as she brought him to climax.

Then, Tessa looked up at him with a look of complete satisfaction. She thought, "This man is mine now, body and soul."

Smab had similar thoughts about his ownership, but their intentions could not have been further apart. In a matter of hours, he had fallen completely for this diminutive vixen, and he felt, without a doubt, that he would do anything she asked of him. Anything.

Tessa was now ready to take advantage of this new-found protector and regain what had been so cruelly taken from her.

She said, "Now, doesn't that make you feel more relaxed? There's something about a sexual release that clears everything up. Now, I don't want to move along too fast, so we'll keep the next part of the game for later unless, of course, you're ready to return the favor now."

Smab's conflict finally gave way as he scooped her childlike body up and laid her on the bed. Then, practically tearing his clothes off, he lay down and pulled her over on top of ready again cock. With practiced precision, she rocked slowly back and forth, taking his hands and rubbing his rough fingers all over her expectant breasts and moist nether regions, bringing him to climax in mere moments.

She thought, "This man is done. Now, we make plans."

A Brownstone Turns Dark

The following day, Tessa left her group behind and made her way to an elegant brownstone a few blocks away. She pulled a key from her purse, unlocked the front door, and walked inside. Everything was just as she had left it the day before. She walked down the stairs to the basement and unlocked the padlock on the door. She heard a muffled noise from the other side but showed little concern for her safety. Once inside, she flicked on the bare lightbulb overhead. It cast long, menacing shadows across the dirt floor. Seated in a chair just under the bulb, with hands and feet tied tightly, was an older man who looked at Tessa in great fear.

Tessa said, "Hello, Mr. Judy. I see you came through the night safe and sound. Sorry about having you bound and gagged like this, but a woman can't be too safe, now, can she?"

Mr. Judy tried to speak but could not, although Tessa seemed to understand his thoughts and answered the unspoken question. "Your wife, saint that she is, especially for bringing us all into this fine home of yours, seems to have taken a bit of a fall. Poor thing cracked her head after she slipped in the bath. Well, at least, she went out clean in body and spirit."

Mr. Judy moaned loudly through his gag, and tears rolled down his face. His head slumped onto his chest; his body shuttered as he wept.

Tessa continued, "Now, this next part is still a work in progress, so you'll have to bear with me for another day or two, then we'll get you all sorted out. I've enlisted the help of a friend to take care of some things in the meantime, so don't worry your little head about us girls; we'll be fine."

Mr. Judy looked at her with renewed terror and struggled to speak again but was consumed with the enveloping darkness as Tessa retreated and killed the light. She thought of Smab's saying about "shining a light in the dark places" and chuckled.

Smab walked into the bar the next afternoon, barely touching the ground. Corene immediately noticed this change in his demeanor and came over to check in.

"Well, someone seems to be in a light and happy mood. I almost didn't recognize you with that grin on your face. I never knew your face could twist like that," Corene said as she chuckled.

Smab was somewhat embarrassed but replied kindly, "That makes two of us. The night was a little more involved than I initially thought, but I got them to the hotel safe and sound."

Corene, not one to miss a chance at advancing a juicy story, "And Smab, is that ALL you did? It seems that grin tells me otherwise. Oh, it's all good, as long as you keep your head about you. And the right head at that!" She chuckled wildly at this last bit as Smabdolem blushed mightily.

Smab couldn't help laughing at himself and said, "For the first time in my life, that is something to be concerned with, but I feel like it's all going to work out fine. Now, leave me be, will you?"

Corene hugged him and said, "Good for you, boy, good for you."

He replayed the night before and tried to make sense of all that had happened. The apparent innocence of Tessa and her friends had been disarming, to say the least, but the scene at the hotel, with all its hopefulness fulfilled, left him not only conflicted but perplexed. How could this tiny but insatiable being get drawn to him in such a way, and there NOT be something else at hand? And with that, his grin was replaced with familiar lines of worry.

Tessa met with her gals at the brownstone and set about plans for the next phase of their operation. She informed them that the big guy was hers to do with as she pleased; all they had to determine now was what that would entail. They had already taken care of the wife, creating an accidental fall that killed her. So all that remained was the play on the husband and, of course, the disposal of both their bodies. This part of the plan is where good old Smabdolem Ik would come in handy. She assured the girls he would have no problem helping them if she kept twirling him around her little finger. Of that, she was most confident.

One of the girls suggested, "What if we used Smab some way to get rid of the guy for us? You could make up a story that he abused you and made you do things against your will. Judging from how easy you wrapped him up, that would set him off like a stick of dynamite."

Tessa smiled at this and replied, "That's an exciting thought, but it doesn't help us get rid of the bodies after the fact. Unless. What if we bring Smab into the house and show him the wife we've already taken care of? We tell him both were involved in the abuse. The husband did the nastiest of things while the wife got off watching it all."

They all felt this would put Sambdolem over the top, and he would do whatever they needed to make amends. But darkness is funny in how it conceals the light of understanding.

Tessa walked into the bar alone, and Smab instantly jumped up from his perch and went to her. "What brings you back here today? You aren't performing again, are you?"

She grabbed a handkerchief from her purse and quickly whipped up some tears, "No, no, Smab, there's something I need to show you, and it's especially urgent. Can you come with me for a few minutes?"

Corene saw this exchange behind the bar and met Smab's gaze, giving him the okay wink.

Smab looked at her, "Okay, let's go, but we need to make it quick."

Tessa thanked him profusely, "Yes, yes, of course. As quick as we can."

The Light Flickers On

They walked quickly in silence down the street, making several turns along the way. Then, as they walked up the steps to the brownstone, it occurred to Smab exactly where they were; this was old Judge Judy's house. He had heard about the judge from Corene, who kept her ear firmly planted on the ground for any dirt that might prove helpful. It turns out Judge Judy was gay and married to a woman who, of all things, was a lesbian. They both existed in the darkest of closets, but word had gotten out to those in the know. Smab had seen the judge come into the bar on certain nights when the entertainment was to his particular liking under the guise of meeting an associate on a work-related level. He didn't know about the wife's other side of life but assumed her to be utterly harmless.

So, when Tessa pulled out a key and entered the house as if it were her own, he was somewhat alarmed. Tessa ushered him in quickly as if she didn't want anyone to see their comings and goings. Then, she led him into the large parlor just off the entrance, where all the other girls were gathered, all very distressed.

Tessa turned to Smab, grabbed him by his large hands, and said, "We need your help desperately. This husband and wife pair took us into their care under the guise of kindness and then tried to take every advantage imaginable when we were most vulnerable. The husband would tie us down and have his most wicked way with us while his loving wife watched from across the room. It was beyond awful."

Smab was taken aback by this revelation and said, "How could that possibly happen? Where are they now? And what does any of this have to do with me?" He was getting visibly angry, just as they'd hoped, but their assumptions would soon prove incorrect.

Tessa continued, "We broke free and overpowered the wife, knocking her on the head while she was showering. Getting the husband under control took all our might, but we finally tied him to a chair in the basement. He's there now, the awful creature."

After hearing this, Smabdolem's face reddened, and his eyes filled with rage. "Take me to him. Now!"

They all headed to the basement, assured that Smabdolem Ik would tear the judge apart with his bare hands. The plan was working out perfectly.

As the light chased the shadows away and Smab saw the judge tied to the chair, a noise started building in his deepest, darkest self. In a rage, he rushed to the chair, grabbed at the judge, and pulled him violently this way and that. Even as they hoped Smab would destroy this man, they quickly became afraid of the rage they'd unleashed. Then, Smab stepped back from the chair, still ranting angrily, reached into his pocket, and withdrew his trusty pocketknife. Then, in a series of lightning-fast cuts, released the judge from the chair. He quickly pulled the judge off his feet, threw him over his shoulder, and carried him back upstairs.

Smab stopped on the stairs and yelled at the girls, "Stay here while I take care of this piece of trash. I'll be right back, don't you worry."

Tessa looked into Smab's eyes, feeling she still had infinite control of this beast. "Thank you, Smab. We'll be right here when you return."

Slamming and locking the basement door behind him, he proceeded to take the judge into the kitchen so he could have a better look at his injuries. Besides being scared to death, he didn't seem worse for wear. He removed the gag and asked after his wife. The judge broke down and told him she was upstairs in the tub, dead, just as Tessa had described. He was inconsolable in his grief.

Smabdolem then returned to the entry area and broke up the place, making it sound like he was destroying the judge with extreme prejudice. Eventually, the crashing sounds died down, and Smab was breathing heavily from his exertions. Finally, he gathered up the judge and walked him out the back of the house, depositing him with a neighbor across the way.

Unlocking the door, he re-entered the basement to confront the girls. They huddled together and cried, expressing their utmost thanks to Smab through their tears. Then, he reached his big, burly arms around the four of them and squeezed. At first, they thought this to be a comforting gesture but quickly realized it was something else entirely.

Smabdolem's rage finally exploded as they started screaming for their lives. He squeezed and yelled at them, "That was quite the tale you told about the judge and his awful wife. The only catch is they're both gay, so the chances of them doing any of those things to you are less than zero. But you. YOU! What should I do with you?"

Tessa was trying to catch her breath to salvage the predicament but to no avail. Eventually, Smab squeezed the four of them into unconsciousness. He then tied them around a pole in the basement, giving them a taste of their medicine, and left them in utter darkness.

When he returned to the bar, he told Corene what had transpired at the judge's house and asked for her advice. "Oh my God, Smabdolem, what those girls go and do something like that for? We have to tell the police right now. Thank the Lord they didn't kill the judge, too, so he can vouch for you. Otherwise, you might find yourself in a deep hole."

Smab replied, "That crossed my mind, for sure. I'm off to the police. I'll be back soon, but who knows how long that will be.

Corene nodded and said, "Smab, you a good man. Now go and take care of this terrible thing quickly as you can."

As he ran towards the police station, Smab thought about Tessa and all that had happened in the last 24 hours. How could life throw so many conflicting emotions at him at once? Indeed, this was a test, but he couldn't say to what end.

Then, as if he was running beside him to gather the police, he heard his old, dearly-departed friend say, "Good job with those tiny terribles today. That's what I meant when I said, 'if you see a dark place, shine a light in there.' They made it very dark for you and that family, but you came along and lit it up for all the world to see."

And like that, all of Smabdolem's conflicting emotions melted away, and he was again at peace. He felt Cora would be pleased.

Dorkus Ilamdril

Dorkus Ilamdril

Looking across the rainforest landscape, Dexomexa notices sun-moon rising as sun-sun is setting in the opposite distance. Xenolabyrinthia has no moons but two suns. Sun-moon is much farther away and casts little in the way of daylight, but still much more than the typical moon on Earth. Sun-sun is the closest of the two and bathes the landscape with heat and light far exceeding anything on Earth. Calling the rainforest a rainforest is a misnomer, as it should be called a steam-forest since the mist that rises above the tall palm-like trees is steam cooling.

"Dorkus, it's time to get out of your pod. Sun-moon is on the rise, and dim-day is just beginning. You don't want to be late for your mission assignment," Dexomexa sing-sang via inner-speak. The Xeno's had advanced beyond the spoken word and primarily used inner-speak, a style of telepathic communication. Their written language, relegated to areas such as signage on space trams and transport pods, was a stylized form of hieroglyphics. "Yes, mother-unit, I'm releasing my hatch now," Dorkus responded.

The hatches were necessary for sleeping as they were the only temperature-controlled zones apart from the common room. Once you awakened in your pod, your next task was to suit up to leave the hatch. From that point forward, your second-suit was the only defense against the two sun's heat and rays. It contained all your life support systems, from hydration to waste management. It was called the "second-suit" because it fits like a second skin.

Dorkus had been training for years to be part of the Alien Exchange Program the Federation of Planets (FOP) created. He didn't know where his assignment would take him, but his excitement about experiencing new cultures and visiting strange locations was constantly building. Finally, they would receive their mission assignments today!

Down at FOP headquarters, Dorkus' case handler looked over some interesting new data from the comms. It was somewhat cryptic, but the words "Illegal Alien Exchange Program" caught his eye. Unfortunately, the message was transmitted using an obsolete radio-wave technology he had only heard about in history downloads. Even so, it appeared the lingo translators had correctly deciphered the contents of the transmission. He also deduced this world must be associated with FOP's Alien Exchange Program, so he set the coordinates for this new planet, Earth, as Dorkus' drop point.

"What do we know about this planet? I've never heard of it before," Dorkus replied.

"We know nothing except they are part of the Alien Exchange Program, so we can assume them to be relatively advanced," his handler responded. "Your primary mission will be to learn as much as possible about this planet and report back. But, unfortunately, we have nothing on them in our data mines, only the transmission received via comms today."

Dorkus zip-tubed back to his common room to say farewell to his mother-unit and make his last-minute preparations. He was told the trip would be long, over 20 milliseconds, and he would feel disoriented upon arrival. Discussions about whether his comm-link would remain viable were left uncertain. He desperately hoped his link would work because if it didn't, he would be at a complete loss when communicating with any beings he encountered. His handler assured him his second-suit would remain intact.

Modern space travel had advanced far beyond the old days of jumping from wormhole to wormhole, witnessing space as a series of elongated bands of light and color rushing past. Now, you could enter the coordinates for your destination directly into your frontal lobe, and when ready, blink twice, and you were there. You must blink twice, of course, as the first blink begins your departure and the other finalizes your arrival. Still a bit clunky but sufficient in most cases. There were no transportation centers like the old airports. You could depart from anywhere, anytime. With sufficient intel, you could determine your "appearance" location within a few millimeters. Lacking proper intel, your destination became a little more challenging. For example, you might wind up inside a building or in front of a shuttle hurtling down the street. Not ideal, but most times, workable.

Such was the case with Dorkus and his assigned appearance destination. Immediately following his second blink, he discovered himself inside a small metal box that felt like it was moving. It was well-lit, and there was one other being inside. That being carried a small transport case of some classification, and when he turned to discover Dorkus, who had instantly appeared, his eyes widened, and he started moving his mouth, producing strange sounds.

"Where the hell did you come from?" the man exclaimed. "What's up with you scaring a guy like that?"

At that precise moment, Dorkus realized his comm-link was not working. He also noticed that this being's second-suit didn't match his skin color and texture the way Dorkus' suit matched his.

"So what in the world are you doing standing here naked as a jaybird gawking at everything?" the man stammered.

Just then, the small room stopped moving, a panel opened in the wall, and the being ran out of the metal room, leaving Dorkus behind. After a moment, he gathered his courage and stepped out of the box into what looked like a very long, skinny room. Many evenly spaced vertical rectangles followed one another along the room's walls, and yellowish light orbs hung above the floor at other intervals. The floor was not the smooth stone of Xenolabyrinthia but rather a soft, squishy material. It felt curiously comfortable under his feet.

Without warning, one of the rectangles opened, and two other beings emerged. One was similar to the being he had first met, but the other was very different. It was smaller, had longer hair, and wore a different type of second-suit. Both looked at Dorkus with wide eyes and hurried away down the skinny room without making a sound.

Thinking he should trace his steps back to where he started, he returned to the small metal room. Unfortunately, the door closed as soon as he entered, and it began moving again. When the door reopened, Dorkus entered a vast space where many other beings were moving randomly. As he walked into the area, these beings instinctively avoided him, never making eye contact or running away in alarm. Curious. He decided to enter one of the invisible streams they were pursuing and see where it led. He passed through several large archways and, finally, through a transparent, rotating wall. This rotating wall had several sections, each containing just one being. He assumed it was a collator or counter of some sort. As the wall rotated, those beings inside the segments departed, and others entered from the opposite side. However, the wall never stopped moving. Almost as soon as he entered, he found himself outside, where many beings and all manner of mechanical devices were running about.

He thought to himself, "I really could use my comm-link now. And my second-suit, while it seems to be functioning well, certainly stands apart from what these beings are wearing." Then, slowly walking down this broad, rock-like path, he noticed some extraordinary beings standing beside a wall, looking very intently at him.

"Hey, cutie," one said, "I like how you're lookin' in your birthday suit. Wanna come inside and have a good time? You lookin' a little lost, honey." This long-haired being was the first being who hadn't tried to avoid him, so he took it as an excellent sign. Maybe he could communicate with it and maybe find a more appropriate second-suit.

He walked over, and the prostitute took him by the hand, smiling into his eyes. "So, you're a quiet one. That's okay. We cater to all kinds, and I do mean ALL kinds."

At this, she pulled him into a small, dark room, pushed him down on a small soft surface, and then sat down next to him. Next, she slowly removed her second-suit as if she was having trouble with it. Then he noticed she had several strange hieroglyphics on her skin. They looked familiar but indecipherable. He reached out his hand to touch them, but the girl jumped back and shouted at him, "Wait a minute, mister, you don't get to handle the goods until I see some cash. For $50, I'll take you around the world." She stood there, looking down at him with a severe stare, awaiting his response.

Dorkus could tell that not having comms could be a disaster ready to happen. So he had to find some sort of Intelli-link to help him communicate.

Thinking he could use sign language, he grabbed a piece of the being's second-suit and draped it across his chest. The prostitute started laughing. "Wow! So you're quiet AND a cross-dresser. It must be my lucky day." Then looking more closely at him, she said, "Hang on a minute, I've got just the thing for you in my closet."

She hopped over him and pulled something out of a small chamber.

When she turned back towards him, he saw another component of a different second-suit. The prostitute pulled him to standing and took the bra he had nabbed earlier. Then she slipped a tight-fitting red dress over his head and attached a spiked dog collar around his neck. "Wow! Now you look like something! Let's hit the street and see what we can make happen." And with that, the prostitute led Dorkus on a leash back out to the street.

As they slowly walked down the street, the prostitute paraded Dorkus. "Check out my new pet. Pretty cool, huh? He doesn't turn any tricks yet, but give me a little time, and soon he'll be the life of the party." The reactions he witnessed from the beings passing by left him somewhat disturbed and concerned for his safety. Some beings got very excited and agitated, while others turned and hurried away with their eyes wide. All his instincts told him to escape this situation as soon as he saw an opportunity, but how?

After a while, the prostitute returned him to her room and sat him on her soft surface again. Then she removed the dog collar but left him in the dress. Sensing the time was right, he jumped off the bed and ran away as fast as his dress-constricted legs could carry him. The prostitute screamed after him, "Wait, where are you going? We were just about to have some real fun. Hey, that's MY dress you have on! You better get back here!" All of this he heard fading away in semi-doppler effect as he raced down the street, unsure where he was headed other than away from her.

After a few blocks, he turned into an alleyway to catch his breath. As he stood gathering himself, he suddenly noticed more of the strange hieroglyphics he'd first seen on the prostitute's skin. Only these were all over the walls. They were rather beautiful, and there appeared to be layered messaging, with one set of glyphs applied over the other. Very strange. His advanced intellect told him these symbols were some secret language fundamental to how these beings conducted themselves. He tried rebooting his comm-link, and this time, miraculously, it garbled out a message. It didn't make sense to him, but at least it was a start. As he stared at a section of the wall, his inner-speak said, "Man who writes on shithouse walls should roll his shit into little balls. Man who reads these lines of wit should eat those little balls of shit." Curious. He must decipher this "shithouse" and learn more. He also discovered that while the comm-link seemed to interpret what he was looking at, his speech-producing protocols remained inoperable.

Unexpectedly, he heard someone yelling at him. He turned to see a significant, dark-complected being with shiny eye coverings and a long coat walking towards him. There were two others in similar dress following close behind. They swayed back and forth slowly as they walked toward him, grabbing their genital areas and gesturing menacingly at him. His "danger" sensors activated protective measures, but like his comm-link, he wasn't sure they were working.

"Yo! What do we have here? Is you a lady or some damn man dressed up like a skank-ass ho?" the leader said, looking over his reflective eye protection. The two others laughed at this for some reason and then quickly stopped as the leader turned and stared at them. "You know this is my territory, right, so you better be moving along. You get me? Or maybe you be needin' someone to take care of you, you know, look out for your well-being and all."

Sensing their demeanor had changed, Dorkus reached out his hand in the universal symbol of welcome. The leading man looked at him for a bit and then took his hand, shaking it vigorously, pulling him against his chest, and bumping and slapping him roughly on the back. "Yeah, I got you. You my bitch now. That's right!"

With that, they all turned and walked down the street toward some sort of waiting vehicle. It was long and black and had large shiny wheels. A pair of fuzzy cubes hung from a small shiny window in the middle of a large piece of glass. In fact, there was glass all around the upper chamber, so Dorkus thought it must be a type of zip-tube transport. The two followers opened a series of small doors, and they all squeezed inside the device. There was a unique aroma Dorkus had never encountered. It smelled burnt and yet somehow sweetly aromatic. One of the followers reached up and turned a small metal tab, starting an engine of some sort, and they were moving down the street in no time. Then the driver reached up and switched on a noise-making device, which was very loud. Dorkus could feel the sound waves pounding his body, making him very uncomfortable. As they rolled down the street, each man started rocking in time with the sounds, looking very menacing as they stared out the glass compartment. Occasionally they would yell something strange out the window at a passer-by who would acknowledge them in various ways. They rode for a few blocks and then turned into another alleyway that led to a large metal door. Momentarily the door slowly opened, revealing a vast, dark chamber. The transport unit pulled into the room, and the metal door squeaked shut behind them. His eyes quickly adjusted to the dim light, and he saw several other people lying around on soft surfaces and other apparatuses inside the room. A cloud of blue smoke was just above these people, which matched what he had smelled earlier in the transport.

One Swell Dude

"What up, bitcheses! Papa's in the house!" the leader yelled to no one in particular. A series of subdued moans and groans echoed back to him. "Come check out my latest talent edition to the scene."

Several languid bodies slowly assumed a standing position and ambled over to inspect Dorkus.

Girl #1 asked, "Is she a she, or is he a she? I can't tell?"

Girl #2 followed, "Whatever flavor it is, it show got a big ol' forehead. Damn!"

Girl #3 added, "Yeah, but it's kinda cute. You know, like an ugly puppy is cute."

They all laughed at that and then slowly found their way back to their reclining positions, the same as before.

Dorkus scanned the room in silence and again took notice of the hieroglyphics contained therein. As he walked towards the nearest wall, he noticed a small open door leading to another room where the walls were covered entirely with strange symbols, many of which looked like various forms of genitalia. As he had seen previously, the messaging was many layers deep, and the graphics were quite varied, but all followed a familiar theme: this thing called "dick" or "cock" seemed to be the key to unlocking it all. He just had to crack the code so that he could understand everything.

Upon entering the dimly lit room, he noticed a line of what he assumed were docking stations lined up against one wall. He could tell they had once been white but were all shades of yellow and brown now, and a distinct ammonia smell emanated from them. Some had what looked like giant pieces of blue mineral nestled in the bowl at the bottom. A shiny handle, whose purpose was unknown, was mounted at the top of each station. He heard one team member enter the room as he studied the units. He walked over to the docking station, unfastened the waist of his second suit, and pulled out a long black extension. Then, leaning one hand against the wall, he sprayed the docking station with a curious yellow liquid.

"Ahhh, yeah! That's much betta. My back teeth was startin' to float," he said laughingly. "Whatchu looking at my man? You better get your eyes back in that big white head of yours. Oh, I get it. You want to compare junk and see who got the biggest Johnson. Awright! Whip it out, then. Let's see what you got."

He motioned for Dorkus to unfasten his second-suit and remove his waste management umbilicus. Confused by this sudden interaction, he felt compelled to try and mimic the stranger's actions as best he could. He pulled the release tab on his second-suit, and retracted his umbilicus, which was quite long compared to the strangers. This development resulted from years of evolution and genetic engineering, providing greatly enhanced wastewater management without needing external evacuation into a docking station.

"Holy shit, man! What the hell is that thing? A damn white anaconda!" the stranger yelled. "Dayam!"

He then ran out into the main room, yelling for the others to come and see. Immediately, all the beings filled the room and began looking at Dorkus and his flaccid umbilicus. The men's faces showed various states of shock and amazement, with a bit of envy. The women were equally awestruck but more out of wonder and sheer admiration. None of them had seen anything like this before, but they couldn't wait to get their hands and other parts on it.

The leader held up his hand to calm everyone down, slowly walked up to Dorkus, and looked him in the eye. Then, with as much respect as he could muster, he held his hand out to Dorkus, "My man, you are true, my man! If I had junk like that, I'd never leave the house!" Finally, grabbing Dorkus' hand in a series of confusing grips and slaps, he shook it vigorously and motioned for him to put his umbilicus away. The girls, who were now quite taken with erotic possibilities, made their way over to inspect Dorkus with newfound respect and admiration.

Excitedly, they all exited the docking station room. Dorkus would have to explore the markings he discovered in more detail later. But, for now, he felt like he was, at last, communicating with these beings on some level, unsure what message he was sending.

The leader and his two associates headed towards the vehicle and grabbed him to come along. "We got's to get you into some nice threads, man. Can't have you walking around in that damn dress 'cause you sho as hell ain't no woman." He directed the associates, "Head down to 'Needles,' and let's get him zoot-suited up and some nice flaps on his feet. Then we can make a plan about what to do with him." All the while, Dorkus looked out the window, seeing secret message after secret message passing by his window. It was so frustrating he couldn't decipher what it all meant.

Pulling up in front of 'Needles,' they departed the vehicle and entered the building. Dorkus spied what looked like the torso of some unfortunate individual, staked on a pole. Its skin was unlike anything he had ever witnessed, soft like fabric but tight still on the underlying body. They were quickly greeted by what he decided was a tiny woman, barely five feet tall, with straight black hair and large glasses, wearing many narrow adornments around her neck, soft tape with evenly spaced numbers. She wore a small pod on her wrist with many tiny metal needles stuck in it. Dorkus felt this had to be very painful, but she showed no signs of distress.

"Kimchee, I want you to meet my new main-man..." the leader started, then stumbled, "what are we calling you, my man? You gotta name?"

Finally! A word he recognized, Dorkus croaked as best he could without his comm-link voice module, "Dorkus."

"Dorkus!? Hell, hung like you is, I don't care what we call you. Kimchee, meet Dorkus. I want you to fix him up in the most fly zoot suit you ever stitched. Now, when you start measuring him for pants, allow plenty of room for that firehose he got dangling between his legs," the leader smiled.

"Oh, you got big wanker, no? We see about that," Kimchee laughed. "Follow me." As Dorkus followed her to the rear of the shop, the boys left, saying they would be back in an hour or so. "Stand up here. I measure you." Dorkus was positioned on a small platform in front of three different mirrors. Looking at himself in the mirrors, he could see himself from almost every side. Kimchee started tugging on his second-suit, confused as to what it was. Finally, she said, "Takey this off! I need measure you without suit on."

Very confused by this directive, he obliged her, removing his second-suit for the first time away from the safety of his sleeping pod, revealing his naked body from head to toe. Even he had not seen his body in full like this before. He was amazed at the proportions of everything and the whiteness of his flesh. His muscles were well-defined, and his body hair was barely visible in certain patches.

"Whoa, you do got big wanker. Like third leg! Big thing, no problem, no problem. We strap to other leg. You rightie or leftie?" Kimchee said in amazement. She spun him around several times, taking many measurements and scratching them down on paper. "You put suit back on now, we done."

Dorkus put his second-suit back on and started wandering around the shop. He had never seen second-suits like these before. So many different colors and textures. His only concern was that he didn't see any waste management technology incorporated into them, which would be a problem. And these bizarre things they put on their feet: shoes. There were so many different-looking versions. It was amazing. And confusing.

The leader and his associates returned with the vehicle a short time later. He spoke briefly with Kimchee, and they departed. The leader said in the car, "Kimchee will have your suit ready Friday morning, which will be perfect. After that, we'll hit all the clubs and see how you make out." Dorkus wasn't sure what "hitting the clubs" meant. Maybe this was some musical device, like the glass-bell ringers back on Xenolabyrinthia. It didn't make much sense to him, but he had no choice except to see where it led.

It was getting very dark now—something Dorkus had never experienced on Xenolabyrinthia. The large structures that towered over them had tiny lights showing from within, all the way into the clouds. Even the vehicles had lights shining down the paths they followed. It was all quite remarkable and beautiful.

"Head back to the crib, and we'll hit it for the night," the leader said.

"Dorkus, you've had quite the day. I'm glad we bumped into you like we did. I see big things in your future." At that, they all laughed loudly.

At the "crib," Dorkus started encountering a very distressing pain. His stomach was very cramped, and his lower abdomen was convulsing erratically. "Yo! Do you need to take a shit, man, or what?! Come on, I'll help you out," one of the girls said, leading him into the docking station room. Once there, she showed him a small room he hadn't noticed before, with a different docking station, this one low to the ground. She motioned for him to enter, but he didn't understand. Then, she started pulling at his second-suit, trying to remove it. He stopped her and released it for her, then she shoved him down on the station and said, "Okay, now you can do your business. I'll be right out here when you finish up." She left, closing the small door behind her.

Scribbles of the Ancients

To his amazement, he noticed hieroglyphics covering the door and walls of the tiny space, so he could finally study them in peace. Of course, there were the usual genitalia depictions, but there was also considerably different wording like he had seen earlier. "There was a man from dumb-dass, whose huge balls were made of brass. And when he'd screw his bitcheses, his balls would bang like thunder until lightning shoots out their ass." His comm-link must be malfunctioning. There is no way they would use metal alloys to create testicles on this primitive planet. They didn't even attempt such a thing on Xenolabyrinthia. And what is this "screwing" all about. And weather anomalies such as lightning shooting out of their anuses, no way. What did any of this mean?

As he studied the graphics, his primal bodily functions returned from their long-dormant state, and he defecated quite prodigiously into the docking station, causing him great alarm. "What the...? That was inside me!? And that smell, oh my." Because he always wore his second-suit on Xenolabyrinthia, which handled all the bodily functions, he had never witnessed any of his waste product. And now that he had seen it, he certainly didn't like it.

Sensing he had completed his business, the girl asked, "You all finished up in there? Make sure you wipe your backside before you get out. And light a match, damn. You stanky!"

Noticing the soft paper next to the station, he pulled on it, unrolling a generous quantity. Was there no end to this infernal thing? But then, he heard from outside, "Yo, don't use up all the paper! Just tear off what you need. You need help?" Without waiting for his reply, the girl entered the small room and took over the paper machine. "Here, wipe your bottom with this." She motioned to his posterior as she did this, and Dorkus did as she directed. "Good, now drop it in the bowl, and we'll flush it all down. Whoo!" She stood him up again, and he refitted his second-suit—what an experience. He couldn't help noticing how she eyed his umbilicus, slowly reaching for it before she caught herself and stopped.

The leader said, "Come here, Dorkus, and I'll show you where you'll be sleeping tonight. It's not much, but it's better than sleeping on the street." He directed him to a small, dark room with several small sleeping platforms on the floor. All but one already had someone lying on top, trying to sleep. In total, there were six people in the pod. "Sleep tight, and we'll carry on in the a.m." Dorkus settled down and, much to his surprise, fell asleep almost instantly. His body was tired, and his mind bewildered. Not being able to communicate was much more challenging than he ever imagined it might be. He wished he had paid more attention in history classes instead of relying on his AI implants to provide all the answers. What he remembered from his recollections just wasn't sufficient for the task.

An hour or so later, amid all the snores and wheezes that filled the room, Dorkus was awakened by one of the girls who had crawled quietly into his sleeping pod. She didn't make a sound as she undid his second suit, and Dorkus, not knowing what she was up to, didn't offer any resistance. Finding what she was looking for, she took his umbilicus in both hands, holding it as if choking up on a baseball bat for a quicker swing, and started going down on it, taking it deeper and deeper into her throat. A strange tingling started in Dorkus's loins, one he had never felt before. After a moment, she paused, looking Dorkus in the eye, and whispered, "How is that, boy? I'll bet you never been treated to that before." Then, smiling seductively, she went back to her business. After a few minutes, the tingling resumed and gathered strength until Dorkus could feel he was losing control of his faculties. Finally, he came into the girl's eager mouth. "Oh baby, that was quite the load! Yummy, tastes like spiced honey!" The girl then smiled at Dorkus as she pulled his suit back on. "Next time, you'll pleasure me. I'll show you how, so don't worry about that." And with that, she crawled back to her pad.

This whole exchange left Dorkus very confused. Over the millennia, scientists had studied the human genome, mapping every possible genetic system they could find. As a result, doctors had long since cured illnesses like cancer and heart disease. In addition, human reproduction had been perfected beyond predictability, and babies could be engineered using artificial insemination and growth chambers.

But try as they did, Xeno's scientists had never been able to crack the most basic primal signals produced by various organs during manual sexual encounters. They knew these signals existed, and they knew how to replicate them with absolute precision, but they could not turn them off, which was their primary objective.

Moreover, they felt these uncontrollable urges could lead to very unpredictable, and therefore undesirable, results. It was as if the male genitalia possessed a second consciousness whose sole purpose was to spread seed. These primal urges have propagated for millions of years, extending the genus. Over time and following scientific discoveries, procreation became recreation, and people performed the sexual act more often than not for sheer pleasure. There had also been cases where criminals performed sexual acts to great tragedy, such as rape and murder, but in terms of overall sex act numbers, such occurrences were low. Ultimately, Xeno's scientists determined some riddles could not be solved.

The sun crept through the darkened windows as Dorkus looked around the room. Everyone was slowly moving about, making moans and groans and scratching various body parts. Then, they headed for the docking station one by one to relieve themselves. Dorkus followed behind and observed as best he could. But, for some reason, these beings became very angry when he tried to watch what they were doing. Finally, one said, "Yo man, keep yo eyes off my junk! What the hell?" Sensing danger, he moved away and waited for the room to clear out, then re-entered and tried to replicate their actions as best he could.

When Dorkus entered the main room, the leader called out, "Come on, Dorkus, we got to get us some grub steak and hit the street."

Grub steak? I didn't know you could make steak out of grubs, those white bug larvae he'd seen on Xenolabyrinthia. And what is steak anyway?

As they walked down the street, one of the associates asked, "Hey D, how'd you sleep last night? Hope them bed bugs didn't bite." At this, they all laughed loudly and fell around as they walked. If he understood them correctly, which was debatable at this point, maybe the girl who visited him last night was a bed bug. She didn't bite, but she undoubtedly could have, as she had a mouth full of teeth. He was curious about what she did to him, though, as he had never experienced anything like the tingling and release she'd produced in him.

Rounding the corner, they entered a small establishment with several gathering spaces along a line of windows opposite a long counter with high seats situated along its edge. The smells inside were delightful and created sudden hunger pangs in his stomach. He hadn't realized until now that his second-suit had not fed him since his arrival. Clearly, the suit was not operating, so he might as well dispose of it. Maybe this "zoot suit" Kimchee was creating for him would perform better. They sat in one of the gathering areas and started looking at what they called "menus." Soon a stranger approached the table and asked if they were ready to order. Each person described to her what they wanted off the menu, and when Dorkus' turn arrived, the leader spoke up and said, "My man will have the World-famous Big Breakfast with all the trimmings." The stranger scribbled everything down on a little pad, turned, and walked away. Soon she was back with an array of hot and cold beverages, followed shortly by large trays of food. It all looked extraordinary and smelled fabulous. Then, all conversations stopped, and they began consuming everything on the plates with strange tools. Very curious. Dorkus tried his best to emulate their actions, but it was much more complex than he expected, as was virtually everything about this strange planet.

"Dorkus, how's that food taste to you?" asked the leader, smiling with a sense of satisfaction. "That fried chicken got a good scald on it, and that waffle, mmm, mmm, good." Then he laughed a little too loudly. "Eat up! We got to hit the street to Kimchee's and get your suit for tonight's show."

Dorkus felt much better after getting food in his stomach. However, he was intrigued by the "the show" comment the leader had made. Was he somehow supposed to be a part of a performance, and if so, what was his role? Maybe his new suit would provide some answers.

Being Fly to the Third Zoot

Arriving at Kimchee's shop, they all piled out of the vehicle and strolled inside. She greeted them and asked Dorkus to follow, "Come, we try on suit now. All done. Carry shoes." She handed him two strange-looking gizmos and gently pushed him to the shop's rear. He stripped off his second-suit, making a mental note to dispose of it later, and Kimchee handed him the bottom part of his new suit. Then, she helped guide him into these new "pants" and dealt with the "zipper" and "belt." Then she handed him the top part of the suit. It was made from a much lighter material with many small, hard-to-manage fasteners down the front. Next, she wrapped a decorative strip of cloth around his neck, securing it with a remarkably elaborate knot. The top part of the suit fitted inside the lower part with the decorative ribbon dangling down the front to his waist. Try as he might, he could not see how this suit would provide any of the functions his second-suit offered. Finally, Kimchee handed him a larger top piece that matched the bottom section. It had only a couple of the hard-to-manage fasteners to deal with, for which he was very grateful. She tugged and pressed on the suit as she spun him around in front of the mirrors, muttering to herself.

"Put shoes on now," she said, handing him the two gizmos he had handled earlier. He looked at her in utter confusion. She pulled him down to a seated position, took the shoes away, and lifted his feet roughly to put them on. First, she applied a skin-tight material to each foot. Then she struggled to shove his unsuspecting feet inside the shoes.

"Now, you proper man. Women fall at your feet," Kimchee said as she admired her work. "Come, show others."

"Whoo-ee! My main man, D! You is sharper than my switchblade, boy," the leader exclaimed. "All you need now is a proper brim, and you are ready to play. Kimchee, hook D up with a sly hat."

Kimchee left to retrieve whatever the leader had asked for and, when she returned, handed him a small, soft bowl. Then, seeing he didn't comprehend what to do again, Kimchee took the bowl from him and put it on his head. She then roughly turned him around so he could see himself in the mirror.

Dorkus saw himself and thought, "What have they done to me? I don't recognize myself at all." This zoot suit was SO different from his second-suit, not only in function but in appearance, that he couldn't comprehend its purpose. It felt very loose in some areas and tight in others, unlike his second-suit, which practically matched his skin. And these things on his feet were very uncomfortable. This whole affair would take some adjusting to.

"Now you is fly! Check it," the leader exclaimed. "All the ladies be fallin' at yo feet tonight!" The associates looked him over, examining every aspect of the suit, tugging on the top part, brushing the shoulders back, wriggling the neck fabric. They all agreed he was "fly to the max," which Dorkus accepted as a good thing. The leader paid Kimchee for the suit, and they all departed.

All That Jazz

The proprietor peered out her office window through a cloud of blue smoke to the jazz hall below. The cafe tables were covered with upturned chairs, and maids were sweeping out the previous night's stinky cigar butts and broken wine glasses. The ledger in front of her looked good, all things considered, but it could always look better. Maybe a bit more water in the drinks, a little more for cigarettes and cigars, and perhaps a small bump in the cover charge. It all adds up. There had to be a way to wring more money out of this joint; whatever that way was, she would find it.

"How are we holding up on wine and liquor? And all their mixers, are we good?" she asked the bartender, who was busily marking the levels in each bottle before "adjusting" their contents by adding water.

"I think we'll be good for tonight, but this is our second "adjustment," so after that, we'll need more stock," the bartender said over his shoulder, never breaking eye contact with the bottle he was filling.

Walking down the back hall to the talent dressing rooms, she passed several playbill posters from better times. Her club had once been a launchpad for new and undiscovered talent. But lately, tastes in music and entertainment had changed, and her establishment felt oddly left behind. Patrons didn't want to sit and watch someone sing or play. Instead, they wanted to jump up and hit the dance floor, performing the craziest athletic moves imaginable. Swing, they called it. But, of course, having couples dancing like that meant you had to have a much bigger space. However, space was limited in her establishment, like most of her other options.

She needed a spectacle, something nobody had experienced before, at least not in these parts. Something, better yet, someone she could control. Burlesque shows were getting increasingly risqué, but even almost complete nudity seemed to have limits in keeping audiences coming back. Sadly, vice wasn't as profitable as it used to be, regardless of what form it took. Or maybe sin had become too predictable and too pedestrian for modern man's sensibilities. But she knew from her own experience that the games people played in the privacy of their abodes made club offerings seem like going to church.

She was greeted by the leader and his band of associates when heading out the back door to the alley to get some fresh air. He was always good for a laugh, and God knows she could use that about now.

"Well, if it isn't Mr. Trouble in the flesh. And I see you brought all manner of trouble along with you for backup. So how are you?" the proprietor said to the leader. "I was just thinking about you and wondering when you'd show up."

"You know me. I always pop up when you can least afford for me to make the scene," the leader responded laughingly. "I've been better than I deserve, but I'd wager, not as good as you."

"Come on in the house and let's talk," she said, welcoming them in. They cracked jokes and told lies about all manner of things as they made their way back to her office.

"What brings you to my door today?" she started.

"I want to introduce my newest associate to you. Name is Dorkus. We found him wandering around lost and offered him our kindness, you know because that's how we roll. He's really quiet. Some might say he is too quiet, but he more than makes up for it in the "gifted manhood" area, if you understand my meaning," the leader said.

"Oh really?!" the proprietor replied sarcastically. "What could he possibly have that I haven't seen or had a hundred different ways myself?"

"D! Stand up and show the lady what I'm talking about," as he gestured to an uncomprehending Dorkus. Then, one of the associates motioned for him to pull his umbilicus out of his new second-suit and show it to the lady. The things these beings seemed most interested in made little sense to him, but he felt he had no choice but to follow through and see what developed. So, he unzipped his second-suit and carefully removed his umbilicus, which was easier said than done.

The proprietor's eyes widened, first in awe, then extreme curiosity, and finally, full-blown terror at the site that unfolded before her. "Trouble, for once in your silly miserable life, you DID NOT tell a lie. But, good God almighty, look at that thing!"

"Truth, that's what that is. Truth!" he cackled back. "When this truth first made itself known to me, I told myself, who can help me make the most of this amazing opportunity? And, of course, I thought of you."

"And how, pray to tell, am I to make something out of this "amazing opportunity" as you call it?" she asked.

"As you may or may not know, I'm a bit of a producer, and I've been working on my own show. Now, this ain't some "whiteface singing and jigging" bullshit. No! I want to create something people ain't never seen! It will combine African dance, Burlesque, and pure no-holds-barred erotica. Costumes, music, erotic dance, sex on stage—real Dante's Inferno shit!"

"Boy, you know you can't be doing shit like that in a club! Once they found out what you was doing, they'd shut us down, lock yo ass up, and throw away the key," she yelled back at him.

The leader merely smiled and said, "That's why they ain't never gonna know what we doing. We's gonna keep it a secret, at least as secret as greasin' the right hands can keep something a secret. Think of all the speakeasies that used to be around here. That shit was illegal as hell, yet more liquor was sold then than before. So you see, this 'bad' idea works to our advantage. People don't like being told they CAN'T do something, especially if they like doing it, and even more if it's BAD! That's TRUTH!"

She wanted to tell him he was crazy as a shithouse rat, but deep down, she knew he was right. She had seen some of the very government leaders who voted for prohibition patronizing their favorite speakeasy, hiding in plain sight. And it didn't matter about their wives leading the charge against the evils of drink, shouting their morality for all to hear. These men knew where to get what they wanted, even if it involved sleeping around. Some actually preferred it that way.

"Okay, okay! You've made a believer out of me. So, how are we supposed to make this production of yours happen?" she asked.

"You let me take care of that. So, we agreed on a deal?" the leader asked, holding his hand out to shake.

Reluctantly, the proprietor reached out, "Agreed."

All Systems Go

"Have you had any success linking up with Dorkus? He's been out of comms reach for 72 hours. It's not like him to miss reporting in," the unit commander prodded emphatically via inner-speak.

The comm-link tech replied, "It's as if his comm-link got severed somehow in passage. I can send neural signals without interference, but it's as if his confirmation protocols are blocked or missing. Very strange. And impossible to reboot without a complete link."

"Can you detect a signal from his second-suit? Is it still intact, and are his life-support systems online and functioning? I think we can assume that since we can't communicate with him, his comm-link translators aren't working, and he can't communicate with anyone wherever he is."

"I have a geolocation on his second-suit, but it's been static for several hours now, so either he removed it for some reason, or he has received a mortal injury. Unfortunately, I cannot confirm his actual status beyond that," the tech replied.

"Keep trying to reboot the suit and let me know the instant you have something," the unit commander said, walking away.

Back at the compound, the leader gathered everyone around and told them of his plans. First, they would convert part of the compound into a makeshift stage to practice their dance choreography and work on other stage-related logistics, such as lighting and blocking. Then he would work with the young girl associates to develop exotic costumes for all the characters. He wanted the outfits to be as revealing as possible, yet what was visible had to communicate a strong African heritage. Finally, they would design and build each character's elaborate headdresses and other body adornments, accentuating their sexual energy.

"D, I have a most exciting outfit in mind for you. You ever seen an elephant?" the leader asked.

Dorkus tried to access information regarding this "elephant" but couldn't access the knowledge. So finally, shaking his head in confusion, he lowered his gaze and stood silent.

"I'll take that as a 'No.' Well, an elephant is a giant beast that roams around down in Africa. They are enormous, bigger than the small delivery vans you see running around. It has tremendous ears and two really long tusks made out of ivory. But what makes this the perfect animal outfit for you is their long trunk. They can move that thing around and grab things with it, spray water out of it, and do all kinds of shit," the leader said gleefully. "So, I'm gonna make the top part of your body look like you're sitting atop this big boy, with your legs dangling down below his large flappy ears, and that big old Johnson of yours is gonna be his trunk. You going to be a white elephant, extremely rare. And extremely potent."

The only part of this exchange Dorkus understood was the leader's excitement, so he nodded in agreement, not feeling he had a choice.

"Truth! Let's get it on then," the leader shouted.

Everyone broke away and started working on whatever part of this production was theirs. Dorkus didn't have a role beyond being the elephant, so he just tried to stay out of the way unless asked to help in some fashion. Thankfully, he was not needed.

After a few hours, when everyone was fully involved with their creation, one of the girl associates approached Dorkus with her outfit. She was the African Queen, wearing an elaborate green turban headdress and long dangly earrings with many gold necklaces hanging around her neck, and to Dorkus' eyes, not much else. Her ample naked breasts, perfectly round buttocks, and manicured pubic region were utterly exposed. Her only other adornments were piercings through each of her wine-colored nipples. She stood before Dorkus and slowly rotated, allowing him sufficient time for a thorough inspection.

"Oh great beast, I am your Queen. I would very much like to ride upon your majestic trunk and take you on a magical tour of my homeland," the girl said as seductively as possible. "There are many exotic tales I can share with you. Come."

And with that, she took Dorkus by the hand and led him to the small back room where she had a small soft surface waiting. Once there, she commanded him to undress. "You must remove all your clothes for this journey, as they will only impede our progress."

Then, eagerly helping him out of his clothes, she grabbed him by his trunk and slowly massaged it with both hands. Within seconds, that tingling sensation Dorkus had experienced with the other girl associate began. His trunk grew, and the African Queen smiled with great satisfaction. Then, she took it in her mouth and started going down on it, stroking it in and out, making the sensations even more intense. Finally, she stopped, looked up at Dorkus, and said, "Now, my beautiful beast, I will mount your majestic trunk, and we'll tour my homeland." And with that, she shoved Dorkus down on the soft surface, straddling his mid-section, grabbed his umbilicus with one hand, and guided it into her eager vagina.

She moaned quietly as she rocked back and forth, then said, "Thou art truly the most extraordinary beast I've ever encountered. Riding upon your great trunk across my homeland is a journey not to be soon forgotten." After a few minutes of rocking, she became very enthusiastic and started screaming aloud. Then, finally, she gasped a few times and fell face down on Dorkus' chest.

Dorkus feared something terrible may have happened to her, but he was afraid to move. Finally, after a bit, she stirred and said, "THAT was fucking amazing!" and rolled off him, leaving him on the soft surface. "Every woman–hell, man or woman–should know how that feels. Here, let me help you get your clothes back on." She was no longer speaking as the

African Queen but as the girl associate. This change struck Dorkus as very odd. Do they have multiple personalities on this planet?

Back out in the makeshift stage area, the African Queen was actively conversing with the leader. Dorkus walked up just as they finished their talk. The leader said, "D, the African Queen here just told me about your marvelous abilities with that magnificent trunk of yours. You will be the center of our "audience participation" segment of the show. For a hefty fee, the exact amount yet to be determined (the leader chuckled), members of the audience can have their own "white elephant ride" on the stage. First, Queenie and all her maids will dance around the scene, singing African chants. Then, the men will twirl firesticks, dancing in the opposite direction, and chant along. Finally, when the guest finishes their journey, which could be short or long, that's the beauty of it; nobody knows, they'll scream aloud, and everything will go quiet. And that, my friends, is when the top will come off the building. Truth!"

The proprietor arrived at the address the leader had given her, thinking, "Where in the hell am I?" Then the large door rolled up, and she saw him standing there, welcoming her inside.

"Welcome to The Erotic Savanah Theater!" the leader said excitedly. "We have so much to show you. Your mind is about to be blown apart like never before."

"You seem mighty sure of yourself. I'll be the judge of whether my mind is blown or not. Now show me what you got," she said somewhat grumpily. She hoped deep down that this wouldn't be another huge disappointment. The club needed a new gig like never before.

Bowing low to the proprietor, the leader said, "Right this way."

Now seated in front of the makeshift stage, the lights dropped from dim to almost pitch black. Then the sounds of African drums started, and she could see torches swirling around, creating flaming circles in the inky blackness. Next, a lone figure emerged in the center of the stage as the lights came up. The proprietor could see it was the new guy, Dorkus, dressed in a very convincing elephant mask. Then she noticed that his trunk was not part of the costume but his huge Johnson. The dancers and flame twirlers circled Dorkus as he slowly rocked back and forth in place. Then the dancers parted, creating a path for the leader to come on stage. He arrived just as the chanting suddenly stopped with a loud "CHA!"

"Welcome to The Exotic Savanah Theater! Join us on a one-of-a-kind African safari where you can indulge in any and all sins of the flesh. Come ride on the great white elephant's trunk while eager Nubians dance in erotic ecstasy. But first, just to set the right mood, let us take part in the African Queen's celebration of fertility, whereby all the dancers will engage in a fevered orgy of the flesh." the leader bellowed. At that, the chanting started again as all the performers gathered around Dorkus. The men arranged themselves back to back, each taking a woman from behind. The women were front to front, with arms draped over the shoulders of each other. Then, on the signal chant "CHA!" the entire circle started thrusting in unison, looking like a single writhing creature.

As the orgy continued, the leader left the stage and returned to speak with the proprietor. "So, what do you think of our Exotic Savanah Theater? You ain't never seen nothing like it, I know."

By now, the proprietor was curiously aroused by the whole production and having an open mind to new and different things; she took this as a good sign. "I must say, this is NOT what I expected, but it sure fits the "I've never participated in anything like that before" category. Do you really think people will come onstage and have sex with that beast?"

"Well, we might have to plant someone in the audience to break the ice with D, but once that happens, I feel like it's gonna be game on, bitcheses!"

"What do you think of doing a test run here at your place? I could invite some trusted regulars with their special friends to a "members only" review, and we can see how it goes. If it proceeds as you think, then we'll move it into the club after that," she said.

"Truth!" said the leader as he excitedly shook her hand. "Let's do it this Wednesday night. That's usually a slow night, so we won't pull your regular crowd away from the club."

Nervously she agreed, "See you here on Wednesday. I'll have the boys bring over some bar stock and set that up. The rest is on you. Got it?"

"Like balls in my bag!" he laughed hysterically.

"You crazy, you know," as she stood to leave.

Cha to Char-boiled

"I've got a lock on Dorkus' second-suit, and I can tell by the lack of medical data I'm receiving that he's not dead, he just isn't wearing it. I've rebooted the suit and run diagnostics remotely, and it checks out. His comm-link is also working," the comm-tech informed the mission commander.

"If he's not wearing it, how can we communicate with him?" he asked.

"We can't. But we can send someone to the suit's exact coordinates and see if he requires assistance," the comm-tech replied. "So, what are your orders, sir?"

"Make it so. I'll inform Dexomexa that we've located her son, and we're sending support," he ordered.

It was now dark again, and Dorkus wasn't sure what was happening, but even in his diminished state of communication, he could feel something big was about to transpire. The leader and all his associates were in a state of high agitation, running back and forth, barking orders, and moving things about. He did his best to stay out of the way. Then the leader walked up, put his arm around his neck, and said, "D, tonight is going to be your big stage debut. You cool?"

Dorkus didn't understand, so he just nodded, like always. It seemed his best defense.

"Man, when you start working that trunk of yours, with all those dancers grinding 'round you in a circle, this place is gonna come undone!" he followed emphatically. "Truth!"

Dorkus nodded again, and the leader jumped away, humming a tune.

About a hundred people of various persuasions gathered around the makeshift stage area. Nobody knew what to make of the scene, so they clung together in pairs or small groups. Then, the light blinked a couple of times, apparently a signal for everyone to find a seat. Finally, after a few minutes, the leader appeared on the stage, standing in a bright white spotlight. He had on the shiniest second-suit Dorkus had ever seen and was smiling from ear to ear.

"Welcome, everybody!" After some brief hand clapping, he started again, "The Exotic Savanah Theater is about to take you on a magical journey to the center of sin! Sinners, are you READY!" he yelled.

More enthusiastic handclapping followed as the lights darkened again. Then, the sounds of African chants and drums started to build, and dancers entered the stage. Dorkus followed along to his position at the center of the stage and started slowly rocking from side to side. He heard snickers and laughs from the crowd but couldn't fathom why. The flame twirlers followed as the ladies danced in place. Even in his confused state, Dorkus could feel the energy building. Suddenly, someone yelled "CHA!" very loudly, and everything stopped. Then, after a few beats, there was another yell, "CHA!". Next, the flame twirlers dropped one end of their fire sticks into a small vessel, making tiki torches out of them. Finally, all the dancers formed their circle of sex around Dorkus, who continued his slow rocking. "CHA!" again, and the male dancers in the circle of sex started thrusting to a steady drumbeat. The beat continued and began to pick up speed. As it did, the women dancers began to moan and groan in ecstasy. After a minute, the drumbeats picked up dramatically, and the women dancers started screaming in orgiastic splendor. Suddenly the lights went black, and everything was quiet for a single solitary moment. Then, just as suddenly, the audience erupted in screams and applause. The sounds this small but now quite enthusiastic crowd made were deafening and somewhat terrifying to Dorkus, who still rocked.

Then the lights blared back on as the leader jumped back up on the makeshift stage. The crowd continued to hoot and holler as he tried to calm them down. After a minute or so, he could finally be heard over the applause, and he started quietly and then yelled, "And that, my friends, is just the beginning!" Applause erupted again, and he quickly regained control by raising his hands and calming them down. "You are now ready for the main event. But this is not just another dance number where members of our troop have all the fun. Oh no! In this segment, YOU can become part of the show if you so desire." The leader turned and winked at Dorkus as if giving him a sign, the meaning of which was unclear. Then he announced loudly, "Introducing Dorkus, the great white elephant! As you can plainly see, this is not your average pachyderm. Oh no, my friends, this is something else altogether. You see, Dorkus trunk here is precisely what you think it is. A GINORMOUS Johnson! And he will gladly offer you a ride on that trunk if you feel up to the challenge. This offer is open to men and women alike but be forewarned. Once you've had THIS white, you'll never be right again." He laughed, then caught himself up and asked, "So who among you is willing, and able, to take Dorkus on his maiden ride?"

The leader looked out over the group, searching for the female he'd planted as his volunteer when suddenly, several hands shot up in the air. Then, thinking to himself, "Shit, this is working out even better than I expected," he pointed to a stranger in the group. She jumped up and squealed with excitement as she ran towards the stage.

"Winner, winner, chicken dinner!" the leader exclaimed.

He welcomed the volunteer onto the stage. She was a dark-skinned Rubenesque girl with a single long braid running down the center of her bare back. An ample bosom was barely contained by her spaghetti-strapped gold lame dress. Giddy with excitement, she practically drooled when she saw Dorkus' trunk up close as she wriggled and twisted around with pent-up desire.

Slowly stepping to the side of the stage, he said, "Let the safari begin!"

The sound of drums started as the volunteer slowly sauntered around Dorkus, taking in every square inch of his body. Then, finally, she reached out, lightly touched his bare chest, and slid her trembling hand down to his now quite attentive umbilicus. Just as she began to kneel in front of Dorkus, he looked up and saw a familiar face enter the back of the room.

It was Eo from Xenolabyrinthia! He thought, "They must have tracked his second-suit and sent him here to check on my mission."

The girl suddenly regained his attention when she grabbed his trunk in both hands and started blowing him like he was a parade balloon. Dorkus looked up plaintively at an amazed and very confused Eo as she took more of his umbilicus into her throat. He had never seen anything like this and couldn't discern whether Dorkus was in distress or if this was part of his mission research. But, ever the academic, he decided this was part of Dorkus' mission and observed quietly from the back of the room.

The girl stood up and looked Dorkus in the eyes, licking her lips as if he was the best meal she'd had in her entire life. Then, she spun around, pulled up her skirt, and guided his trunk into her steaming cunt with practiced precision. Finally, the crowd started chanting, "Dorkus, Dorkus, Dorkus!" as she rocked back and forth, eyes all but rolling back in her head. Next, after a minute or so of rhythmic rocking and chanting, she came with a full-body shudder, her essence squirting all over Dorkus' trunk and legs.

The crowd went wild as the now exhausted girl pulled away from Dorkus. The leader jumped back on the stage and, putting his arm around the girl's shoulder, helped her off the stage. "TRUTH! That's what you just witnessed. TRUTH!" he exclaimed. "I hope everyone had a good time tonight. We'll be going on another safari soon, so keep your eyes and ears open." Then the actors left the stage as the drums started, and the crowd got on their feet and started dancing wildly around the room.

Eo followed the group to the dressing room. Once inside, he handed Dorkus his second-suit that he'd retrieved earlier and motioned him to put it on. The instant he pulled the suit on, he could tell it was functioning again. He had never felt such relief in his short life.

Using inner-speak, Eo asked, "What was that performance I just witnessed? Is this part of your mission research? And what was that being doing with your umbilicus?"

"You ask good questions, as always," he replied. "When I appeared here several days ago, none of my second-suit's systems functioned. No comm-link, AI translators, waste management, food supplements, nothing—which made communicating with these beings almost impossible, but after some close calls with other beings and some rudimentary language interpretations, the leader you saw on the stage took me into his pod, and here I am."

"We surmised that might be the case after we lost contact with you. Unfortunately, it took a bit of work to locate and reboot the second-suit, and by the time we sorted that out, we could tell you had removed it," Eo said. "So the only way we could reach you was to follow the second-suit and see where that led. Luckily you and the suit didn't get separated."

Cosmic Interplanetarianisms

By now, the rest of the troop had noticed Eo and Dorkus were together, and Dorkus had put his strange suit back on. Finally, the leader approached and spoke to them, "D! Who is your friend here? I didn't know you had any relatives in town."

Finally able to use his comm-link and translators, Dorkus talked with the leader. "Leader, this is my associate Eo. He joined me here and helped get my second-suit functioning again. He has come from very far away, as have I, to learn more about your planet's customs."

"Far away? You mean like New Jersey or Philly, or farther away than that?" the leader asked, looking somewhat confused by Dorkus' sudden ability to communicate.

"Let's just say farther away than that," Dorkus replied. "I'd like to ask you some questions. First, the routine we just performed, what was that about? Is it a sporting event of some kind? And what was that girl doing to me on the stage?"

"D! That was TRUTH. That's what that was! That girl was living her wildest fantasy right there for all to see. Shit, sex is the oldest game there is. And my man D, whether you know it or not, you are quite the sex machine. People would pay good money to ride on that big-ass Johnson of yours. Do you folks not go in for boning back home?"

"Boning? No, we don't go in for boning, as you say. The need for sex, as you demonstrated tonight on the stage, has been replaced by other, less messy ways of procreation," Eo replied.

"Procreation?! Man, that was RECREATION, not procreation! She was getting her brains fucked out, exactly how she likes it!" the leader said, incredulous at what he'd just heard.

"Thank you for clarifying that for us. I'm curious about the strange language I've seen used here, a form of advanced hieroglyphics, I think.

Can you tell us about that?" Dorkus asked.

"High-ro what? Man, show me what the hell you talking about," the leader said, getting more agitated.

Dorkus led him to the bathroom and showed him the graffiti on the walls. He pointed out specific bits and pieces to the leader and looked to see his response.

"Strange language?! Man, that's just some stupid shit people scribble all over the place cause they crazy. Ain't no secrets here, just some fool's bullshit. So, what the hell?" the leader said with equal parts disgust and amazement. He turned and walked away, muttering under his breath.

"You've been most helpful. Thank you." Eo said.

Then using inner-speak, Eo said to Dorkus, "This civilization is not what we thought at all. However, the old game of sex seems to be alive and well. Since I have never experienced sex, and you have, could you describe how it made you feel?"

Dorkus thought for a minute and then responded, "The first time I encountered it was different from what you saw tonight. The girl beings truly enjoy playing with the umbilicus and seem to crave it very much. When the first girl took my umbilicus into her mouth, repeatedly sucking and stroking it, it created a new and strange sensation in my loins. A tingling of sorts. Then, most surprisingly, she produced an emission that she said: "tastes like spiced honey." This emission left me feeling somewhat tired but strangely satisfied. So I'd classify it as enjoyable, even though things can get messy, as you witnessed tonight. I suggest we do further research before we abandon all hope."

Giving Dorkus' response due consideration, Eo agreed they would investigate further. Maybe by learning from a much earlier form of being, they could finally crack the primal urge code that had eluded them for so long.

They found the leader and told him they'd like to remain in his pod and learn more about sex. A calculating smile slowly crept over his face as he considered this turn of events, then replied, "So, you two would like to learn more about the big nasty, huh? TRUTH, my brothers. Truth!"

Claudia Felonia

Claudia Felonia

Claudia Felonia sits alone in a windowless room. Some would think it antiseptic and sterile, even mechanical, devoid of human touch. But the air is redolent with lilac, lavender, and other florals, with only a trace of fecal matter and formaldehyde. This "transit station," as she likes to think of it, is where she is most at ease, most herself. Her clients are lifeless, literally. Any concerns they may have possessed in life have long since departed. Any dealings with those of higher status and their judging glances. Their whispers of condescension. None of that exists here, only the silent power of death before life is made eternal.

"There, there now. You look like you've just closed your eyes a bit for a well-deserved nap," Claudia says to the body she is preparing for burial. "That lip gloss brings out your natural color, and as my mother used to tell me–god rest her soul–you should always look your best, no matter the occasion. I try to follow her sage advice. I mean, who wouldn't want always to look their best? What would be the point of that? Surely no good could come from letting yourself go to seed, not caring a wit about who saw you in a sad state of neglect. So, nope, ALWAYS look your best, even if you're not feeling your best. Oh, and that dress they picked out for you is simply perfect. I saw one just like it the other day at Pearlstein's and thought, that sure is a gorgeous dress, but when would I ever wear such a thing? Why I'll bet you'll be the toast of the town when you get on the other side. I can see it now, those pearly gates swinging wide, all that golden sunlight bouncing around, wrapping you in a heavenly halo, angels and cherubs singing in the background, and not a care in the world because you're not in the world, you're in heaven. Oh my, what a glorious time that will be."

Exit Speech

Claudia Felonia is a curious creature. Painfully shy around the living, almost to the point of paralysis. But put her among the dead in her role as a restorative makeup artist (also known as a desairologist), and she can chat for hours about anything, everything, and nothing. Her mind jumps from thought to thought, like a pinball bouncing off the bumpers in a noisy arcade game, as her mouth issues forth an endless stream of play-by-play gibberish. She is a master of one-sided conversations, and the fact her audience can't interact is a definite plus, as they would undoubtedly disrupt her already random train of thought, causing it to jump the rails.

Claudia is also highly devout, and her belief in the afterlife and what it will be like is unshakeable. She attends church every Sunday, always sitting alone and contemplating the shape of things beyond this mortal coil. All those she has lost over the years will be there, patiently awaiting her arrival. And, of course, they will be in the best possible health because this is heaven, after all, so you can only be your best self there. Even her friends once afflicted with debilitating diseases like polio will sing and dance around without a care. Incredible, she believes.

Such is her belief in the hereafter that she started writing personal notes to departed loved ones and concealing them on the persons she is preparing for burial. Tucking these letters under their crossed hands or in a coat pocket, she hopes these notes will find their way to their intended recipients.

"Dear Mrs. Elise, I am entrusting you with this message for my sweet mother, who awaits you in heaven. Her name is Mary Felonia. I'm sure you and she will become fast friends. She should be easy to find in the directory after you pass through the pearly gates, or I'm sure an angel could help you locate her cloud. Please tell her that I am well, and I think of her always. Thanks in advance for your help in delivering this message to her. You are truly an angel now. Until we meet again, faithfully yours, Claudia Felonia."

Funeral directors have much to deal with, from regulatory documents to family directives and supply chain issues regarding coffins or urns. So, they consider themselves truly blessed when they have a specific talent consistently performing as expected. Claudia is just such a monster talent. She is always eager to lend her expertise and can always be depended upon, even if interactions with her are, well, odd.

The funeral director said, "Claudia, I have an exceptional client for you to work on today. She was involved in a ghastly head-on car collision, ejected from the car straight through the windshield. I recommended to the family we have a closed-coffin ceremony, but they wouldn't hear of it. So, you have your work cut out for you. We have some not-too-recent pictures of her for you to review. Time is also of the essence as the service is tomorrow. I know you prefer to work alone, so I'll leave her with you. Let me know if there's anything you require."

Claudia meekly responded, "Thank you, sir. I'll do my best, as always."

As the door clicked behind the director, his footsteps echoing into fading silence and the quiet solitude of her inner sanctum reestablished, she began her work.

"Well, you've gone and made quite the mess out of yourself! However, I'll wager you didn't suffer long, which can only have been a blessing. I've often wondered what's the last thing to go through a person's mind before they die, but I guess in your case, it was that car windshield. Oh, I know that's a bad joke on my part, but if you can't laugh at yourself, who will do it?" Claudia chuckled.

"Let's get you all cleaned up, and then we can start putting you back together. I saw this thing on the telly the other night. It was an electric broom; only they called it a vacuum cleaner. It sucks the dirt right off the floor! And it has all these hoses and attachments for doing all manner of things. It looks like a crazy octopus or something, but it seems like one giant hassle to me. Give me a good old broom and a dustpan, and I'm good to go."

"My, that's quite a gash on your cheek there. I'll have to sew that up, then use some of my special wax to smooth it out. After that, I'll give you a new coat of paint with my trusty airbrush, and you'll be better than new."

"Your hair's a bit of a fright, too, since that windshield glass removed half your scalp. But we can use a wig to get you back in shape there, so no problem. My mother used to wear wigs all the time. She would take her hot curlers and roll up her wig just as she wanted. She loved seeing all sides of it without having to trust a mirror. Then when she had everything just so, she'd brush it out and plop the thing right on her noggin. She tucked in a few stray hairs and, voila, good to go."

"I see you had quite the manicure going there. Too bad you lost several fingers on one hand, though. It looks like a good time to break out the old gloves. I've always loved the feel of new kid gloves. That leather feels like butter, and you can get them in any color you can imagine, even some you can't. Or I could try one of those new prosthetics they have for just such an occasion, and then we could paint you good as new. They now have so many great nail colors, not just primary red or natural. You can go as crazy as you'd like. The other day, I saw this guy at the market; he was a piece of work. He had let his nails grow so long that he had to walk around with his hand in a sling. And those nails looked like some crazy vines coming off the ends of his fingers. They wrapped around one another like a grapevine wreath or something. I don't know how he did anything for himself. I'll bet wiping his backside was a real challenge. Maybe he has one of those new-fangled bidets that squirt water up his bum. That would be something to see. I've always wondered when you might want something like that in the bathroom. I can't imagine there's much call for it, but then again, you never know what some folks are into in the privacy of their own homes. People are just strange birds, don't you think?"

"Looks like that nose could use a little help, too. But again, nothing some well-placed cotton can't set straight. We have to pack it in there to get the shape we want, and "Boom!" you've got a new nose. Your eyes look a little sunken, too, so we'll add some eye caps, glue everything shut, and finish them with lovely new lashes. We'll need to fill out your cheeks with some cotton since you're looking a little on the gaunt side. You can't have people thinking you were malnourished or anything like that. I had the best meal of my life the other night at this all-you-can-eat Chinese place. Sweet and sour everything, chicken about a dozen different ways, all kinds of soups and rice, it was something! And, of course, fortune cookies! Mine said, "You will meet someone soon who will depend on you for their happiness." I'm guessing that must be you! How did they know?"

A Body of Correspondence

After a few hours, Claudia had put her client back together so well that she looked even better than before her untimely demise. Unfortunately, this is not a unique situation, especially when the photos she's provided have some age on them. Most families are happy to see a younger version of their dearly departed, thinking, "She never looked that good in life; at least she can look that way now."

Claudia always ends her time with her clients with a special request. "I'd like you to deliver a message for me when you get to the other side. I'll tuck it right here under your crossed hands, so it will be the first thing you see when you open your eyes. You can't miss it."

"Dear Mrs. Crawford. I am entrusting you with this message for my sweet father, who eagerly awaits your arrival in heaven. His name is Lester Felonia. He was always shy around people down here, but I feel certain he's become quite the social butterfly in heaven. At least, that's my hope and prayer. He should be easy to find in the directory after you pass through the pearly gates, or I'm sure an angel could help you locate his cloud address. Please tell him that I am well, and I think of him often. Thanks in advance for your help in delivering this message for me. You are indeed an angel now. Until we meet again, faithfully yours, Claudia Felonia."

Claudia stands and stretches her aching body back into shape, as she's been sitting now for several hours. Then, smiling, she surveys her work one last time before bringing the director in for a look. "Nice job, Claudia! Thank you, Claudia!"

Unbeknownst to her, a nefarious character of the janitorial sort, Sid Feckman, had been watching her chat away for much of the time she worked on Mrs. Crawford. In his twisted little brain, he thought playing a trick on Claudia might be fun the next time she came to prepare a body. That would make her think twice about rigging up messages to be delivered in the great beyond. What he should have considered was what else Claudia Felonia was capable of doing.

Tower to Launch Pad

Sid Feckman went about his work at the funeral home pretty much as he did about life in general: put in the least effort required to stay alive. What's the use of trying to get ahead? That only creates a harder fall when the whole thing hits the shitter, and everyone knows it WILL hit the shitter. Count on it.

Sid wondered, "How can I put the fear of God in this God-fearing woman? Of course, in her mind, these folks don't become angels until after they're buried, so I'll have to figure a way around that somehow. Maybe I could throw my voice and make her believe the body is speaking to her when she makes her final request of them. I'll bet that'd freak her chatty little ass out."

Then a brilliant thought occurred to him, and for once, he was thankful for his checkered past. If he could get his hands on a two-way radio, like the police use in their patrol cars, he could place a little speaker right under the head of the body where they rest on the preparation table. Then he could speak right to Claudia as if the body were alive. But, of course, their lips wouldn't move, so he'd have to observe closely and speak when Claudia momentarily turned away during her activities. So now all he had to figure out was what to say. Oh, and get his hands on a radio. That might prove a bit more of a challenge.

As luck would have it, Sid's challenge of getting the radio became a little easier when one of the ambulance drivers he knew delivered a body, and Sid noticed the two-way radio they used to talk with their dispatchers. So he casually asked, "Hey, I've been thinking about getting one of those fancy radios you use there. Can you tell me where I might find such a thing?"

The driver looked him over suspiciously and then answered, "Well, you might want to wait until the next version comes along. These units are a little sketchy, especially if you're on the outskirts of town. But if that's not a problem for you, you might be in luck because we are installing newer, stronger radios next week. I think I can get my hands on one of the old ones. So, what's it worth to you?"

Sid tried to conceal his excitement and said, "Well, since you're just going to dump them anyway, why don't you just give it to me?"

Incensed, the ambulance driver said, "And why don't you just jump up my arse then?"

Sid quickly regained his footing and said, "Hold on now, no need to get your Dickies all in a twist. How's $25 sound?"

"Well, if it were $50, that'd sound much more like it," the driver replied.

Sid shook his head hesitantly and said, "You drive a hard bargain, but I'll take it. Tell me when you have it, and I'll get you the money."

"Deal," the ambulance driver said, shaking Sid's hand.

Now that he had that problem sorted, it was a simple matter of what to say when the opportunity presented itself. But then again, maybe it wasn't that simple. First, he had to figure out how to install the speaker under the table so no one would see it. Of course, that meant working in the morgue at night when no one was around. NOT his idea of fun. But he felt it would all be worth it to scare the bejesus out of Claudia.

A few days later, the ambulance driver was back making another delivery for the morgue. Again, he met up with Sid and sewed up the radio deal.

Sid had been thinking about how all this would work. His perch just off the morgue area was very concealed, and he could make it even more so with some ingenuity and some old sheetrock. Ultimately, it occurred to him that if he was talking into the radio in such proximity to Claudia, she might hear him speaking aloud and over the speaker. Not good. So, the idea of building a small closed-off area took shape. He'd add some old blankets to soundproof it and a tiny peephole to watch Claudia, and he'd be in business.

Running the wires was a little more challenging. Luckily, the tile floor in the morgue had a removable grate that covered a large drain cavity running from the table to the wastewater treatment area outside. So all he had to do was lift the grate panels, run the wires underneath, and have them exit beyond where Claudia might detect them and into his hideaway.

It was a longer night than he had expected, but finally, Sid had everything installed and sorted out. About halfway through, he asked himself if all this would be worth it, but he figured he was committed and forged ahead. Damn the torpedoes.

His wait was shorter than expected as a new client was due to arrive the next day, and the director had called Claudia specifically to handle the challenge. An elderly burn victim from an apartment fire. She would require all of Claudia's skills and creativity. And it would not be quick. But luckily, she had a few days before the memorial to do her magic.

The director escorted her into the mortuary where the body lay, covered. As he pulled the sheet back, Claudia let out a small but audible gasp. She had seen burn victims before, but this poor soul was almost unrecognizable. All her hair had burned off, her eyelids blistered and cracked, and large areas of her upper body looked like fully cooked meat taken off a grill. "Oh my, she must have suffered terribly before succumbing," Claudia said, almost in tears. "It will take a lot to bring her back, but I feel like we can make her presentable to the family for their goodbyes."

The director looked at her with great admiration, "I thought if anyone could handle this case, it was you. Thank you in advance for whatever you can do here. As always, I'll leave you with it. Let me know if you need anything at all."

Claudia gently set her tools aside and slowly walked around the body, examining her from every angle. Luckily, she need only worry about the top half of her body, as the rest would be concealed within the casket. But that was little consolation, as what remained was in horrible shape. She pulled out the photos of the person and reviewed them. She was attractive, with bright eyes, full lips, and long blonde hair—a matron in some upper-class family.

"Well, no use beating around the bush; you're a hot mess, at least you were. Now you're just a mess. Let's start by giving you a good bath and removing as much burned flesh as possible. That way, I can see what I need to rebuild with wax, cotton, and whatnot," Claudia said.

This work was tedious and gruesome, as large chunks of her flesh fell away under gentle water pressure and the lightest scrubbing. At times like this, it pays to have a strong constitution and a healthy detachment from one's work. The body wasn't a real person but rather an inanimate object you were charged with making look better. And, they couldn't feel pain, even if you did.

"Oh my, there's not much of you left, is there? But at least your underlying skeletal material is intact. It reminds me of an art show I saw on the telly one night. They were making a sculpture of a little bear, and the artist had to make this thing they called an "armature" out of wire. It looked like a skeleton but not nearly as detailed as you might think. So then they just globbed all this clay on it, and surprisingly it started to look like something. So that's what we have to do with you. We'll build up your tissues with layers of cotton and, finally, cover them with a smooth layer of wax."

"This reminds me of making my layer cake the other day. I love Red Velvet Cake with cream cheese icing! Yum, yum! Of course, it makes watching my figure that much more of a challenge, but you can't be good all the time. At least it's not Devil's Food cake," she said, chuckling at her dark religious humor.

"There was this politician on TV the other night, talking about all the "pork" in some bill he was against. I thought that odd because, judging by his looks, he seemed to be all about the pork—big ol' jowls hanging off his face, tiny little porcine eyes staring at the camera. Just mash in his little pug nose, and you got yourself a County Fair Blue Ribbon winner!"

"I love going to the fair: all the noise and the smells. You see stuff you don't see every day. All those crazy side shows, giant pumpkins or watermelons, beautiful animals, ugly people. And the rides! As Mama used to say, "It takes all kinds, and they're all right here."

After a couple of hours, Claudia stood back and reviewed her work, "Well, we're making progress, but we've still got a long way to go. I need to get some air and make some water, but I'll be back. Don't go anywhere," she chuckled.

Sid had been watching from his perch for much of this time. He saw this break in the action as his opportunity to start messing with Claudia. So he took his position behind the wall, fired up the radio, and put his eye on the peephole. It wasn't long before Claudia came back.

Claudia sat down and said, "I just had the best BM ever. I'd been feeling a little constipated, you know. So I bought some of that laxative you hear about on the radio, and "BAM," it all broke loose. Whoo wee!"

Then the motionless body spoke in a falsetto tone, "You silly cow! I don't want to be hearing about your stinky BM."

Frightened, Claudia almost fell off her stool and muttered, "What in Jesus' name?"

The body just lay there in silence. Claudia stepped closer and examined the mouth to see if anything had changed since her first inspection. As far as she could tell, nothing was different, yet she had spoken.

"Whoa! Maybe that laxative worked too well and shook something loose in my brain, too," she said.

"Stop your jibber jabbering, will you, and get me put back together," the body said, again totally motionless.

"OK, that's it! I'm going to take a walk, and when I return, none of this will have happened. All these chemicals must be getting to me," she said as she backed away from the body.

Sid could hardly contain his glee as he watched her scamper away in fright. His scheme was working out even better than he had dreamed.

Claudia sat alone under a shade tree, somewhat rattled, and tried to sort out what she had just experienced. Nothing like this had ever happened to her before. And even though her belief in the afterlife was unshakeable, she was convinced this encounter was something other than that. Very much other. After a few minutes, she noticed Sid exiting the mortuary. She thought this very odd, as she had not seen him enter when she was working. He stepped out and looked around suspiciously, then laughed as he walked away. He hadn't seen Claudia sitting there, but she had seen him.

"That sneaky little bastard! I'll bet he's behind this little charade. Well, two can play this game," Claudia said as she stood to head back inside.

One requirement for doing Claudia's work is extreme attention to detail. To most people, a nose is a nose, but to her, no two are remotely similar. Of course, that goes for any other feature, so when she returned inside, she examined the body thoroughly from head to toe. At first glance, everything seemed as it should be. But when she got down and looked carefully at the body from the side profile, she noticed something had been duct-taped under the head of the table. She bent down to look and saw it was a small speaker! Then she glimpsed a concealed wire running down the floor drain and leading into the darkness. She followed this wire and discovered Sid's secret hideaway, radio, and all. As she crouched down in the little hideaway, she noticed the peephole. Looking out the peephole, she saw her worktable clear as day.

"Why, that little rat bastard! Does he think he can scare me like that and get away with it? When I'm finished with him, being scared will be the least of his concerns," she thought.

Before leaving the hideout, she cataloged where everything was located. She imagined where and how Sid would perch on his apple box to look out the peephole. The angle of his head as he looked through the hole. Which eye he might favor as he did so. How he would use the radio to spook her.

Every detail she could imagine.

Then she went outside the hideout and repeated this cataloging of information. How could she conceal herself, so he wouldn't see her reenter the room? How close could she get to the peephole before he noticed her? How could she use this surprise to her advantage?

All these data points were thrown into her mental soup pot and left to simmer. She would serve the resulting stew to Sid, quite cold. And with great relish.

A Stab in the Dark

A week or more passed before Claudia was called back to work on a body at the funeral home. During that time, she worked out how she would deal with Sid.

For all her devout beliefs in the hereafter, where good people spend eternity surrounded by singing angels and golden light, you could be forgiven if you assumed she would be benevolent and "turn the other cheek" regarding Sid's transgression. She had undoubtedly heard this lesson should be the preferred approach. It was simply the Christian thing to do. Godlike. But, like many people asserting the Christian mantle, Claudia liked to pick and choose her beliefs, taking into account her unique system of right and wrong. Hers was an odd mixture of old testament wrath and over-the-top vengeance, with a halo.

The director led her into the morgue, saying, "this case is not as bad as the last one you dealt with, but still quite a challenge–a suicide by shotgun. Luckily, he pointed the gun under his chin, so it only took off the back of his head and neck rather than blasting the whole pumpkin to bits."

Claudia was somewhat shocked by what she saw. There was a rather large hole in his throat; otherwise, he looked intact. But things were quite different when they rolled him over, and she saw him from behind. The entire rear section of his skull was missing, and the spinal column was missing entirely down to his upper shoulders.

She exclaimed, "My, to end your life that way. It makes you wonder what was going on with him."

The director quickly answered, "Embezzlement. Curiously, from his ailing mother. Impatient? Insecure? Both?"

"Well, we'll never know," said Claudia, quietly signaling her desire to move on. "I'll get started on him unless there's more I need to know."

The director quickly added, "Nope, that's it. Service is tomorrow. And, as always, thanks in advance for a job well done."

Blushing slightly, she replied, "Thank you most kindly."

Then faking she had forgotten some necessary supplies, she left the morgue. She walked out, sat under her tree, hidden from the door view, and waited. Her wait wasn't long, as, within minutes, Sid slithered his way into the morgue. Claudia waited what she felt was an appropriate amount of time, and she reentered the morgue.

"OK, let's get you cleaned up," she said to the corpse. "Then we'll put your neck and head back together." Luckily, there were prosthetics, essentially plastic skull caps, for such cases as this.

As she started to roll him over, Sid saw his chance to freak Claudia a bit and said, "Hey, be careful how you handle me back there. Don't go sticking things where they don't belong."

Claudia feigned being shocked and let the body drop back into position. But, then, she said quite indignantly, "Why, I never! You should be ashamed of yourself, thinking impure thoughts like that."

Sid replied, "Impure?! Why don't you climb up on top of me, and I'll show you something impure." Then he laughed as menacingly as he could.

As Sid was having fun with Claudia, she quietly made her way over to his secret area, being sure to remain in his blind spot. She stood stock still, listening intently for any movement from Sid on the other side of the partition. She knew he would be straining his eye, searching for where she went in the room. Then, without warning, Claudia jabbed a long knitting needle straight into the hidey-hole and right into Sid's awaiting eyeball. At first, the needle felt stuck there and didn't move, so she gave it a quick whack with the palm of her hand, and she heard a slight "crack" as the needle jabbed its way through Sid's skull. (Little did she realize she was performing a transorbital lobotomy on the feckless Feckman.) Then, all she heard was Sid falling backward and hitting the floor. He didn't cry out or make a sound of any kind.

The last thing to flash through Sid's mind was, "where in the heck did she go?" Then there was this unexpected sting from something he couldn't identify, and suddenly, his mind went utterly blank.

A Knitted Brow

Walking around the partition, Claudia saw Sid lying on the floor. Except for the large knitting needle sticking out of his eyeball, he looked at peace, like he was taking a well-deserved nap. She looked more closely and noticed the needle had just missed his eyeball and instead had skirted right through the socket into his skull. To her great surprise, there was not a drop of blood, and Sid was breathing normally and didn't seem to be in distress of any kind.

Claudia said, "That'll teach you to scare the daylights out of people, you jackleg. So, what should I do with you? Of course, I could always pack you into a cardboard box, feed you into the incinerator, and cremate your worthless carcass while nobody was around. But it looks like you won't be causing me any more trouble for a while, so I'll see how things play out."

She reached down and pulled the needle out of his eye, being as careful as possible. To her relief, he didn't flinch in the least.

"I'll leave you here and go about my work. Sooner or later, you'll wake up, or someone will discover you. By then, I'll be sitting at home, free as a bird," Claudia said.

She settled in and started talking with the corpse, "That guy over there has always been a pain in my neck, playing jokes on me, moving things when I'm taking my breaks. And that latest trick, making me think you and others were talking, well, that was just a step too far. A person can only stand so much, and then, as Popeye says, "I can't stands no more." The truth is, I'm not quite sure what happened to him when I jabbed the needle in there, but whatever it was, it put him down for the count."

The corpse lay quiet, just how she liked—no surprise retorts or jokes, just a calm, still death. Finally, after 30 minutes, she stood and looked over her work. "You don't look half bad for someone who tried to blow his dang head clean off."

Then, she sat down and wrote her requisite note to loved ones in the great beyond. "Dear Mr. Riley, first, let me apologize for the disturbance today while I was preparing you for your departure. I have resolved the problem, and all is right with the world again. I am entrusting you with this message for my dear aunt, who awaits your arrival in heaven. I know you committed suicide, and there might be some issues with clearance once you get to the pearly gates, but hopefully, they'll get you all sorted and let you pass. I'll wish you good luck in that regard. Her name is Betty Felonia Peace. She should be easy to find in the directory after you pass through the pearly gates, or I'm sure an angel could help you locate her special cloud. Please tell her that I am well, and I think of her often. Thanks in advance for your help in delivering this message to her. You are truly an angel now. Until we meet again, faithfully yours, Claudia Felonia."

She tucked the note under Mr. Riley's hands and patted him on the head. "Good luck then. I'll see you again one of these days."

Finally, she walked to where Sid was sleeping and checked on him. He had not moved a muscle since she had removed the needle. She checked to make sure he was still breathing, and, much to her relief, everything was satisfactory. Then, pulling the partition wall aside slightly, so the director might notice him napping on the job, she walked out the door.

About an hour later, the director checked on Mr. Riley. "Once again, Claudia has performed a miracle." Then, he heard a faint moan behind him. Turning, he saw Sid lying on the floor in a perplexed state. Apparently, he had been taking a nap and was now disoriented. He stooped down and tried to awaken the still body. "Sid, what are you doing sleeping on the job? I should dock your pay for that."

Sid looked at him without registering his presence in the least, and it took only a moment before the director could see something was undoubtedly wrong. Maybe he had a stroke. Or a heart attack. Try as he might, the director couldn't clear Sid's mind to determine what was happening. Finally, after a few minutes, he hurried away to call an ambulance so they could check him out.

After a quick examination, the nurse said, "We've checked him out from one end to the other, and there is nothing physically wrong with him. His vitals are all fine, although he evidently likes to hit the bottle. Otherwise, he appears to be in good shape. It's like his mind reset to that of a small child or a mongoloid. At least he isn't violent in any way. I've never seen anything like it. How is he normally?"

The director responded quickly, "Pretty much the opposite of what you see before you. He was always conniving schemes and bullying people, playing treacherous practical jokes, and generally being a pain in the arse. Do you think he'll snap out of it?"

The nurse replied, "It's hard to say. If I were a betting person, I'd bet against it. There's nothing evidently wrong with him that might improve with time, so I don't want to get your hopes up."

That night, Claudia sat alone at church in her regular pew, listening intently to the preacher drone on about God's guiding grace. She was admittedly thankful to God for guiding her hand in dealing with Sid, making him a docile creature again. Then, when the time came to kneel for the Lord's prayer, she recited in her most devout manner:

Our Father, which art in heaven,

Hallowed be thy name.

Thy Kingdom come.

Thy will be done in earth, as it is in heaven.

Give us this day our daily bread.

And forgive us our trespasses,

As we forgive them that trespass against us.

And lead us not into temptation,

But deliver us from evil.

For thine is the Kingdom,

The power, and the glory,

For ever and ever.

Amen.

She thought the whole bit about "forgiving trespasses" was not to her liking, especially regarding Sid Feckman. But then she thought about the "lead us not into temptation" section and felt better about herself, as she had undoubtedly led Sid away from any further temptation, at least regarding playing tricks on her.

Then she said a solemn, "Amen. And amen."

James "Smitty" Smyth, Jr.

James "Smitty" Smyth, Jr.

"Smitty! Get yourself away from those goats! What have I told you about fondling those poor critters?"

Mamaw uncorked a stream of "God help us" sputters as she swung her straw broom in Junior's direction.

"Aw, Maw, I was only funnin'," James Jr. squirmed. "I treat 'em real nice, nicer than that old ram does. He just jumps on and starts humping. I like to talk with them, you know, pet them, get to know them."

Mamaw teared up. Where had Smitty's life so tragically taken a turn? Then, like a train picking up speed, the instances started coming to mind.

Maybe it was that time she dropped him on his head when he was just a tiny nubbin. Of course, that cow stepping on him probably didn't help much, either.

Or it could have been even earlier when the ol' Duroc sow was rooting around in the cabin and knocked over his crib. That youngster suckled on her teets like he was one of her little piglets.

Then, of course, there was the mule-kicking.

Here's Smitty, trying to paint the old mule's hooves a shade of purple from berries he'd picked off pokeberry bushes when the dang mule up and kicked him in the head. Not once, but twice! So I asked him, "Jesus, boy, there is no lesson to be learned from the second kick of a mule. What's wrong with you?"

Thinking back on how her life had turned out, she couldn't help but feel she'd been tricked somewhere along the way.

On the other hand, Smitty didn't see anything wrong with his actions or how his life was going. Ever since he'd slipped into "Little Jimmy's" saloon over in queertown a few months back, his affection for goats and other warm-blooded animals shot up like sixty. That night, amid the smoke and alcohol, the unbridled male testosterone, he found his life's purpose. His eyes opened wide to a world of possibilities as he saw men drop the braces off their shoulders and let their pants hit the floor. He saw dudes grabbing each other between their legs, dropping down on their knees, and having their ways with both ends of each other, something he found curiously exciting. The sound of their gruntin' and groanin', yowlin' and hollerin', got his blood boiling. His knickers got tight around his little untested wanker, so he started playing with it, not knowing what else to do. In short order, this activity became his most favorite pastime—and never more than a short arm's length away.

What little formal education Smitty had experienced, he accomplished in a one-room schoolhouse with only ten people, all of whom were girls (except for him). But, as he grew, he started seeking answers to what he felt were some of life's elusive mysteries. Like when asleep sometimes, why would his willie get oak hard when dreaming about farm animals? Or when Mamaw had laundry drying on the line out in the yard, why did he have an irresistible urge to steal her bloomers and model them for all the woodland critters?

Only knowing girls growing up, he took a feminine view of things, especially those of a sexual nature. He liked the way girls looked and acted. They were always prim and proper, not trying to pick a fight just for the sake of it like some of those stupid town boys. Since the girls didn't seem to mind, he was more than willing to play dress-up or any other kind of game they chose to entertain themselves. The more substantial girls (his Daddy would call these girls "killing-hog sized" while Mamaw called them "stout") disliked Smitty simply because he looked so much better than they did under a scrim of make-up.

Junior's Origins

Ima Stranger, a.k.a. Mamaw, came to this great land on a boat from England, believing it would be the adventure of a lifetime. She was part of a Catholic church group whose mission was to "save the heathens" on this new, wild, and savage continent. Little did she know that many of the savages she would try to save were fellow passengers traveling on the same boat with her. One of those passengers would prove to be her greatest spiritual challenge and make her rethink her life from the get-go.

It was chilly when she descended from the ship, the early morning frost starting to melt away. The smell of garbage filled her nostrils—an unsettling combination of body odors, a bouquet of rum, mildew, and old food. And that was the paying passengers. The below-deck animals, God bless them, were even worse.

She headed into town with her bonnet ratcheted down, good and tight, her hands nervously rubbing her rosary beads. Whenever she was anxious or unsure, her hands would start working the beads, fortifying the moment.

Ima made her way down to the wharf mercantile, thinking, "Surely they'll have some nice things a lady of refinement could put to good use, like a bar of scented soap." But, as she swung the door open, tinkling the little "Welcome!" bell overhead, she realized she was too optimistic about the so-called enterprise. She surveyed the dark innards of the store, including a motley pack of men clustered tight around a wood stove, practically hugging it. Most had their shirts off, leaving their rib-lined torsos and paunch bellies open to the warm air. A few had even dropped their pants to the floor. She didn't dwell on the whys and wherefores, but it seemed a bridge too far for a mercantile open to the public.

It's not every day a lady takes in a scene like this. Nor is it likely that a man frequenting such a place would ever witness such a figure of feminine refinement crossing the threshold. Nevertheless, James Smyth felt this was a sign from somewhere–maybe from up above or maybe from down below–and he clumsily gathered himself up to greet Miss Stranger.

"Well, hello! What can I get you? Name's James, by the way," he drawled in a gentlemanly manner. He appreciated how her bonnet wrapped snugly around her ears, held in place with satin drawstrings and needlepoint fringe. Just perfect! He thought—maybe I could borrow that same bonnet one day and wear it around town. Come to think of it, that dress looks dandy good, too—I'd take it up in the back a little, but that would be easy peasy.

Ima rubbed away on the beads. "P-pleased to meet you, James. As you may have guessed, I'm new around here. I need to get a few things to set up my room at the church where I'm staying. For starters, I'd sure like to see your flowered soaps and some fabric for making dresses."

James excitedly thought to himself: she can make dresses! Hot damn almighty, she can make me a dress!

"Yes, ma'am, step right this way."

She followed James to the rear of the store, refusing to glance at the scrum of men hunched around the stove.

To call what Ima saw displayed as a "choice" was being very generous with the definition, as she had only two options: red and white or blue and white gingham. And, of course, an odd assortment of flour sacks with botanical imprints, some of which contained rotten cornmeal with maggots inside. She sighed heavily. "Oh my! W-well, I'll take three yards from each bolt as a start. Do you have any sewing supplies?"

"Oh yes, ma'am. Right over here," James replied. "Do you need thimbles, needles, and thread?"

"Sure do," Ima whispered to herself.

James gathered everything and wrapped it in brown paper while she cautiously proceeded past the stove to the front of the store. After taking her money, he bid her a good day.

Back in the daylight, Ima looked appraisingly at her new surroundings. The England she'd left behind was a frightful and dirty place. Oily, greasy coal dust covered every surface, as well as an ever-present sulfur smell. Walking below an open window, you could get doused with last night's bedpan waste. The very air showered the senses. And the sheer number of people could be overwhelming, especially to someone as introverted and nervous as Ima. At least, she didn't have to contend with all that in this new port of call.

Mugwumped by Assisi

So, you might wonder exactly how she got from there to here.

As is often the case in such a story, it involved a man, but not in the traditional sense, as you might assume. Father Featherbrain was his name, the local priest at her church. He was the most significant man in her life. He instructed Ima concerning the Bible, showed charity for those less fortunate, and maintained virtue above all else. He listened intently to her confessions, making mental notes of concerns, and helped her deal with her considerable insecurities. He guided her down the path of righteousness, away from the dark side. Or so she believed. In her eyes, he was a saint, on the level with St. Francis of Assisi.

While he may have been a saint in her eyes, he was something else entirely too many of the young acolytes in his parish. To them, he was Father Fucks-you-in-the-Brain. He liked nothing better than to get a glass or two of communion wine in his belly, fire up the incense braziers, and start diddling the young boys. First, he'd grab them roughly by the back of their heads and pull them under his crimson robe, where his erect holiness awaited their undivided attention. Then, he'd recite to them all manner of scripture as he worked the boy's heads around, poking and probing most furiously. Every now and then, he'd encounter an unruly, ungrateful miscreant who thought a nasty bite would be an appropriate way to disengage from the rubric. These cases required administering the holy wand in a more disciplined and direct approach, starting at one end and finishing at the other.

At this juncture in our story, the phrase "The Lord works in mysterious ways" boots itself into play. Father Featherbrain found himself on the dodge from some influentials within his parish, the target of a series of unfortunate whisperings and clandestine meetings. Only the Bishop, of similar personality and sensibility to the pastor, could offer him a pathway out of his current box canyon, that being a hastily thrown-together mission trip to the new world.

As luck would have it, in one of her many confessions, Ima informed the priest that she wished to do more to help all those poor souls she saw in need. As a result, Father Featherbrain reached out to her and asked if she would accompany him on this critical mission to do God's work and act as his lead liaison for the church once they arrived in America. Of course, she was most humbled and a little bewildered at the thought of being considered for such an important task. But, after a long run of praying and bead rubbing, she agreed to go along on the journey.

So it was a curious encounter when Father Featherbrain first met James Smyth after his church group settled into their new accommodations. Ima introduced the two after James delivered some food staples they'd ordered for the church. James immediately sensed that he and the righteous one had a strange attraction. The appeal was curiously unsettling for him, as the last thing he pondered was going to church. All that crazy talk about sin and redemption didn't plan out with his worldview. And that nonsense about living a life of pain and relative suffering now so's you could frolic about in eternal joy and happiness in the hereafter sure as heck didn't make any sense. He wanted his frolickings today; thank you very much!

Father Featherbrain instantly recognized a fellow compatriot in James and truly admired how he carried himself, with his narrow hips swaying back and forth. And his way of dressing seemed most praiseworthy, with his embroidered overalls and bright white spats covering his yellow work boots. Most daring indeed. He had to find a way to spend more time with this showboat of a creature, and he thought he knew just the way to proceed.

Ima proceeded with her work organizing a community school at the church. She worked with the pastor to develop the lessons and set about getting the word out to the local families and nearby settlements. On the pastor's suggestion, she asked James if he might help her put together a little posting and mention the school to families who came into the mercantile.

"Father Featherbrain would be most appreciative of any assistance you could provide and would offer up prayers on your behalf," said Ima. "You know everyone in the region, and your involvement would be a blessing."

"Well, if the good Father is involved, count me among the willing!

I'll spread the word to all my regulars and see what we can get done," James responded. His mind ran double-time to determine how he and the saintly one might find themselves alone for some quality "get to know you" time. The thought of being all tangled up in that red velvet robe he always wore when he preached made his poor head get all light and fluffy. They could have their own "communion," breaking and eating the flesh, just maybe not in accord with the good book.

As sure as day follows night, Father Featherbrain's scheme played out perfectly. First, James and his posse of friends helped get the children lined up for school. Next, Ima went about devoutly teaching the lessons, leading the little ones on the path of righteousness. It seemed like God's important work was being done. All the while, the devil plotted and planned.

To express his sincere appreciation, the pastor invited James to a unique service so he could thank him personally. Unlike most church services, though, this one was completely private, just the two of them. It was not exactly a confession for Father Featherbrain, more like a communion with benefits. He poured the wine, lit the candles, and burned incense. An eager expectation of the night's fellowship filled the small room at the rear of the church. Father Featherbrain wore his most ornate robe and intently looked forward to bringing the "good news" to James in a furious manner.

James arrived right on time, waltzing into the church, humming a spirited tune. He wore his most impressive finery and even moved his weekly bath up a couple of days. James could hardly contain his enthusiasm as he giddily followed the pastor to the back of the church, where they entered the dimly lit back room. Feeling electrified by the soft glow of the candles, he noticed all the little details. In addition to the wine, candles, and incense, the pastor had some of those little white crackers James had seen Ima serving the children during communion. They call it the "youChrist" or something like that.

"James, thank you so much for agreeing to meet with me tonight. Your work on behalf of the church has been a godsend to all. And no one appreciates it more than me. So I'd like to express my deepest appreciation to you, starting with a toast," the priest said. "Lord, we raise these glasses of holy wine to James, one of your most diligent and deserving servants."

As the wine made its way down James' gullet, his mind started working on how to move this little get-together along. Draining the glass in another gulp, he set it aside, moved directly in front of Father Featherbrain, and slowly started pushing him back against the small communion table. The pastor, picking up on James' direction, cleared the table with a quick swing of his arm, clutched James about the head and shoulders with the other and pushed him down to his knees. Then, throwing the crimson robe over his back, James enthusiastically set himself to the task at hand, causing the priest to reach heights of ecstasy never achieved before.

Father Featherbain thought, such a willing and capable disciple!

After taking the priest's holy essence in full, James emerged from under the robe and, in a move that caught Featherbrain somewhat by surprise, spun him around and shoved him over the table. His holiness was unaccustomed to such treatment, but he quickly saw where enlightenment led. James started with a gentle rhythm and promptly picked up the pace, compelling the pastor to sing "God Save The Queen" at the top of his lungs.

After a few minutes of boisterous activity, all was quiet again, and the room shimmered with an otherworldly glow. A winded Father Featherbrain poured another round of wine and offered another toast. "What God has brought together, let no man put asunder. To our clandestine union! May it endure forever, world without end."

James had never felt more incredible pride in his work. And with the cloth to boot! Suddenly that whole "Do unto others as you would have them do unto you" jazz made perfect sense. So maybe he was a Christian after all. And so began James' religious period, embracing his new-found calling with all the vigor he could muster.

Feeling renewed in faith, the good priest started making plans to keep his flock under control. First, he and James would get together regularly for confessions and communions. Then, he and Ima would work out plans for bringing the little ones along, teaching the Golden Rule like never before.

A Marriage Made in Heaven

One day, Featherbrain had a vision out of the blue, not unlike Saul, on the road to Damascus. He would arrange for James and Ima to be married, thus assuring he would always have his most trusted disciple nearby.

Ima had never really thought about getting married before, as she viewed her lifelong relationship with Jesus as such. However, when Father Featherbrain extolled the benefits of being a married woman, she began to come around. Companionship. Security. Fidelity. And if she was so inclined, a little clutch of her very own to raise in the faith. And she could sense the pastor felt James was the best possible choice for her, although she wasn't exactly sure why.

James was equally baffled as to why he should get married, remembering all the good times he shared playing with girls back in his academic years. Then, he thought better of it. Instead, he envisioned how he and Ima could play dress-up, exchange make-up tips, and talk about the latest fashions for the mercantile. He saw how it could be a helpful thing. She might even have pointers for him in dealing with the priest and his holy spirit.

Since neither Ima nor James had any family to speak of, Father Featherbrain performed the small service with just the three of them in his small room at the back of the church. Ima had never seen this room before, but she felt somehow that James had, which made her feel a little more comfortable about everything. They exchanged vows, each gave the other what passed for a wedding ring, and that was that. It was a short and sweet affair.

So, Ima moved into the small apartment above the mercantile with James. She was pleasantly surprised by how well he'd decorated the place.

Lacy curtains and clean, painted floors. Even fresh-cut flowers in an old whisky bottle were on the small oval table. And apparently, he had already bought her some clothes as several dresses were hanging neatly in the wardrobe. And they were just her style! What a sweet man!

James was increasingly giddy with excitement to have Ima living in his place. He unpacked her few belongings and helped her locate the essentials, such as the washstand and bedpan. He was particularly excited when she noticed his homemade dresses hanging in the closet, and she appreciated their designs. An excellent sign, indeed.

As part of his religious work with James, the priest told him how he would have to consider and even facilitate specific sentiments with Ima. For example, sex. James would no doubt have to deflower Ima, as she was most assuredly a virgin. While this seemed a little off-putting to him at first, he quickly came around when the pastor suggested they could dress up and play "country doctor," which would put things in a better mental frame. After that, he would have to be exceedingly gentle and encouraging, and nature would hopefully take its course.

And so it was that nine months later, little James "Smitty" Smyth, Jr. arrived on the scene. He was not precisely an immaculate conception but damned nearly, as James and Ima had had sex only once. Sex was NOT what Ima had signed on for, especially in the manner James liked to entertain. For his part, James took this in stride, as he always had other fields to plow and seeds to sow. Nevertheless, father Featherbrain remained a central pillar of their lives, and once Smitty arrived, he became an unofficial godfather.

Smitty strutted his stuff so much like a miniature James it was uncanny. His mannerisms. His walk. His talk. The things he pondered. Ima tried her best to bring him up and keep him on the straight and narrow path, but he kept veering off the moment she took her eyes off him. She often looked towards heaven and thought, somehow, this whole affair with James Sr.

was to test her faith.

Eventually, with differences too much to gloss over, Ima and James Sr. decided to part ways. Thinking some distance from temptation might help Smitty, she relocated to a small cabin on the outskirts of town. While it troubled Ima considerably to reach such a decision, James Sr. took it all in stride, just as he had every other "normal" type of social adjustment, as in the end, it all meant little to him anyway.

As James Jr. matured, his true nature became even more apparent. He was a sweet boy, and just like his Father, all the girls at school loved him for how well he understood their feminine wiles. However, the few bruiser boys in his class thought he should be beaten and teased daily, so they obliged.

The Original Moon Shot

Occasionally, you hear about inventions (or conventions, depending on the subject matter) that make you think, "How did anyone ever think to try that for the first time?" Like eating the first raw oyster or frying up pig intestines to make chitlins. Or eating snails or grasshoppers. Someone had to be the FIRST person to try a particular "that," and so it began.

Well, Smitty intersected with just such a time. It started innocently enough when he got ahold of Mamaw's well-worn rosary beads. He decided he would wear them high up on his thigh. He'd seen some of the dancers down at Little Jimmy's wearing garters under their skirts and felt it would be enjoyable, and besides, it felt good. Smitty's dress was an old flour sack he'd found in the barn. He cut some armholes and cinched the tent tight around his waist with a piece of twine. He liked how the beads rose up, pressing gently and reassuringly on his inner thigh.

Things got even more interesting when he tried to ride one of the pigs in the sty. Jumping up on the pig's back, wrapping his legs tightly across the critter's generous girth, he held on tight as the squealing and thrashing began. This activity continued for a short time, with Smitty's little ass-crack bouncing up and down on the Duroc's spine and those rosary beads getting pushed further up his thigh. Then, suddenly, Smitty felt an electric sensation he'd never experienced before. His eyes popped open wide, and his brain exploded, asking, "What just happened down there, and why am I smiling?"

Hopping carefully off the sow, he stood transfixed. His eyes were wide; his mouth turned up at the corners, his inner workings extremely confused. Then, slowly he pulled up his bag skirt and bent over only to witness the rosary beads partially dangling out of his bum. He wasn't sure exactly what had happened back there, but he liked it. Hmmm, how many beads were up there? He decided to slowly pull them out. As each bead passed his previously virgin sphincter, he felt a marvelous sensation. This new feeling bordered on a religious experience in his still formative brain. New-found respect for his Mamaw welled up inside him, and he felt that maybe he, too, had a spiritual bent that he hadn't realized until now. He must investigate and conduct additional experiments. Who knew what otherworldly spiritual pyrotechnics might be awaiting his discovery?

As James went about this line of inquiry, other genetic traits became evident, billowing to the top. The phrase, "Like father, like son," jumped to life in his experimental adventures.

And so the circle of life continued, world without end.

Izzy and Shelley Ibrahim

İZZY AND SHELLEY İBRAHİM

"Get those backdrops lined up and sandbag 'em so they won't fall over on the dancers. And somebody, man the spotlight and make sure it's going to track Izzy around the stage," Jacques Benoit, the director, yelled into his megaphone. "Double-check the riggings on the clouds as well. We don't want them all tangled up with the dancers on their swings."

Shelley yelled back, "On it," and he jumped into action, climbing the ladders, checking the riggings, and adjusting the spotlights. A man of few words, he let his actions speak most of the time.

While his reputation as a director was that of a giant, Jacques Benoit's physical stature was diminutive, as he barely topped out at five feet; Napoleon had nothing on him. You could always count on seeing his black beret cocked to one side as if that made his brain more creative. And his glasses pinched his nose, making his face seem somewhat cartoon-like. He had been at The Delirium Theater for a short while, but his impact was profound. His use of mechanics, as well as beautiful forms, had no equal. Nobody knew he had Shelley Ibrahim to thank for much of this, though he rarely did.

Shelly planted another idea in Jacques's head: "I think if we ran a zip line from one corner of the stage to the other, we could have a dancer fly across the stage like a bird. Of course, we'd have to fashion a harness out of leather and feathers, but it could be amazing. We could add pulleys on each end, like you see on clotheslines, and move them back and forth."

Jacques looked above the stage, trying to envision this new set-up, and after a minute, said, "Yes, I was just thinking that very same thing. It could be very dramatic, and I don't know anyone else who has ever done that." This lie, of course, was just another to be added to the mental ledger Shelley kept in his head. Nevertheless, he had to give the director his due. He was always willing to take credit for someone else's ideas.

"I'll get with Izzy, and we'll start working on the costume and harness," he replied. Izzy was Shelley's mother, a beautiful fan dancer from the Middle East (who most people thought flew over on a magic carpet). Shelley's father was unknown, as Izzy was stunningly beautiful and equally promiscuous. As a nymphomaniac of the highest order, she tested and teased the virtue of any man or woman with no specific allegiance to either side of the coin. Her dark almond skin, raven black hair with just a hint of cerulean blue, high cheekbones, and eyes seemed to pierce the fabric of time and space. Shelley was born in the back of a theater when Izzy was only 17.

From birth, Shelley was mechanically inclined and liked to take his few toys apart, even as a small child, to see how they worked. Then, as he grew, he combined bits and pieces from various toys to create something unique.

Feathers were a source of constant amazement to him, especially the iridescent peacock feathers used to create the dancer's fans. He loved nothing better than to take a handful of feathers and unfurl them slowly under his nose. He could picture these majestic birds slowly strolling about in exotic gardens. The feathers' softness and texture, combined with the endless palette of color, gave him goosebumps. He felt an almost erotic attachment to that little fluffy part of the feather, which attaches to the bird's skin. It was as soft and satisfying as a first kiss.

"Shelley, sweetie, what have you got rattling around in that little brain of yours today?" Izzy asked when he entered her dressing room. She still danced and was often in the lead position on the stage, even though she was in her late-30s and considered an antique by the other girls. But the audience adored and revered her. It was as if she drew some magical power from the footlights, the heat rising from them making her movements with the fans at once intoxicating and alluring—her musky redolence filling the theater. And when the spotlights singled her out, revealing her almost nude body, glistening with a hint of sweat on her well-toned muscles, the tasseled nipples of her pendulent breasts twirling behind the feathers, the theater would spontaneously erupt with applause.

"I'm going to create the gift of flight for you," Shelley told his mother. "No longer will your heavenly beauty be held hostage to this earth. Instead, you will soar above the stage like none before. You will flutter and flit like a garden fairy, casting your divine spell on all who lay eyes upon you," he said, grinning.

"Oh, you crazy little wizard! I'll no longer need magic carpets from my homeland," she said, thrilled. "When shall we get started on this fabulous illusion?"

Smiling proudly, Shelley replied, "I'll need to run to the hardware store to gather all the pulleys and ropes and stop by the tannery for some sturdy leather for the harness. Then, we can take your measurements and start working on patterns. First, we'll do a rough mock-up of everything to make sure it works. Then, we can start making everything look fabulous."

Competition in theaters was intense; everyone was always looking for the next big show, idea, or talent. Fame and fortune could sweep in overnight and disappear just as fast, so whenever word of something "new and different" hit the street, it spread like wildfire. Unfortunately, ideas were more complicated to protect than money, as there were no copyright guarantees or laws strong enough. Secrecy was the best defense, but even that had a minimal shelf life, sometimes only days or weeks. Usually, the "new thing" took the form of a singular person or a song/show production, but someone could also create a unique piece of technology every now and then. So the clock had already started ticking on Shelley's "flying dancer" idea, and he hadn't even left the theater yet.

Victor Horgiot, a man of means and even more considerable meanness, got wind of Shelley's invention. He owned a local bank, a chain of hardware stores, and a fledgling import/export business down at the docks. Between these enterprises, he had an eye or ear on everyone in town, and that's how he liked it. So, speaking into the phone, he asked, "What's that, you say, Nathanial? He's building a rig so a dancer can fly over the stage while others are dancing below?"

Nathanial was one of Victor's most trusted snitches, working at the hardware store near the theaters. His clandestine network of stagehands and delivery people gave him a steady stream of information. "That's what he said. He also said old Jacques got excited about it, claiming credit for the idea himself. But he didn't think it up; it was Shelley Ibrahim. You know, Izzy's son," Nathanial explained.

"Did he show you a drawing or anything about how this contraption might work?" Victor asked.

Nathanial replied, "No, sir. He keeps his ideas locked away in his brain until he gets them sorted, then builds them. I've never seen a drawing for anything he's designed."

"Well, we'll need to keep an eye on young Shelley and see how we might unlock his little noggin," Victor replied.

"Let's use your best-fitting corset as a starting place for the harness.

Then we can add straps and supports as needed," Shelley directed. "Once we sort out the basic set-up, we can make a much stronger version of kid leather and dye it to match your skin."

Izzy beamed with pride at her son. "My sweetie, you are so clever. How do these wonderful thoughts come into your mind?"

Shelley replied, "It remains to be seen how wonderful this thought is, so let's get started, shall we?"

"This red one with the cutouts for my breasts fits best. It snugs up against my ribs and extends to just above my thighs," Izzy said. "The lacings are all in the back."

Shelley took a long, measuring look at the garment and said, "Put it on and let's see where we might attach some straps for your arms. But first, we'll need to create a solid spine to connect the feathers and the support rope. It's a good thing you're so petite."

Once Izzy got into the corset, Shelley attached his rough mock-up of the harness, which included a large ring for attaching a single rope. He then had her lie down on the floor and, using a block and tackle system suspended from the ceiling, began to pull her up off the floor. She struggled to maintain balance as Izzy's weight shifted to the harness. Her legs flailed about, and her arms started circling.

"Whoa, whoa, whoa! Okay, we'll need to add a few more supports so you can manage your flight once in the air. So I'll lower you down, and we'll add some temporary supports and try again," Shelley mused.

Back on the ground, Izzy removed the corset and left to get dressed in something more comfortable. Now that he saw how a live person moved in his harness, he could use his large mannequin to work out the alterations. Of course, the weight wouldn't be the same as Izzy, but he felt it was close enough to make it work.

While Shelley worked on his harness for Izzy, Jacques worked on his own balancing act. Victor Horgiot had reached out to him, and he wasn't sure why, but he knew well enough the man wielded considerable power. So, sensing an opportunity, Jacques spied on Shelley and Izzy, "Shelley, how are you coming along on our flying dancer harness? Do you foresee any difficulties you can't sort out?"

Shelley responded, somewhat taken aback by the "OUR flying dancer harness" comment, "We encountered a few problems, but it's nothing a little time and some noggin scratching can't sort out."

Feeling very pleased with this news, Jacques replied, "Very good, very good! Keep me informed on your progress so I can decide how we might incorporate this bit of magic into the show." At this, he clicked his heels, turned, and shuffled away, humming some silly show tune as he went.

Back in his office, Jacques returned Victor's call, "Mr. Horgiot, what a pleasant surprise to hear from you. Sorry for the delay in my reply, but as you might expect, the demands of the theater are legendary." He wanted to impress upon Victor what an important person he was and what an honor it was that he returned his call. "How may I be of service to you?"

Victor smiled, thinking, "What an arrogant little shitbag." He said, "Well, I understand you are a busy man, and I appreciate the callback. As you probably know, I am a massive supporter of the theater, not just yours but pretty much all of them. I've heard through my sources that you are about to unleash yet another spectacle on your audiences, and I wondered if we might discuss this and see if I might help you move the endeavor along?"

Caught off guard, Jacques thought, "How on earth does he know we're working on something new? No one has talked about this outside the theater." He replied as obsequiously as possible, "Thank you, Mr. Horgio, for your patronly support, past and present. Because of erudite individuals like yourself, we have succeeded and thrived where others have tragically failed. I'd greatly appreciate an audience with you to see how we might collaborate on some future magic."

"Perfect. I'll see you at the club on Friday for lunch. Noon work okay for you?" Victor said. "Just give them your name when you arrive, and they'll show you to my private dining room."

Feeling sufficiently respected, Jacques replied, "Excellent, sir. I'll see you there and then. Take care."

Behind the Scenes

What Jacques didn't realize about Victor's support of the theater arts was the true essence of that support. It was a cunning combination of blackmail and extortion, with a hint of outright intimidation. Theaters received various "protections" from Victor in exchange for large monthly payments. Things being what they were in the theater world, finding some secret relationship or fetish that you could exploit wasn't hard—a kept woman or man, a penchant for sucking on toes, the pain inflicted by whips and chains, whatever. It was simply a matter of finding these frailties and applying the appropriate pressure. Over time, he essentially owned these theaters, at least in terms of power, if not on paper.

Victor sat back in his oversized leather chair behind his equally large desk and contemplated his next move. He vividly recalled a one-night stand long ago with Izzy Ibrahim, giving him a brilliant idea. He remembered what an insatiable sexual appetite she had and her sheer creativity in that regard. One couldn't even fantasize about the things she did with, and to, him. So perhaps now would be an excellent time to make her re-acquaintance.

Shelley popped into Izzy's dressing room to deliver a large bouquet of roses. "The florist just dropped these off for you. The sender told him to wait for your reply. Any idea who sent them around?"

Opening the small folded card, she read, "From your one-time lover and long-time admirer. I would appreciate the honor of dinner with you this Thursday evening. Please reply in the affirmative to my courier. Until then, your patron, Victor Horgiot."

"What a surprise this is. I hadn't thought of Victor since before you were born. That was so long ago." Izzy replied. "What should I tell him?" Shelley considered the request for a moment, then said, "Tell him you'll meet, and we'll see where it leads. He is a rich and powerful man with a dark side. It's best to know which side you're dealing with."

When the courier returned with the good news, Victor was quite pleased. He now had two critical pieces to his plan in place.

"Okay, I've made the modifications to the harness, and it's time to give it another test flight," Shelley said to Izzy. "With the new supports, you should be able to maintain your balance and move around easily. I've also put up our zip line and pulleys so we can see how they hold your weight. We may need to add some turnbuckles to create more tension, but we won't know for sure until we get you off the ground."

Slipping her petite frame into the new harness was a little more challenging with the latest additions, but she eventually got everything where it needed to be because she was so bendy.

"Well, let's see if this idea of yours is going to fly," Izzy laughed.

Shelley hoisted her off the ground, and much to her surprise, she felt quite stable and could breathe easily. Then, she began performing various airborne tricks, flapping her arms like a bird, kicking her legs like she was swimming, and could even arch her back like she was diving.

"This is amazing! It feels completely comfortable and leaves my arms and legs free to do whatever I want," she said.

Izzy giggled with glee as Shelley lowered her back to the floor. "My little wizard! You have created something truly magical. I must think about how I can move with this newfound freedom."

Shelley felt justifiably proud, "I can see the finished costume in my mind.

You will be a spectacle." He determined they needed a few turnbuckles and other items from the hardware store. He wasn't ready to tell Jacques about their success yet, hoping he could keep it secret for a bit longer.

Nathanial greeted him as he entered the door, "Hey, Shelley. How's that new contraption of yours coming along? You got Izzy flying like a bird?"

Shelley replied, "Not just yet, but we're getting close. I need some stout turnbuckles and some larger pulleys. And what kinds of kid leather do you have in stock?"

"No problem. Let me show you what leathers we have. We can get dyes, too, if you think you'll need that," Nathanial gestured. "I'll grab the other hardware while you look these over."

When Shelley left the hardware store, Nathanial called Victor with an update. "Mr. Horgiot, Shelley was just here getting more supplies for his flying dancer contraption. I think he's getting close to having everything sorted out, although he was a bit cagey about telling me anything."

"That's excellent news, Nathanial. Thanks for the update," Victor responded, smiling. Then, hanging up, he contemplated how his upcoming dinner with Izzy might proceed. Undoubtedly, she would know the status of the flying machine. All he had to do was get her to spill her guts. He knew from experience, though, that might be easier said than done.

Now that he had a working prototype, Shelley could get down to the fun part of the project: design. He loved the feeling of creating something that had never existed before. His biggest challenge was remaining patient and taking his time sorting everything out. He could close his eyes and see the finished product, but it was quite a leap from imagination to reality, so he had to plan accordingly.

Shelley met up with Izzy to show her the leathers, feathers, sequins, and all, and to talk about the next part of the process. He would have to disassemble her favorite red corset so he could use it as a pattern. He felt this was a small sacrifice considering what they would achieve in the end, and luckily, Izzy agreed.

"Oh, I'll be sad to see such a precious and provocative thing taken apart but look at the fabulous something it will become. It will be like the phoenix rising from the ashes," she said.

This vivid image provided Shelley with a flash of inspiration. He could use brilliant red and orange dyes for the leather and the feathers on the flying harness and create an elaborate headdress for Izzy to wear, transforming her into a flaming bird character. In addition, she could wear red fishnet stockings with long flowing feathers attached down the rear seam and arm-length gloves fixed in the same manner. Finally, he could line the entire piece with sparkling yellow and silver sequins.

Excitedly, Shelley said, "A phoenix! That's a fantastic idea. I can see the finished product in my mind now. I'll get started right away." He picked Izzy up and spun her around the dressing room. Then, setting her back down on the ground, he kissed her on the cheek, grabbed the materials he'd brought, and dashed out the door.

Jacques knew he had to keep pressing Shelley on the flying harness, especially now that Victor had learned something special was in the works at the theater. But he also knew Shelley well enough that if he pressed him too much, he'd clam up and not tell him anything. It was exasperating to deal with such a temperamental creative sort. On the other hand, he should be grateful to have the opportunity to share the stage, so to speak, with someone of his immense stature—the worthless ingrate.

He popped into Shelley's workroom and asked, "How's it going in here? I see you have lots of raw materials and other random things lying around. I hope there's a plan underneath all this." To his untrained eye, it looked like complete chaos.

Shelley responded begrudgingly, "I have the vision down in my mind, which is truly the hardest part. So now it's just a matter of making it happen. But it takes time to work out all the kinks. It's not like buying a costume off the rack."

"Of course, of course. Creative juices and all that. You mustn't rush the process. Oh no! But if you could buzz me when you think you might have something to see, that would be great. We have someone who might invest in our idea: Victor Horgiot. Do you know him?"

"Everyone knows Victor in one way or another. My Mom told me of a one-night fling she had with him way back before I was born. How does he know we have something he might want to invest in?" Shelley squinted.

"I'm not sure, but when I have lunch with him on Friday, I plan to find out. We're meeting in his private dining room at the club. Very uptown." Jacques replied, as smug as he could make it.

At this, Shelley's alarms started clanging. The invitation to have dinner with his mother the night before could not be a coincidence. The only other person who could know what they were up to was Nathanial at the hardware store. But of course! Victor owns the hardware store. Nathanial could be a set of eyes and ears for him, routinely reporting anything out of the ordinary to Victor. He'd have to be very careful in any conversation with Nathanial.

Dim the Lights

In her dressing room, Izzy was thinking back to that one night long ago she had spent with Victor. She'd had hundreds of male and female lovers since then, but he'd always had a particular fascination as he was her first male lover. Even at her young age, starting when just 17, the allure of sex was overpowering, but Izzy had never pursued anyone of the opposite sex. So that night, she decided to focus on her pleasure like never before, and since he seemed a most willing and capable partner, not to mention almost a decade older, he would oblige as best he could.

Stopping by her dressing room after the performance, he said, "Dearest Izzy, my name is Victor Horgiot, an unworthy theater patron. Your display tonight has left me in a state of exhilaration. It would honor me if you accompanied me to dinner so I might repay you in some small way for the pleasure provided by your visage. Please say you will dine with me."

Izzy had never encountered such an emotional reaction before and was unsure how to respond. And yet, there was something beautiful about this man, though she couldn't say what. "Of course, I will accommodate you in your time of emotional need. Let me change out of these things into something more appropriate, and I'll be right out."

Bowing deeply, Victor replied, "Thank you graciously, my goddess. I'll bring the carriage to the stage door and await our departure."

Some other dancers came over as soon as he left to congratulate Izzy on her prize catch. This news pleasantly surprised her as she had no idea who Victor Horgiot was. However, when she heard he was an only child and heir to one of the city's most enormous fortunes, she decided fate must have something special in mind for their rendezvous. And so, she determined to make the absolute most out of this chance encounter.

Victor met her at the stage door and escorted her into the carriage. She had changed into a stirring "little black dress," accentuating her decolletage to a most significant advantage and displaying her well-toned muscular legs well up her thigh. Then, borrowing the finest toilet water from one of her older dancer friends, she dabbed herself where she knew it would produce maximum effect.

"You are an absolute vision. Thank you for agreeing to dine with me on such short notice. I can only imagine how full your dance card must be, so I consider myself most privileged," Victor fawned.

"It is my pleasure, Mr. Horgiot, I assure you," Izzy demured, batting her smoky eyes in the darkened carriage. "It is true my dance card is often full, but not so as you might think."

Dinner at the club was everything Victor had planned and imagined it could be. Fine wine, great food, intoxicating laughter. She was a living, breathing fantasy, and he was the sole beneficiary. He sensed a lust and vigor in her that belied her petite frame. The combination of time and alcohol only intensified these signals emanating from her dazzling eyes and beckoning lips.

"The only thing that could make tonight even more magical would be an aperitif on my balcony overlooking the city. Shall we?" asked Victor most eagerly.

"I agree there is more magic in the offing, so let's go about making it happen," she replied in her most sultry tone.

The wine had done its trick and unlocked what precious few inhibitions Izzy had, and when the door opened to Victor's apartment, she made her first move. As Victor walked over to the bar to prepare their drinks, chatting nervously over his shoulder, she slowly undressed, dropping garments as she walked towards the divan beside the French doors leading to the balcony. Then, when he nervously turned around with fresh drinks, the vision of her lying back on the sofa in the Lord's most spectacular glory took his breath away.

Sitting up as slowly as smoke rising from a doused candle, Izzy said, "Why don't you join me over here so we might get to know each other better? There is much you still need to know about me and I, you. But, first, let me help you out of these wicked clothes."

Before he could fake a protest, she stood and put her hand over his mouth, calming his actions. Then, as slowly and seductively as her hands could work, she undid his tie, belt, buttons, and finally, his sanity. Suddenly, overcome with lust and longing, he scooped her into his arms and took her into the bedroom.

He dropped her onto the bed, ready to mount her when she elbowed herself to a sitting position. Not wanting to lose control, she calmed his urges and slowly knee-crawled back onto the bed, beckoning him to join her there. Following her lead, he crawled onto the bed, where she quickly threw him down on his back and mounted him like a stallion. His mind was running completely unbridled now, and it was mere moments before he climaxed uncontrollably into her writhing body. Sensing this would cause embarrassment, Izzy moaned quietly and slowly started rocking rhythmically, as if this was all a part of the plan, taking his mind and body where she wanted to go. Victor's brain collapsed entirely as his carnal desires took control. He rolled her onto the bed and started thrusting again from behind, doing everything he could to make her come. As she was about to climax, she arched her back, reaching behind Victor grabbing his buttocks, and pulling him mightily into her. He grabbed her firmly as if holding on for dear life, and after what seemed a short eternity, she released him and pulled away.

Mistaking this break as a pause to catch their breath, Victor collapsed on his back on the bed. Unfortunately, this action seemed like an invitation to Izzy to entertain other fantasies. First, she slowly crawled up to his waist and took his now flaccid member into her hot mouth. Next, she methodically worked his willing penis back to full attention, simultaneously cupping his balls and tweaking his anus. Then, as he was about to make a move to mount her again, she quickly flipped her body around, straddling his face with her rose-colored, dripping-wet vagina. (Curiously, at that most improbable moment, his brain interceded, causing "A rose by any other name would smell as sweet" to arrive in his mind.) Finally, she exploded in screaming ecstasy as he instinctively licked all around her twisting clitoris.

And then, silence.

Exhaustion had never occupied this location in Victor's mind before. As for Izzy, it was a frequent circumstance, the only exception being this time it was with a single man and not multiple female partners. While Victor had the honor of being her first male partner, he quickly became just another number as she tried from that night forward to fulfill her insatiable sexual appetite.

Snap Out of It

Snapping back to the present moment, Izzy wondered about whatever had happened to Victor. He had never called on her again, even though she regularly saw him at the theater. But, of course, it wasn't long after that magical and transformative night that Izzy had a new set of circumstances to deal with: she was pregnant with Shelley at the ripe age of 17.

Coincidentally, Victor had his own set of unique circumstances to deal with: his two overbearing, ultraconservative parents. So when he told them of his infatuation for Izzy, and they learned of her vocation, to say they were perplexed would be the understatement of the ages.

"Have you lost touch with your faculties? You can't be frolicking about with this trollop off the stage. I don't care what height of delirium she may excite in you. You are heir to one of the great fortunes in this city, and you must act accordingly," his father bellowed from his fleshy-cheeked, Rosacea-flushed face.

"Dear, dear. There are any number of suitable debutantes from the finest families from which you may choose. Why must you fixate on this girl of no social standing whatsoever?" his mother inquired in her most ingratiating voice.

"She is a singular talent, of that there is no doubt," Victor pleaded. "She can transport her audience into another realm of ecstasy few even knew existed. I bear witness to it."

"I am familiar with this "realm" you so casually speak of, as it can be entered into via any number of doors down in the red-light district," his father testified. Victor knew his father paid handsomely to have a courtesan at his beck and call, and the hypocrisy enraged him. "We will speak no more of this, which is final. Am I crystal clear?"

Victor was indeed crystal clear, as he had witnessed his father's clarity on any number of subjects in his 26 years. "Yes, Father, I am crystal clear as you wish."

Arriving at the club created a strong sense of deja vu in Izzy. The scent of well-oiled oaken halls, wax candles, and eau de cologne transported her back to her previous encounter with Victor. She was escorted back to Victor's private dining room. As she entered, he rose from his chair with a flourish, kissing her on both cheeks and shaking both hands as if they were long-standing friends.

"My dear Izzy, you are captivating as ever. If only we could all age as gracefully as you," Victor shrugged with a twinkle in his eye.

"You are too kind, Victor, but I thank you nonetheless for your most thoughtful remarks. I was pleasantly surprised when I received your flowers and the invitation to this lovely luncheon. Thank you in advance for what I am sure will be another memorable occasion," Izzy said, smiling seductively.

Blushing beyond control at this, Victor quickly retreated to his seat and bid her to take a seat. "I've taken the liberty of ordering our lunch so that we might get down to the business at hand. I hope you enjoy steak and lobster."

"Lovely!" Izzy replied.

Victor got straight to the point, "I have watched your career for these many years. I have always admired your passion and fire on the stage. You seem to feed on some invisible energy within the theater."

Izzy replied, "The stage is where my true self is most at home. The shimmering heat from the footlights, the glassy-eyed looks of anticipation and desire, the rising and falling of tensions—these are what I live for."

Victor replied, "I understand from my well-placed sources that you are working on a new addition to the show. Can you tell me more about it?" A look of concealment crept over his face like a passing shadow.

Shelley had told Izzy to be careful about speaking to anyone about their plans, as someone could easily steal their idea. But looking into Victor's eyes, she sensed an opportunity to turn his inquiry to her advantage. She had seen that carnal desire in his eyes many years ago and knew how best to manipulate it.

"It seems nothing can remain a secret in this small community. Indeed, we are working on a unique business opportunity. Once I explain it, you may want to invest as a silent partner," she replied.

"I'm intrigued. Continue, please," Victor said.

"I recalled the first time we met today, and the wonderful evening it was—the combination of unbridled passion and theater of the mind. Our most base animal instincts were laid bare and acted upon to absolute effect. Then I thought, what if we offered this "passion service" to a select clientele as a fully formed production, like theater, but for a private audience? We could consult with these clients about their fantasies and create an extravagant show to deliver this unique live experience. It could be a part orgy, part fantasy, part whatever. No two performances would be the same. Of course, this production would come at a very high price, but as you can attest, well worth the investment. What do you think, Victor?" Izzy said as she settled slowly back into her chair.

Victor's mind was running amok, thinking of any number of wealthy friends who would pay untold sums for just such a night. This idea was so much more remarkable than a flying dancer costume as to be ridiculous. "I am indeed intrigued by this idea, and an investment in such a production company, if you will allow me to call it such, would be my privilege."

Izzy flashed her most radiant smile, "Excellent then. I'll consult with my creative partners and be in touch very soon. Now, enough talk of business. Let us toast our much-anticipated reunion. Cheers!"

Meanwhile, Shelley had made significant progress on the flying dancer harness and was ready for Izzy to take another test flight. He still had to dye the leather and feathers and add the sequins, but he had finalized all the structural elements, which should work perfectly. He found Izzy in her dressing room, having just returned from dinner with Victor.

"How was everything with Victor? Did he ask you about the flying harness?" asked Shelley.

"He didn't mention that specifically, but he did ask what we were up to, and in a moment of divine inspiration, I turned him quite easily to our advantage," Izzy replied. She guided Shelley quickly through her "private theater" idea, embellishing as she went along, and ended with Victor being a silent partner to provide funding and a list of potential clientele.

"Wow! That is quite the business venture. And this crazy idea just popped into your cute little head out of the blue," asked Shelley with apparent disbelief.

Smiling as if caught with her hand in his pocket, she hesitated, "Well, truth be told, this is an idea I've been formulating for some time. I didn't share it with you because, until that very moment with Victor, I didn't see how it could conceivably work. As I explained my thinking, you should have seen the drama unfold in his eyes. If I had asked, he would have walked off the rooftop's edge."

"Well, that makes success with our flying harness even more critical. It will become one of many such fantasy-driven devices," Shelley said. "Let's get you suited up and try it out again."

This time the harness worked perfectly, and Shelley could maneuver her back and forth across the stage and turn her 180 degrees at the end of the loop. She had complete control of her arms and legs and could easily breathe. Now came the fun part: decoration.

Back on the stage, Izzy said, "That was incredible. I felt as free in the air as I do on the stage. When will you have all the feathers and other adornments ready? I can't wait to show Victor this latest development."

Shelley tensed, saying, "We need to be very careful now and not let Jacques know we have a working prototype. He's having lunch tomorrow with Victor, and I'm confident he'll ask the same questions he had for you. So when he asks me how it's going, I'll tell him we're still working out some kinks but making progress."

Jacques popped into Shelley's workroom the following day, exactly as anticipated. "Please bring me up to speed on the progress of our flying harness. I have my lunch meeting with Victor Horgiot today, and he will inquire about it."

Scratching his head as if he were at a loss on how to respond, Shelley said, "Well, we're taking one step forward and then two steps back, you know, but we'll get there. We're just not there yet."

Very agitated by this information, Jacques spun about and left, cursing under his breath in French as he stomped away. Shelley, on the other hand, was quite pleased.

Victor arrived early for lunch and was ready and waiting when the hostess announced Jacques Benoit. "Welcome, Jacques. So glad you could make it. How are things moving with your new offering down at the theater? I hope you're making significant progress."

Sputtering slightly, Jacques replied, "Well, we are moving forward, but as is often the case with brilliant new ideas such as these, there is much trial and error, and sadly the errors are winning the battle for the moment. But, fear not, we shall prevail."

"What seems to be the problem? Is it something a timely investment might overcome, or is it something more?" Victor asked.

Jacques replied, sensing an opportunity to line his pockets, "A timely investment would move things along at a more suitable clip. I sincerely appreciate your adeptly identifying the problem and offering a solution. I think a $10,000 investment would break the log jam."

"Let's not get the cart before the horse just yet. First, I'd like to see this opportunity for myself, and then we can discuss my investment level. So when would be a good time to stop for a look-see?" Victor asked.

Sensing he was about to lose control of things, Jacques pivoted as best he could. "Well, we'd certainly like to make that happen and will make every effort to accommodate such a patron as yourself. But we'd need certain assurances that our idea remains safely in our possession once revealed to you."

Victor bristled at this and responded curtly, "I'll have my lawyers draft some language to that effect, and we'll go from there." Then, quickly looking at his watch, he pushed his chair back and, much to Jacques's surprise, said, "I just remembered I have an essential matter to attend to down at the docks. Sorry to break our lunch off so abruptly. Good day director." With that, Victor exited, leaving Jacques quite baffled. And somewhat perturbed.

A Slow Boat to the Congo

In his office, Victor called Carl, his head of logistics, and told him to come by his office as soon as possible. He then started swearing out loud, "That little Napoleon shit smear! I'll give him some assurances, the likes of which he's never seen. I'll box his ass up and ship him off to the Congo. He'll fit in with those pygmies we ran into."

Carl rapped on the closed office door and entered. "Hey, Boss. It sounds like you've got a personnel problem to deal with."

"Yes, his name is Jacques Benoit, the director at The Delirium Theater.

Unfortunately, he thinks he can dictate terms for my investments in his pathetic little theater. He will soon learn nobody dictates anything to me. I was hoping you could take him away on our next boat to the Congo and dump him off with the pygmy chief as my gift to him for his faithful service."

Carl smiled and said, "I'm sure we can arrange secure passage for Mr. Benoit on the next steamer down. Consider him already delivered."

Shelley was busy putting the finishing touches on the harness and supporting garments in his workshop. Everything looked even better than he'd imagined, and he couldn't wait to see Izzy decked out and ready to fly. But, unfortunately, Jacques was approaching from way down the hall and wasn't happy from the sounds of it. So, quickly hiding the costume, he busied himself with other work and waited for Benoit's arrival.

"Shit, shit, shit! I think I have genuinely dropped a rope around my very own neck. My meeting with Victor did NOT go as planned. Oh no, far from it," he said in complete panic mode, frantically pacing back and forth. "He wants to see the idea, and when I asked for legal assurances that he wouldn't try and steal it once he saw it, he got very agitated and left quite abruptly. We are genuinely over the barrel, and I feel it starting to roll."

Shelley looked at him with amazement and, trying to collect his thoughts, offered up, "Maybe there's still a way we can salvage the situation. Izzy had dinner with him last night, and she seemed pretty happy after the meeting. Maybe she can help us turn Victor around."

Shock crossed Jacques' face like a thundercloud, "She what!? Why would Izzy be having dinner with Victor Horgiot?"

Shelley replied, "Well, he sent her a dozen roses earlier in the week and invited her to join him for dinner at the club. So evidently, they had a relationship of some sort a long time ago."

Once again misreading an opportunity, Jacques responded, "Yes, yes! We can make this work to our advantage. Where is Izzy?"

"I guess she's in her dressing room," Shelley said, feeling uncomfortable.

"Follow me," Jacques demanded.

They sprinted down the hall and across the back of the theater, bursting into Izzy's dressing room, where she stood half naked. She didn't think so much as to blink at the intrusion, nor did Shelley seem shocked, as he had seen his mother naked numerous times, but Jacques, on the other hand, was quite embarrassed. He had never seen such a beautifully erotic creature.

"So, so sorry to barge in on you like this. Please, please forgive me, but I am in dire need of your assistance. I understand you and Victor Horgiot had dinner last night, and it went well. At the risk of being intrusive, can you tell me why he reached out to you?" he sputtered as he looked away.

Casually, Izzy found a robe and wrapped herself up, and settled back into her dressing room chair. "I was as surprised as anyone when the flowers arrived, as I haven't seen Victor privately for many years. Then I remembered what a magical night it was so long ago, and I thought I might as well see what he had in mind. He asked about the theater. And he wanted to know about anything new we might have in the works. I told him you were always working on something or other, but I am only a dancer on the stage and can't exactly say what it might be. Shelley smiled inwardly at this exchange and had never felt more incredible pride in his mother's ability to lead men astray. He knew precisely what she and Victor had discussed; it was much more than a flying dancer costume. So much more.

"Do you have plans to see him again? Soon, I hope?" pleaded Jacques.

"No, we left any future meetings in his hands. I have no claim on his time or emotions, but if he calls again, I will gladly go," Izzy said with a note of finality. Then, quickly standing, she said, "Please excuse me now. I must get dressed for rehearsals."

"Yes, yes, yes. So sorry to have interrupted," Jaques begged as he backed into the hallway.

Outside Jacques' apartment, it was well past two in the morning when Carl decided the time was right to shuttle Jacques away to his new destination. He and his accomplice quietly climbed the fire escape stairs and entered an open window to the living room. They could hear the regular tempo of deep snoring down the hall. He crept down the darkened hall, placed a few drops of ether in a handkerchief, then quickly held it over Benoit's suddenly-surprised face, and he was out. They rolled him up in a small oriental rug and proceeded right out the front door of the apartment building; their only witnesses were the dim streetlights and wharf rats.

Later that same morning, Victor paid Jacques a visit on the steamer. "When we last spoke, Mr. Benoit, you asked for assurances from me regarding your new invention. Well, you can rest assured you won't need to worry about the theater any longer, as you are bound for the heart of the Congo, where your next performance will depend entirely on your creativity and pluck. No poaching ideas from talented stagehands. No fancy dancers to boss around and treat like your personal property."

Jacques listened intently, eyes filled with terror, then pleaded, "What do you mean by all this? You can't ship me away and think no one will notice. I am an important person, and there will be an investigation. People will ask questions. Furthermore, what is this business about the Congo?"

"You failed to realize that, essentially, I own the theater where you are employed. That's the beautiful thing about being a silent partner. So, people looking for you will be told you decided to take a sabbatical rather spur of the moment to refresh your creative spirits in some exotic land. Then, one thing will lead to another, and you will disappear, never to be heard from again."

"Surely we can come to some arrangement. This affair is beyond the pale of human decency," Jacques pleaded. "I'll do whatever you ask, just set me free, and we'll start anew. I'm begging you!"

"You see, that's where you made your mistake. I'm not human, at least not as you ascribe to being human. I didn't get where I am today by being decent if what I desired required employing other means to accomplish it," Victor bragged. "Much as I hated that bastard before he died, my father pounded that into my head daily."

Stepping through the bulkhead door, slamming it behind them, and spinning the hatch closed, Victor and Carl exited. Jacques started screaming, but there was no one to hear his cries. At this particular moment, Jacques wished he wasn't creative, as his mind started envisioning what would happen to him upon his arrival in the Congo. Unfortunately, none of these thoughts fell into the "exotic vacation" category.

Victor informed Shelley and Izzy of Jacques's sudden departure through an intermediary. Then, as an added surprise, they were told they would now be in charge of operating the theater.

"I guess Jacques has finally been hoisted with his own petard, to quote the bard. Couldn't have happened to a nicer fellow," Shelley said gleefully. "No more need for hiding our plans out of fear he'll take credit for them."

"Yes, yes, yes! We can do whatever we want now," Izzy said excitedly. "My mind is running wild with new ideas. Let's finish our flying costume and show it to the other dancers. What a fantastic development!"

Even though word had come to them through an intermediary, Izzy and Shelley knew who was behind this development. So it was of little surprise when Victor arrived at the theater later that day. Izzy was the first to see him and hurried over to greet him.

In Full Feathered Flight

"Welcome, Victor. So nice of you to stop by the theater on such a momentous day. We are just about to unveil a new costume to the rest of the group that will transform our production. Please be seated while we attend to the last few details," Izzy said, directing him to a seat in the center of the theater.

Victor did as she asked, but before she could get away, he inquired as to who the gentleman was assisting her. When he first laid eyes on him, it was as if he saw himself many years ago. "Oh, that is my dear son, Shelley. He is a genius with things mechanical and decorative." Then, turning, she shouted for Shelley to come over and meet Victor.

As he approached Victor, Shelley was taken aback by his appearance, seeing what he might look like in 20 years. "Good to meet you, sir. I'm Shelley. My mother has told me a little about you, so it's good to meet you in the flesh. We are very excited about the costume we're about to reveal for the first time. I think you'll be impressed."

Victor quickly collected himself, "Good to meet you, Shelley. I await seeing your creation with much anticipation. Please go about your work."

Izzy slipped into her unique fishnet feather stockings and arm-length gloves while Shelley readied the harness and accompanying headdress. After Izzy was fully dressed, Shelley stood back and admired his work. She was the most exotic, erotic vision he had ever created. The combination of feathers and sequins combined and her nude breasts and midriff on display were intoxicating. She stepped into position at the rear of the stage, and Shelley attached the rope to her harness and reeled her skyward. Then he killed the stage lights, so the theater was completely dark. Next, calling out a command to the assistant manning the spotlight, a single intense beam of light hit the curtains. The curtains pulled back, revealing Izzy suspended well above the stage, slowly starting to dance like a bird in flight. The flaming red feathers and diamond sparkles created a spectacular effect. Then she started moving across the stage and eventually out over the first few rows of seats, slowly spinning as she progressed. After that, she became much more visible, and Victor leaped to his feet and started applauding.

"Bravo! Bravo! Amazing! True to your word, no one has ever conceived such a dazzling display," Victor gushed as he sat down, still clapping.

Shelley came out from behind the stage as Izzy continued to flutter overhead. "Thank you most kindly. I agree it is something to behold, and no one makes it work better than my dear mother. She was born for this."

Victor agreed, "She is entirely charming and, at the same time, utterly erotic. I can hear the crowds erupting now as she begins her performance. Spectacular falls well short of describing the overall effect."

After Shelley lowered Izzy back on the stage and got her out of the costume, the three met again. Victor's mind had been running wildly ahead, developing many plans of how they might employ this new device. But, little did he know, Izzy had her own list of derivatives, all of which would shock and pleasure Victor.

"Did you notice the uncanny resemblance between Victor Horgiot and me?" Shelley asked Izzy. "It was like looking at myself in an older mirror."

Izzy smiled knowingly, "Yes, I did notice that. Of course! I'd have to be blind not to see it. But, you know, I started thinking back to that first time I met Victor when we were both much younger, and I started doing some math, which you know is not my strong suit. I was just 17, he was 26, and I had never been with a man before, as girls were my only sex partners until then. It was with him that I discovered my true nature. That sex was my ultimate performance, my reason to be." She walked around, nibbling at her fingertips, "It was just under nine months after that night that you arrived. Victor never called on me again, and I went on to have numerous sexual encounters with men and women alike. So, it never dawned on me until I saw the two of you together that he might be your father. It was amazing. I could tell right away that he had similar thoughts."

Shelley was quiet for a bit and then spoke up, "So what do we do with this new development? Do we pretend nothing's changed, or do we engage with him further and see what evolves?"

Izzy replied, "I'll reach out to him for another meeting to discuss running the theater, as well as my other big idea, and see if he makes any mention of you and his possible relationship. If he does, we'll see where that leads. On the other hand, we'll follow that path if he doesn't ask anything more about you, which he may do out of fear. Either way, Victor is our ticket to better times, don't you think?"

"As crazy as it sounds, I agree that's a good plan," he said.

"Now, let me tell you about my extraordinary idea for our new private theater parties. As I was suspended above Victor, rotating overhead as if weightless, another use for the flying device popped into my brain. Bear with me as I describe it, for it is somewhat complicated, but I think you'll get the gist of it," she said.

She then proceeded to describe a series of what Shelley would later refer to as sport hammocks, which were, in fact, sex hammocks. The best-seller became the "Cockscrew Hammock." With this device, the female partner sits astride an opening in the center of a small square hammock platform suspended by a single rope. The male partner lies directly below the hammock where his erect penis awaits. The hammock is rotated many times, creating a twisting, spring-like tension in the rope. The female then lowers onto her waiting partner, and the hammock is released, which starts to unwind, to dizzying climactic results.

As Izzy finished describing her new products, with the most delicious twinkle in her eyes, Shelley responded, "It never ceases to astound me how enthusiastic you become when talking about sex. And the ingenuity you bring to it is extraordinary. Have you considered what we should call this private theater of yours?"

Giggling with glee, she replied, "Yes, as a matter of fact, I have. But, like the hammocks, it isn't straightforward, so hang with me as I explain. First, I learned about this thing called the "Id." The "Id" is the part of our psyche, hidden in our unconscious, that is the source of instinctive impulses and urges to seek satisfaction and pleasure. When I heard about this, I finally understood what drives me so. Not only me. Everyone has these urges and impulses to seek pleasure, even you, but each person's urges are unique. We are all entities or vessels for these thoughts of the "Id." That led me to the word "identity," and through some creative wordplay changed it to "Id+Entity" and finally, The Id+Entity Theater."

Shelley's reaction was a mixture of awe and amazement. "Curiously, it all makes perfect sense."

Izzy continued, "In our private theater productions, customers of any sexual orientation can act out their wildest fantasies. First, we'll meet with these ultra-wealthy clients to learn their desires for the occasion. Then, under your direction, our group will design every aspect of their fantasy, creating costumes, sets, and whatever is required. Some of these creations will be unique versions of our sex swings and other products we might develop. Finally, we'll incorporate the client's guests into the show as they see fit. Short of criminal rape or murder, anything goes."

"And where pray tell, do we get these clients? This offering isn't something we can shout from the rooftops or stick up on a playbill," Shelley asked, sensing Izzy already had an answer for that as well.

"That is where our newfound friend Victor Horgiot comes into play. When I painted this picture for him over dinner, using the broadest brush imaginable, his eyes lit up with excitement and possibility. He knows these people of great wealth, and he even has insight into some of their singular sexual desires, although how he knows these things is a mystery to me," she explained. "He would also help us to put a value on these productions. Since each show is a one-night affair and highly individualized, the ticket price will be very high. Even so, he does not see this as being a problem.

Rich people are not concerned with something as mundane as money–they seek pleasure at any cost, and we can deliver like no one else."

Shelley reached out and hugged Izzy, picking her off her feet and twirling her around. "You are a genius. Absolute genius. And this side hustle is in addition to our regular theater productions?"

"Yes! Think about it. Those clients we entertain privately will also want to bring others into their circle of friends, and the main theater offers that opportunity. Their friends can see and hear our productions in the comfort of The Delirium. Afterward, discussions about what we can deliver privately will go much better, as they have already seen a sampling of our production. It is the ultimate referral network. Well-monied and highly discreet," she said, finishing with a flourish.

Meanwhile, It's Good to Be God

Down south in the Congo, Jacques was dealing with a production scenario of his own. So when Carl unceremoniously dumped him off at the pygmy village, he thought he was dead on arrival. But a curious thing happened, and it was the only time in his life he was genuinely thankful for his diminutive stature.

The pygmies who met them at the river took possession of Jacques, with hands and feet bound. He thought this somewhat ridiculous, as where would he run down here? Back at the village, they dumped him in a dimly lit grass-topped hut. He could smell meat cooking on the open fires outside and heard the murmur of people chatting away in a language he didn't recognize. Chickens and dogs roamed freely. Small children ran naked, chasing one another, laughing and screaming as they went.

After an hour or so, the village chief came to see this new arrival, wearing an elaborate headdress and a simple loin cloth. His ears, cheeks, and nose were pierced with what looked like bones. Highly stylized tattoos covered most of his body. Jacques noticed a deficiency of teeth when he opened his mouth to speak, which offered him a somewhat bizarre comfort since he thought these people were cannibals.

Standing as best he could, Jacques spoke, "How do you do, kind sir? I am Jacques Benoit, your somewhat itinerate guest from the United States. How do you do?"

Jacques was only a few inches taller when he stood before the chief, but this was remarkable in the chief's eyes. This white man was one of them, in stature at least. He did smell offensive, but that was nothing a good dirt bath couldn't fix.

"Ooolalookalu! Kimabasa?" the chief said, rising to his entire four-foot-five-inch height. He then bowed low and awaited a response from Jacques.

"Uh, um, well then, thank you?" he sputtered. Then gesturing his hand to his mouth, he asked, "I have not had anything to eat in several days. Might you have some food and drink that I might partake in?"

"Shumukalamuka! Yah!" the chief replied. He then turned and left, barking orders once outside the hut.

In short order, several dark-skinned ladies appeared, long breasts swinging and sagging almost to their waists, carrying bowls of something. He looked into one bowl and saw what looked like a monkey paw floating in a broth and various roots. They also handed him a large coconut with a hole chopped in it. Then, smiling the same toothless grin as the chief, they set the offerings down and backed out of the hut.

"Th, thank you most kindly, ladies. I'm sure this will be delicious," he replied in his most mannered voice, barely concealing his inner terror.

Outside the hut, the chief talked about this strange new visitor with his council members. He told them he thought this man could be their long-lost god, Smee-yap-na-boo, who was said to be very light-skinned and spoke in unknown tongues. They all looked upon this news in amazement and awaited further instructions from the chief. Then, he said they would build a significant ceremonial hut for Smee-yap-na-boo so that he could teach them the world's ways.

As Jacques struggled to keep the monkey-paw soup down, he reflected on the last week's events. Maybe he wouldn't be in this predicament if he hadn't been such a world-class prick. But, as quickly as that thought appeared, he brushed it aside as ridiculous—everyone else was priggish, jealous of his creative prowess, and simply out to get him.

"Izzy Ibrahim, I'd like you to meet Mrs. Lucille Rockerbilt. "Rocky" is a long-time acquaintance, and we share similar sentiments regarding adventures of the flesh. I've told her about your Id+Entity Theater, and she'd like to host a production at her 5th Avenue apartment. Rocky, you and Izzy will meet and discuss all the details at your convenience," Victor directed.

Lucille enthusiastically replied, "So wonderful to meet you, Izzy. Victor has told me about your creativity in the realms of the exotic and erotic. I can't wait to get started on our production. It will be a small guest list, with only 20 or so attendees. I have been fascinated with the artist Hieronymous Bosch and his wonderful painting "The Garden of Earthly Delights." I brought a print for you to have for reference. This painting should allow us to create many diversions, don't you think?"

Looking at the painting, Izzy felt she had met a truly kindred spirit and replied eagerly, "Of course, of course. Will the guest list include men and women, or all one flavor, as it were?" Looking at the print, ideas of eggs and exotic costumes filled her mind.

"Both, of course, in equal numbers. There will be a mix of sexual orientations, with some gays and lesbians included," Lucille responded.

And so the first production of The Id+Entity Theater was underway. Izzy and Rocky became fast friends, and their joint production was the talk of the monied populace.

Shelley took his mother's ideas and brought them all into being, no matter how insane or unlikely they sounded at first blush. Her visions for erotic pleasure were second only to Shelley's ability to fulfill them.

With this newfound leverage, Victor became even more powerful and expanded his business network worldwide.

Even Jacques Benoit experienced a renaissance of sorts down in the Congo. First, the chief finished building a shrine for him, thinking he was their long-lost god Smee-yap-na-boo. Then, using his newfound godliness to full effect, he combined wild hand gestures and drawings in the sand to communicate his thoughts and directions to his tribe. In short order, he was able to create The Jungleland Theater and began producing a fantastic set of creative productions. On the rare occasion he thought of his past life and how Victor Horgiot treated him, all he could think was, "It might be good to be king, but it's great to be God."

Iris and Beatrice Ohdeshitzo

BEATRICE OHDESHITGO

As her eyes slowly sweep open, she notices it's 5:30. A glance to her left confirms that her lover (also her husband, how convenient) is still asleep in the bed next to her. Looking straight up at the ceiling, she visualizes the bedroom from several angles and then determines her opening movements. Slowly, she pulls the covers back and rises to a sitting position on the edge of the bed. Next, she thinks, "Pause so the camera can dolly around for a better view." Then, after what she feels is an appropriate time, she quietly stands, walks into the bathroom, and closes the door.

Beatrice says to herself, "That felt like a good take. The setting was perfect. You'd swear it was an actual bedroom, not a set in a more significant movie production. My actions were deliberate and natural, and my co-star played the part of the sleeping husband to absolute perfection."

Feeling the cameras had been reset by now for her return to the bedroom, she slowly opens the door and walks back to the bed, gently lying beside her husband. Her hair was perfect, her makeup was evenly applied, and her sheer cotton nightgown was strategically messy. When he awoke, he would see her looking as fresh as the morning dew.

Ready, Action

Ever since Beatrice heard Shakespeare's opening monologue in "As You Like It" in high school, she imagined her life as a continuous movie production.

"All the world's a stage,

And all the men and women merely players."

That would be her life. Every move would be calculated, internally scripted with nuance and meaning, and played with as much passion as she could. Sadly, there were no "Take 2's" in this production, so she must always be on her best game, or the drama would not unfold accordingly.

Roll Cameras

Beatrice's husband slowly stirs, and she readies herself for the next interaction:

Husband moaning: "Morning. What time is it?"

Beatrice: "Oh, it's six o'clock. Did you sleep well?"

Husband: "Yep."

The husband throws the covers off, sits on the edge of the bed, stands, scratches his face, then his balls, and walks into the bathroom.

Beatrice thought, "That was almost a perfect take. The only part I'd edit was the ball scratching. I've never understood why men have to do this all the time. It must be some genetic link to an earlier, vine-swinging ancestor."

Moving the cameras in her mind, she assumes her next position outside the bathroom door, where she hears the tinkle of water. "Shall I make you breakfast, or will you be meeting someone?"

As he shakes the last drops from his free willie, her husband says through the bathroom door, "Breakfast would be great." He then turns on the shower.

Beatrice takes that as her cue to move on to the next scene. "Well done. Perfectly natural in every way. Just the right amount of embarrassed familiarity and institutional memory."

Walking down the dark hallway, she notices the first golden-yellow streaks of another sunrise filtering through the blinds in the kitchen. She pauses, closes her eyes, and can see the perfection as if staged by the best Hollywood set decorators. The sparkling glassware and bone china lined up on open shelving. The Bakelite canisters are stacked orderly, from low to high, with labels facing out. The kitchen knives are beside them, neatly stored in their unique butcher-block stand. The countertop and table are wiped clean, and a single rose bud in a small crystal vase completes the scene. The floral wallpaper reflects and enhances all her feminine characteristics.

Beatrice pauses just outside the door, collects herself, and enters. "Ah! Hello, Mr. Sunshine. It's good to see you again. I hope you had a restful night." This monologue always makes her chuckle, but she can't say why. Switching on the overhead light, she moves to position #2, the refrigerator. Opening the door, she is greeted by well-stocked shelves, neatly ordered as if in the nearby supermarket, all labels facing out for best visibility. Considering her options with appropriate time for reflection and satisfaction, she grabs the eggs and a rasher of bacon.

Then, moving to her next spot, the stovetop, she places the items on the counter and reaches overhead for her cast-iron skillet. She holds the pan up in front of her, examines it critically, then says, " Nothing cooks eggs and bacon like a good old cast iron skillet. And nothing gets my man of a husband ready to make the bacon like a hearty breakfast."

Putting the pan down on the cooktop, she thinks she may have been a little too repetitive with her wording, with too many "bacon references," perhaps. She must get that early morning monologue down with more panache. While it's not the start of the day, it's a vital bridge connecting the beginning to the first main scene: breakfast.

She hears the patter of feet overhead, two pairs: one her daughter and the heavier set, her husband. Walking back into the hallway, where her mind's eye cameras await to capture this interlude, she yells lovingly up the stairs to Iris, her daughter, "Breakfast is almost ready, Iris. Make sure and bring your book sack down when you come, please."

Iris moans, "Yes, Mom. I'll be right down." This interaction is followed by the sounds of drawers being yanked open and partially closed, complaints of an inaudible nature, slamming of the bedroom door, and heavy stomping as she comes downstairs.

Beatrice appraises her daughter's performance, "I think she may be a little overly dramatic this morning with all the drawer banging and door slamming, but then again, she is a pre-teen, so she must be given great latitude to play the role as she sees fit. We'll check out her wardrobe choices and then proceed accordingly."

Cue: Dialogue

Iris saunters in, dressed in a lovely floral pattern dress and black slippers, "G'morning. What's for breakfast? Oh no! Eggs and bacon, again? Why can't we have something different for once, like waffles or pancakes? Or chocolate cake?"

Smiling as if she has anticipated this hormonal outbreak, Beatrice replies, "Honey, you know we only have waffles or pancakes on the weekend or for special occasions. And cake for breakfast, never. I could make you some hot oatmeal. Would you like that?"

"Ugh! That's even worse. I'll just eat some eggs," Iris moaned.

Beatrice thought, "Such drama, such dissent. And so early in the morning! She will be a great actress one day. I guarantee it. My dialogue in this part of the drama was spot on. Just the right amount of motherly resistance but delivered lovingly."

Beatrice's husband appears, "What's all this complaining about breakfast? You should be glad your Mama takes such good care of you. When we were your age, we pretty much fended for ourselves."

Beatrice thought, "Well, that wasn't quite 'I'll give you something to complain about,' but very close. Nobody plays the stern father figure like my man. And it comes so naturally to him."

Iris replied with a slight hint of shame, "Yes, Daddy. Thanks for making breakfast for me, Mama."

"You're welcome, sweetie. It's my joy and pleasure to dote on you and your father," Beatrice gushed.

She fell back and watched as Iris and her husband finished breakfast, basking in the glow of a well-played scene. The tinkling sounds of knives and forks on china always made her feel fulfilled. This quiet consumption of sustenance would lead to another perfect day for both of them. How could it not?

Her husband slid his chair back and dropped his napkin on the empty plate in one fluid motion, always an athletic spectacle from Beatrice's viewpoint. "Thanks, hon, that was very tasty. I'm off to see the wizard. Have a good day at school, Iris," he said as he pecked them both on the cheek.

Iris said, "Thanks, Daddy. Love you," will all the heartfelt sentiment an untroubled childhood can produce.

After a beat, Iris resumed character, speaking in a dull monotone, "Mama, I need money for school. We're going on a trip to the museum to see some old exhibits about Egypt. Tickets are $5 per child."

Bea took this rare moment of unscripted improvisation and quickly responded, "Oh, Egypt! Sweetie, that sounds so exciting. You'll see all those mummies and their shiny gold sarcophagi thingies. And beautiful jewelry. I saw an extensive write-up about it in the paper the other day. Does your teacher need any help? Maybe I could come along as another chaperone."

At this, Iris moaned long and loud, "M-o-m! Please no! You'll embarrass me in front of all my friends."

Beatrice issued a hurtful reply, "Honey, you know I'd never do anything to embarrass you. I just thought you might like it if I was helpful to your teacher. She has so much on her plate and taking a bunch of kids to the museum is no small feat. I'll get my purse and give you the money."

Beatrice reviewed the interaction as she left the kitchen, "That felt solid. The conversation could have gone any number of directions, but we kept everything between the guard rails, and Iris didn't freak out.

Returning to the kitchen with her purse, she fished out a five-dollar bill and handed it to Iris. "Be sure and give that to your teacher. When are you going to the museum? I need to put it on the calendar."

Iris said, "Next Tuesday."

Beatrice saw a motion out the kitchen window and noticed it was the school bus approaching. "Okay, sweetie, the bus is here. Gather your things together. Have a wonderful day."

Iris slides her chair back, grabs her back sack, and floats out the door in a blink, yelling to her Mom, "Love you."

A quiet settles over the house as the bus pulls away. Beatrice looks around and delights with the opening sequence of the day. The next scene will be challenging, with so many variables and different characters to keep straight. She's never been happy with her performance in this setting, but maybe today will be different.

Cue: Pork Chops

Beatrice sees herself walking down the sidewalk to the corner market. She has on her best Sunday dress, her hair wrapped in an elegant scarf, her shopping bags neatly folded under her arm. Her steps are bold and confident. She is a woman on a mission, and that mission is to do some shopping.

Seeing her reflection in the storefront window, she stops, removes her scarf, straightens her hair, and enters the store. She is immediately greeted with the din of store sounds. Soft music playing from some unseen source, customers talking in pairs about prices for this and that, and of course, the occasional "special deal on whatever" announcements blared over the intercom. Beatrice gathers her thoughts, grabs a shopping cart, and begins the task at hand.

As she approaches the meat counter at the back of the store, she notices they have a new butcher. And he is gorgeous! Young and well-muscled, his hair has just the right amount of Fopp hair product and a smile that lifts you off your feet. My interactions with this character must be perfect.

Beatrice approaches the counter and taps on the small bell to get his attention. "Hello there. I haven't seen you here before. I'm Beatrice; nice to meet you. I hope you can help me with some nice pork chops."

The young butcher replies, "I'm Jimmy. Good to meet you as well, Beatrice. Let me show you what we have on those pork chops."

As he turns and leaves the counter to retrieve a tray of meat from the walk-in freezer, Bea has a moment to do a more fulsome appraisal of Jimmy. "Ooh, such nice broad shoulders and a thin waist, and that tight derriere makes me want to reach out and pinch it."

As if someone slapped her across the face, Beatrice winces thinking such erotic thoughts about a complete stranger.

Jimmy returns after a moment, carrying a large tray with freshly cut pork chops piled high. "These are fresh cut this morning and should make for a tasty meal. How many would you like?"

Beatrice regains her composure and says, "If you could wrap up four for me, that would be great. Thank you."

Jimmy picks what he feels are the best four chops, wraps them in brown butcher paper, checks the weight and scribbles down the price, then hands them over to Bea.

His fingers touch hers for the briefest moment, but it's as if Beatrice is struck by lightning. Her mind jumps to a scene where she and Jimmy are in a darkened hotel room. She has never seen this place before, but already it feels familiar, as if they have been there many times. They lie in bed, having just satiated their sexual thirst for each other, talking quietly and smoking cigarettes. Beatrice thinks, "I don't smoke cigarettes, and I certainly don't cheat on my husband with a butcher. Or do I? This scene is so foreign to me; I'll have to improvise as best I can."

She flashes her most seductive smile at Jimmy and says, "Thank you kindly, Jimmy. I look forward to seeing you again. Take care."

Jimmy smiles and returns the look in kind, "Thank you, Beatrice. I'd like that. I'm new here and don't know my way around, so maybe you could help me get to know the area a bit."

Beatrice thinks, "This is all moving so fast, I'm not sure what my motivation is here, but I can feel something powerful is going on." Then she says, "My market day is Friday, so maybe we could grab a coffee or something, and I can share what I know about the area."

Jimmy says, "That would be great. Thanks again. Take care."

Beatrice resets the movie in her mind's eye. She is walking in a dream now through the narrow aisles of the market, grabbing cans of this, bottles of that, out of sheer boredom. Finally, her list is complete, and she's out the door, headed home. That was quite an unforeseen piece of scripting.

The Sudden Improv

Beatrice thinks, "My performance was spontaneous, and I deem it appropriate, but then again, it's hard to know without understanding the larger context of the drama. Maybe this is one of those instances where the audience is taken on a wild ride they never imagined, where the heroine acts with reckless abandon. That would be a new experience for me and would no doubt push my acting abilities to new and untested limits. I'll have to give it a think. Maybe I will be like Lady Chatterley's Lover, taken with a man totally out of my social realm in a predicament that'll heighten the overall plot."

Meanwhile, Jimmy had his own internal wonderings, "Beatrice is a different bird, but she's easy enough on the eyes. I bet she would be a wild thing if you ever got her out of that strait-laced, goody-two-shoes mindset. But, on the other hand, she seems eager to please, which is always a good sign, so we'll see where it leads."

Back home, Beatrice looked around her bedroom, trying to make sense of this new production wrinkle. Her husband's dirty Dickies were hanging off the hamper: half in, half out–resulting from a much-practiced backhand toss from the bedside. Her makeup counter was orderly, some might say to a fault. Everything was just as it should be. So why did Beatrice feel something was off? What was she missing?

She was brought back to the present moment by the sound of Iris entering the front door, just home from school. She could hear the familiar clunk of her book sack hitting the stairs and the clopping of shoes as she entered the kitchen for her after-school snack.

"I'm upstairs, sweetie. I'll be right down," Bea yelled into the stairwell.

Entering the kitchen scene, Beatrice noticed Iris already had bread and jam on the counter and was busy making her sandwich. Beatrice thought, "What a self-reliant little princess you are. Your parents must be so proud." She said, "How was school today? Is there anything exciting to report? Did some new boy catch your eye?" She chuckled at this last bit, knowing full well that Iris was at that age still when boys were the ickiest things imaginable.

Iris moaned back, "M-o-m! Gross!"

Beatrice followed her volley, chuckling, "Well, one day, that will change, and you'll think boys are the greatest thing ever created. And that's when the real trouble will start, so I must be ready to assist you however I can."

At that precise moment, the scene of her with Jimmy at the hotel replayed itself, causing her to lose focus momentarily. Iris noticed this unexpected quiet and asked, "Mom, are you okay? You look like you just saw a ghost or something."

Beatrice replied, "Oh, I just remembered something I should have picked up at the market today," as if nothing else was the matter. "Here, let me get you some cold milk to go with that sandwich."

Beatrice dropped back into her traditional role, washing dishes at the sink, as Iris prattled on about school and what her friends were up to. Usually, quiet time with Iris was the highlight of her day. But today, she was struggling with the scene. She couldn't focus on her dialogue; she didn't know where or how her actions were being captured. Everything was a jumble in her brain.

Then she told Iris, "Sweetie, I am suddenly feeling a little tired. I think I'll lie down for a bit and rest up. Get started on any homework you might have, and I'll check in on you later, okay?

Iris looked at her Mom, feeling a bit panicked. She could not recall a single time in her young life when her mother had napped or laid down to rest in the afternoon. "Oh, okay. Hope you feel better soon."

Beatrice lay down in the darkened bedroom and tried to rest, but her mind would not be denied. It kept playing the scene with Jimmy over and over. Finally, she got out of bed and headed out for a walk. "Iris, sweetie, I'm going to take a walk, but I'll be back soon. I'm locking the door behind me."

Iris replied, unconcerned, "Okay."

Outside, the sun felt warm and welcoming on her skin. A gentle breeze blew, and all seemed right with the world, but in her mind's eye, she knew otherwise. "This new direction has me troubled. I can see where it would open up a world of opportunities, but it also holds great peril if I can't pull it off convincingly. The idea of having a relationship with a lover never crossed my mind, but since meeting Jimmy, that's all I can think about. I must be careful about our next interaction and ensure I pick up on all the right cues."

Looking up from her wonderings, she suddenly found herself outside the market. "How did I get here? That was not my intent when I left the house." Quickly she gathered herself and was relieved to see she had her purse. She walked into the market, browsing about the shelves and end-isle displays, like any other trip, yet knowingly destined to see Jimmy at the back of the store. Luckily, there weren't many other shoppers at this time in the afternoon, and she noticed he was perched on a stool reading the paper, smoking a cigarette.

Beatrice walked up and said, "Hello, Jimmy."

Jimmy looked up, surprised to see it was Beatrice speaking to him. "Well, hey there. I wasn't expecting to see you again so soon. What can I get for you?"

Beatrice said, feigning embarrassment, "Oh, I forgot an essential ingredient for the pork dish I want to make, so I had to return for that. I thought since I was here, maybe we could chat for a bit. You don't seem to have customers lined up."

Jimmy looked back into the processing area and nodded to the other butcher that he was taking a quick break. He took his bloody apron off, hung it on the cooler door, and met Beatrice on the other side of the counter.

Beatrice said, "Can I get you a pop, or would you rather have coffee? Or something else, perhaps." She thought, "that felt like an excellent way to start things off, friendly but inviting, maybe even alluring. His response will be critical to my next sequence."

Jimmy said as he smiled, "A pop would be great, but let me take care of it. What'll you have? Coke? RC? You look like a Nehi grape gal to me."

Beatrice smiled back, "Yes, a Nehi grape would be perfect. Thank you, Jimmy." She thought, "He's following my lead perfectly and interjecting his own brand of spontaneity. I like that."

Jimmy grabbed the drinks, paid for them, and motioned Beatrice to follow him. "Follow me, my lady. I have a special table for two out back. It's quite lovely, as you'll see." He chuckled as he said this last bit, and Beatrice picked up on his witty sarcasm.

He opened the door to the alleyway and presented his "special table for two" to Beatrice. It was an old shipping palette mounted atop an old beer keg. Two rickety folding chairs set amongst an assortment of empty liquor bottles and cigarette butts completed the tableau.

Beatrice laughed as she said, "This is special. It has that well-used look, so hard to maintain these days." She thought, "Just the right amount of flirt. Drop the line in the water and watch."

Jimmy laughed, "Yes, not just anybody can pull this look off, and I must commend you, Beatrice; not every lady sees the appeal of such a special place."

Beatrice thought, "Well played, Jimmy, well played." Then she laughed and said, "So tell me, Jimmy, where do you live? Nearby, or are you one of the long-distance train commuters?"

Jimmy replied with a directional glance upward, "Well, you could say I live very close by. Right over the market. That lovely window box you see filled with dead plants is mine."

Beatrice looked up and was suddenly shaken by what she saw. She recognized this detail, but from inside the apartment. What she envisioned earlier as a hotel room was Jimmy's bedroom, right above them. If Jimmy had asked, she could have told him where everything was in that room. Instantly, she thought, "This plot twist is quite unexpected. Improvisation is the key to advancing the scene further."

Beatrice said, "That certainly is convenient, but it must be noisy living above all the hustle and bustle."

Jimmy replied, "When the shops close for the day, this area gets plenty quiet. Of course, you hear the taxis and delivery vehicles all hours of the night, but it's not too bad." Then, sensing a chance to advance the drama, he said, "Would you like to go up and see it? You might offer me some decorating advice."

Scene Switch: Interior of Apartment

Beatrice's evaluation of this offer was at once instant and daring. "I'd love to see it. I'm sure your sense of decor is better than you allow yourself to believe." But, she thought, "Be careful now, you want to appeal to his sense of pride and chivalry, but you don't want to put yourself in harm's way."

Her internal cameras immediately reset, capturing them from overhead as they moved from the table into the dark, narrow stairwell leading up to Jimmy's apartment. The double padlocks on the door should have been a clue to Beatrice that she had already abandoned her fears about being in harm's way. Jimmy smiled over his shoulder at Beatrice as he quickly snapped open both locks and opened the door.

When Beatrice crossed the threshold into Jimmy's apartment, it was as if she was stepping back in time. She instinctively knew where everything was as if she had been here many times before. The small cash tin he kept on top of the icebox. The ever-present six-pack of bottled beers inside. His straight razor and soap brush on the sink in the small bathroom, just off the bedroom. And, of course, his double bed looking out at the dead plants in the window box. A wobbly ceiling fan spins overhead, barely stirring the dank air. She saw shadow figures of her and Jimmy engaging in the most erotic sex she had ever imagined, things she had never dared with her husband of 15 years.

Jimmy watched Beatrice closely and could tell her mind was running wild. Little did he know just how improbable that run would be. "So, what do you think? This is what you get without a woman's touch on things."

Beatrice didn't acknowledge hearing Jimmy and began walking straight to his bedroom. Then, after pulling down the seedy roll-up blinds, she sat on the lone chair in the corner and began undressing. First, she slowly removed her shoes, then stockings, leaving her garter in place. Next, she undid the bow around her waist and pulled the dress off over her head, revealing her slip and bra. Finally, Beatrice looked at Jimmy with a seductive glance that spoke without words, "Shall I continue?"

Jimmy stood amazed at what had just transpired, but only for a moment. Then he slowly walked across the room towards Beatrice. He stood before her as she undid his undershirt and pulled it off his head. Then, slowly she undid his belt and pulled his pants down, revealing his growing excitement.

Beatrice thought, "I may have gone over the top with this scene. It's all body language and no dialogue, which is not my forté, although Jimmy seems to be picking up on his cues without any prompting. Best to keep going and adapt the script as needed."

Jimmy picked Beatrice up in his arms and carried her gently over to the bed, laying her down soft as a feather, so her legs hung off the edge of the bed. Then he knelt in front of her spread legs and removed her panties. Beatrice's eyes were wild with fire. Slowly he kissed and caressed all around her pubic area, something Beatrice had only ever fantasized about. Each caress was like an electric shock through her system, undoubtedly leading to a blown circuit. She began writhing about on the bed and, after a moment, screamed out in ecstasy as she came.

Then, looking down at Jimmy, she pulled him over onto the bed, rolled him over onto his back, and straddled his legs. Slowly pulling his boxers down, she revealed his growing excitement. She took his manhood into her mouth and slowly began working her will on him. It was only a minute before Jimmy climaxed. Beatrice looked up from her perch at Jimmy's cock and smiled.

Beatrice thought about what had just transpired, "That scene seemed very intuitive and natural and simultaneously very unfamiliar. Jimmy played his part perfectly. Now, all that's left is the sing-sing, big finish."

Cue: Trumpets and Flugelhorns

Jimmy looked at her with a sense of awe. His prediction that she would be a wild thing was so under the mark as to be ridiculous. This woman was a she-devil. There's no turning back now.

Beatrice took in Jimmy's smile and crawled up on his now-depleted member. First, she reached back and undid her bra, pulling it off and dropping it over Jimmy's eyes. Then she leaned forward and buried his bristly face between her warm and wanting breasts. Then, as if called to attention by some greater force, Jimmy's cock assumed its hardened position, and Beatrice reached down and pulled it into her awaiting vagina.

Jimmy's mind was reeling now. "This woman is too much. And to think, I thought she was this uptight little housewife."

Beatrice now viewed this scene from every angle; she saw absolute perfection. Her erotic tendencies and supporting actions were spot on. Their bodies delivered all the dialogue in perfect synchronicity. The light filtering through the dirty windows was perfect. All that remained was the challenging post-coital scene.

Jimmy sat up quickly and grabbed Beatrice as he came a second time. He gasped for breath as he hugged her close to his chest, burying his head in her hair as it fell around her shoulders. Then, he slowly pulled back, rolled her over onto her back, and lay beside her. Finally, he reached for his cigarettes and offered one to Beatrice, who, uncharacteristically, took one.

They lay back quietly, smoking in bed, replaying the scenes that had just occurred, and enjoying the afterglow of bodies well spent.

Beatrice thought, "My work here today has reached a new plateau. I took a risk, and the rewards were more than I ever dreamed. I took an unscripted scene and made it my own; body and soul. I wasn't simply playing a part of a lover; I was that lover."

Then, just as quietly and deliberately as she had undressed earlier, Beatrice put herself back together and, after a quick splash of water on her face, bid Jimmy farewell.

It was late afternoon now as Beatrice walked back home. She envisioned the scene as her husband walked through the door, hugging her and kissing their daughter on the cheek, like a thousand times before. He would ask about her day, and she would reply that it was another glorious day. Only the well-trained cameras in her mind's eye would detect the untruth she delivered, but that was fine. It's her drama, after all.

Finally, it's the end of the day, both are ready for bed, and the scene has moved back to where it all began: their bedroom. Beatrice snuggles into her husband's arms and kisses him. "Good night."

Beatrice reviews her final directorial comment for the day.

Fade to Black

Her eyes dance behind her eyelids as REM sleep sets in.

"Wait a minute, what is this dream?"

Fin!

www.ingramcontent.com/pod-product-compliance
Lightning Source LLC
Chambersburg PA
CBHW070504300726
48975CB00007B/2320